# Long Ago and Far Away

Mark Pimentel

Fulton Books, Inc.
Meadville, PA

First originally published by Fulton Books 2019

ISBN 978-1-63338-844-4 (Paperback)
ISBN 978-1-63338-845-1 (Digital)

Printed in the United States of America

# PART 1

# Chapter One

Albert Einstein, without intending to, provided the theoretical possibility of time travel in his famous papers: "Special Relativity and General Relativity," published in 1905 and 1915, respectively. When he realized that time travel could exist within the constructs of his theories, he dismissed the idea as impractical. If he had lived another sixty years, I could have shown him just how wrong he was.

You see, I'm a physics professor at Harvard University who has discovered a practical application to time travel and have kept this little secret to myself...well, myself and Ron. Let me tell you my story. I'll start from the beginning.

My name is Mark Peterson. I am one of six children (three younger / two older) who grew up in Winthrop, Massachusetts, a small seaside town right outside Boston. It's a peninsula that juts out into Boston Harbor and the cold Atlantic. Boston's Logan Airport sits right next door in East Boston, a short distance across the inner harbor. Sylvia Plath, the Pulitzer Prize–winning poet lived here as a child from 1936 to 1942. JFK's grandfather Patrick Joseph Kennedy owned a house in Winthrop, and the future president of the United States played on her shores. I would be remiss if I didn't mention that Mike Eruzione also hails from Winthrop. He was the captain of that spectacular United States Olympic hockey team that beat the Russians and went on to win the gold medal in 1980.

The town is densely populated but still has its green areas, including a nine-hole golf course and its many parks. Winthrop maintains a small-town feel with its shops and markets and sidewalks that connect quaint neighborhoods. Boston Harbor surrounds the greater part of Winthrop, providing breathtaking views of the water; and as you look west, you can take in the Boston skyline.

I loved growing up near the water. I learned to swim when I was young and spent many a day at the beach. With a large family and many kids in the neighborhood, I was never bored. We had fun outside and never wanted to go home, unless of course we needed to eat—and still sometimes that wasn't a good enough reason. We ran around in ninety-degree weather during the summer and went sledding when temps dipped down into the single digits in the winter. We had fun, plain and simple. There was always a group of us to play basketball, street hockey, chase, or any number of games kids played in the sixties and seventies.

We were all in good shape back then. There wasn't a fat kid in our neighborhood. Today obesity runs rampant, even in the youth. Kids don't get as much physical exercise as we did.

They still play some of the games we played but also devote huge amounts of time to their electronic devices, playing video games and texting.

We lived in a low-income neighborhood and never had much money, but we invented our own fun for free or at a very low cost. This activity not only created a physically fit kid but also developed social skills and increased imagination, which old Einstein said is more important than knowledge.

Throughout my childhood years and adolescence, I lived my life as many other boys did—having fun and getting into trouble. There were the rites of passage like learning to ride a bike, my First Holy Communion and discovering Santa Claus was a myth. I never broke a bone but required many stitches for the plethora of scrapes I gained along the way. I had a paper route, played Little League baseball and was a member of the Boy Scouts. There were best friends and fights with those friends, summer vacations and returning to school in September, laughter and tears, schoolwork and after-school play, Christmas presents and bitter disappointments—the typical experiences that make up the woven fabric of one's youth. And as I stumbled through those years, I began noticing the girls.

# Chapter Two

In ninth grade, I met a girl who would forever change my life. We were in the same English class during the 1972–1973 school year. Her name was Lena Mendleson, the girl I loved and then lost so many years ago. She would stay on my mind for years to come. Her memory was seared into my consciousness and forever tugged at my heart.

I was so smitten that I knew I had to be with her. I wasn't sure how I was going to do it, being as shy as I was, but somehow I had to ask her out—and I did. The seven months that followed were the best time of my life. Everything fell into place. The rest of the world could have fallen down around me, but as long as we were still together, then all would be fine. Have you ever felt that way? Have you ever had the feeling that everything outside the world of *you and her* is virtually irrelevant? That's the way I felt about Lena. I couldn't have been more in love. My world was complete, and I was in need of nothing else to make me any happier—nothing at all.

Of course, if everything ended in a "*happily ever after*" fashion, the rest of my story would not have to be told. On a cold day in January, Lena ended it. She said she had fallen out of love with me. I couldn't believe what I was hearing. That's when my world came crashing down. I walked home numbed from the cold but more so from the shock of what I was still trying to comprehend. I honestly never thought I would be without her, and suddenly I was. To say that I was devastated and terribly alone would be a gross understatement. I would tell people years later that she didn't break my heart— she ripped it out of me.

The rest of my high school years were lonely ones. I didn't care to go steady with any girl; my heart was broken, and my mind was still on Lena. So I hit the books hard, trying to bury the pain. College was fast approaching, and I wanted to make something of myself.

In 1976, I graduated from Winthrop High then went on to study physics at MIT. Because I graduated with honors there, Harvard University offered me a scholarship for my postgraduate studies. Shortly after finishing my PhD, they asked me if I wanted to stay on. I was more than happy to sign on at Harvard—are you kidding, a professor at Harvard University! Shit, John Adams and John Kennedy graduated from those hallowed halls. I'd be teaching some of the intellectual giants of the future and would have free reign with physics research at the most prestigious and well-funded university in the world. Eight years later, I was tenured.

# Chapter Three

The great achievements of man are often arrived at not without the loss of those things which he holds most dear.

—Mark Pimentel

I met my wife during those early years as an assistant professor. I was having a bite to eat at a little coffee shop in Harvard Square. Robin was in a booth near mine. She was strikingly attractive: slim figured with auburn hair and piercing blue eyes; she was a looker. It started with some small talk and ended three hours later. We arranged to meet again, and the rest, as they say, was history. We dated for six months and then married. I was thirty-one and she twenty-five. The year was 1989.

At first, Robin continued with her career in finance; then she slowly weaned herself away, wanting to settle down and have a family. We bought a beautiful three-bedroom colonial in Danvers, Massachusetts, and began to work on that family. After several frustrating years of trying to conceive, we decided to adopt. Adoption is a long, paperwork-filled process that takes months and sometimes years to complete. We were somewhat lucky because within ten months we had our child. After two trips to Russia, we brought Hannah home, a beautiful sixteen-month-old baby girl. It was February of 1994.

We were very happy as the years passed, and Hannah grew. I was content with my position at Harvard, publishing more than I needed to and the young students—that were going to change the world—kept me on my toes. Little did they know that one day I would, in fact, change the world…at least for me.

# Chapter Four

Albert Einstein theorized that space and time were aspects of the same thing—linked, if you will, as one. This concept is termed the space-time continuum. Because of the effects of the gravitational forces of bodies within space, Einstein also theorized that the space-time continuum is a curved pathway, not straight as others assumed. That is to say—as you travel through space and time, you travel along a curved path that could eventually connect back with itself.

In 1935, Einstein and another scientist named Nathan Rosen realized that the theory of general relativity would allow for bridges or shortcuts between space-time. Of course, they were coined Einstein-Rosen bridges. Einstein did not actually believe these theoretical bridges could exist in any practical way that would allow for time travel. Today, these bridges are known as wormholes. In theory, the wormhole could allow passage of an object through this short cut, thus linking up with its past or future.

# Chapter Five

It was 1997 now, and I had begun research in what I described above but on a much-smaller scale. My work was in the microworld of atomic and subatomic particles. This branch of physics is called quantum physics or quantum mechanics. I was attempting to send single particles of light (photons) through wormholes so as to provide a path to the photon's past. Even with a fair amount of time allotted for experimentation, my research and any conclusive findings would take years. That was okay because I was a plodder. If you weren't a plodder, scientific research wasn't the job for you. So I was quite content at Harvard, plodding along and enjoying my work. I was respected by the faculty, well-liked by my students, and very excited about the time travel work I was doing.

# Chapter Six

Sometime in 2001, the arguments began, and as the years and months went by, they became more frequent. In hindsight, it was easy to see it all play out. Spending so much time at work slowly eroded my marriage. A marriage needs to be nurtured, and I was not taking the time to provide that nurturing. I slowly became more and more distant to my wife, and I stopped spending time with Hannah. I was much more content at school than I was at home. As they say, I was married to my job. So the fights began as little spats and gradually became more frequent and more heated.

One late afternoon, after a long and frustrating day at school, I came home and walked into a storm. The argument started slowly but grew into a fury—the type of fight where you say and do things that you don't always mean—things you'll regret later. At its pinnacle, Robin screamed, "You care more about your career than you do your family! Hannah hardly knows you for Christ's sake!" This struck a nerve, and without really thinking, I replied, "Fuck you!" slowly and forcefully enunciating each word. And then I lost it totally. I picked up and threw one of the kitchen chairs to the floor and then stormed out of the house, slamming the door behind me. After three hours of driving around, I came home and slept on the couch. We didn't speak for four days. When we finally did, we both agreed that we had lost our love for each other and it would be best to go our separate ways. After fifteen years of marriage, it was over. I had failed at the most important job of my life.

A month later, I moved out of that large dream house in Danvers and into a small second-floor apartment in Cambridge, Massachusetts—closer to Harvard. It was April of 2004. Eventually my wife and I became better friends than we were as lovers, and my relationship with Hannah improved. At first Hannah blamed me for everything. She would say things like "You don't love Momma" and "You don't love me." This hurt me, but I expected it—she was only eleven years old, and I had heard about this in other marriages that ended in divorce. Hannah gradually began to love and accept me again, and this was in no small part due to my wife who explained things to her about parents divorcing. I was thrilled, of course. I never wanted to lose my little girl's love. After three months away from the house, I was seeing Hannah every other weekend, and we both enjoyed the time spent together.

# Chapter Seven

I adjusted comfortably with my new digs, and things were going smoothly at work. In fact, I was in the lab much more often. Now that I had more time to myself, my research was moving along at a much-quicker pace. I was also more relaxed without the stress of my marriage, so I had managed to quit smoking. I had been smoking since I was young and was very proud of myself for giving it up—any former smoker will tell you how tough it is to quit.

I've heard it said that as many as 90 percent of all people are not happy at their jobs. What did Thoreau say? Something like most men live quiet lives of desperation and then die with their songs never sung. I felt very fortunate not to have slid into that rut. I never took for granted the fact that I had a job I truly loved, not to mention that I was rewarded biweekly with a juicy paycheck.

In early March of 2006, I completed my research on quantum time travel. I published my work and was congratulated by Harvard and the scientific community. There was talk that I was being considered for the prestigious Albert Einstein Medal—this would be quite an honor.

The physics department threw a little celebratory party in my honor, which meant a lot to me. My ex-wife even called to congratulate me. But what meant the most was my daughter telling me that she was so proud of her dad. She was thirteen years old now and growing up fast, but she'd always be my baby girl, and what she had to say would always be very important to me.

My findings were important in the field of quantum mechanics but not revolutionary. The results were anticipated. Time travel at the quantum level was theorized long ago but of course had to be experimentally proven. I had done this, and my name would be noted in history, but I hadn't changed the world with my work. What would be considered revolutionary would be time travel on the macro scale, or in other words, *human time travel.* This is what I planned on tackling next. Actually, I had already begun!

# Chapter Eight

My Monday morning class, following all the attention I received the previous week, was quite remarkable. Before I could get started, a student raised her hand.

"I have a question, Professor, but first I just wanted to congratulate you for your work that you are being recognized for here at Harvard."

She began to clap, and the rest of the students in the hall followed suit. There were whistles and shouts of bravo also. As the din slowly died down, I thanked the students for their praise. They were once again seated except for the young woman who had raised her hand.

"Is it possible, sir, that your work in the quantum field of time travel could eventually lead to human time travel?"

Of course I believed it was possible. In fact, I believed that I would create a time machine (excuse the pun) in the not so distant future and travel through time myself. None of this could be revealed to my students or anyone for that matter. This work was in progress now, and I never intended to share it with anyone. The world wasn't ready for this revelation—how could it ever be?

I knew many of the students by name but couldn't recall hers.

"Excuse me for not knowing your name, would you share it with us?"

"My name is Martina, Martina Eden. I'm a freshman, sir."

"Thank you, Ms. Eden, I'll remember it next time. And thank you for your kind words, I truly appreciate it. To answer your question, no, I do not. Among other reasons, I share Einstein's belief that time travel cannot be accomplished in the larger world because

16

of the many paradoxes that it would create. These paradoxes illustrate how time travel is impractical. One such paradox, most of you are probably familiar with, is called the grandfather paradox: a person travels back in time and kills his grandfather before his father is born. This would prevent him from being born, therefore the time machine could never have existed and time travel could never have taken place…so," I went on, "if this scenario is possible, then time travel is impossible. Does everyone understand this?"

No hands went up, so I continued.

"Let's put the paradoxes aside momentarily, just for the sake of argument. Let's say that somehow we can work around them— explain them away somehow. Then in theory only, and I repeat, in theory only, time travel could be accomplished in the larger world the same way I have shown it possible in the quantum world—by way of CTCs [closed time-like curves], and wormholes. Does anyone know what a CTC is?"

A student on my left named Alfred Beasely raised his hand then answered. "A CTC or a closed time-like curve is a loop in the space-time continuum. That is to say, in theory, as you travel through curved space-time, you could theoretically connect back to where you started. Einstein's general relativity theory allows for these loops in space-time. So in theory, one could travel back to his past along the loop."

"Very well stated, Mr. Beasely, thank you," I said. "What about a wormhole?" I asked. Martina raised her hand again, so I decided to let her answer. "Martina, see, I remembered your name." This got a laugh from her and many others in the hall.

"A wormhole is a connection between any two points along the circumference of the CTC. The significance of the wormhole is that it creates a shortcut in the CTC, allowing for quick passage into the past or the future."

"Very good, Martina."

I then went on to use the classic apple and wormhole as an example to drive home the point.

"Think of your entire life and your movement through the space and time of this life as existing along the perimeter of a round apple. You are a little worm working your way around the apple, working your way through life. But now you take a shortcut and burrow straight through the apple's core, effectively creating a passageway to another time period of your life—to the past or perhaps into your future! Once again, Einstein's theories allow for this, but even if we could create a wormhole and safely travel into the past or future, the resultant paradoxes would render this time travel impossible."

I then went on to discuss my work in quantum mechanics.

"The quantum world is made up of tiny entities like atoms and even smaller particles like photons, which I've worked with in my research. The photon is a minute particle of light that does not conform to the classical laws of physics. In classical physics, one object cannot occupy more than any one position at any given time. In quantum physics, a quantum particle, such as a photon, can exist in more than one position at any given time. How is this possible?" I asked rhetorically. "Because it has a dual nature. A photon possesses wavelike properties as well as particle properties. Any one fixed position cannot be determined. It actually can exist everywhere at once. This makes time travel possible in the smaller world—the quantum world. So the original particle can exist in several, if not, an infinite number of positions simultaneously. What I have proved in my research is that time travel can be accomplished at this tiny level. I have sent photons through wormholes, created in the lab, so that these photons may link up with themselves—in their past."

The lecture became a fifty-minute discussion on time travel. I intended on presenting a ten-minute summary of my research, then to discuss the next chapter in the text, but this did not happen. It was fun though, straying from the intended path and breaking up the monotony—the routine. In fact, I decided on briefly discussing other paradoxes that would prevent time travel in our next lecture.

"I see that this interesting concept we call time is almost up for us. So before our next meeting, I'd like you to do a little research on other paradoxes that would prevent time travel. Get familiar with them because I'll talk about these paradoxes in our next lecture. Oh, and don't forget your regular syllabus homework as well."

I actually received a standing ovation when I finished. This was the second one I'd received in less than a week, and it felt good.

When all the students had filed out, I moved away from the lectern and sat down at the desk, clasping my hands behind my head as I leaned back in the chair. What I couldn't tell the students was that although paradoxes do prevent human time travel, there were ways to circumvent the problem. I knew this, but hadn't worked it out completely.

# Chapter Nine

As the years passed, I hammered away at my research, working out the many obstacles that would prevent human time travel.

I found myself immersed in my work, closer than ever to making my dream a reality. In 2011, my breakthrough year, I discovered something that shattered every theory of how time travel worked. It was just a theory and yet to be proven, but soon I would confirm it. The epiphany or revelation I had was this: when you travel to a time period where you already exist, you don't arrive as a separate, identical you, but instead, your present-day self supplants, or in other words, takes over the body of your earlier self! Therefore, this proved that the quantum world and the macro world adhere to similar but separate laws of physics. The human body can travel through time like a quantum particle can but is prevented from existing as more than one of itself. This must be God's way of keeping the world in a normal state, so to speak. This is extremely significant because it prevents the paradoxes that would result if a time traveler arrived as a double or twin of himself. For instance, there would be no twin to kill his grandfather and fulfill the grandfather paradox.

Also at this point, I was close to developing a wormhole for the machine that would allow for safe and practical time travel. The problem that many physicists have is creating a theoretical Lorentzian wormhole that would stay open and allow a time traveler to pass through it. Most models predict a collapsing effect inside the throat or tunnel of the wormhole. The Lorentzian model is a theoretical life-size wormhole unlike the subatomic Euclidean wormhole of the quantum world that I worked with in my earlier research. Kip

Thorne, a renowned theoretical physicist at the California Institute of Technology, was on the right track when he theorized that if the wormhole was static or unchanging in time, then it would contain exotic matter. This matter has a negative energy density that would allow the wormhole to stay open during a time travel event instead of collapsing like many theorists suggest. I used his research and extrapolated data from my micro-work, allowing me to predict outcomes for larger particles using very similar theoretical models.

# Chapter Ten

In the fall of 2012, the time machine was getting close to completion and the theory was all but worked out. My final calculations had to be completed and verified, but I was having trouble with the higher math. Although I have a solid math foundation, I realized that I would need some assistance from Ron Sarno, my colleague and friend. As I thought about this, I glanced over at my Einstein poster on the wall above my desk. *The Great One,* as I sometimes referred to him, stood there looking perplexed. The caption read, "Do not worry about your difficulties in mathematics, I can assure you mine are still greater." Even Einstein needed help with complex math occasionally.

Ron is a professor in the math department here at Harvard and also happens to come from Winthrop. The odds of two professors that teach at the same college who also hail from the same town must be astronomical, but sometimes truth is stranger than fiction, as you will see.

We first met at a charity golf tournament and since then have become good friends. He is a younger junior professor who was just recently granted tenure. We now golf and go out together occasionally, and it's always a good time. Ron has that youthful spirit and enthusiasm, a breath of fresh air for me, and in a way keeps me young. He's smart as a whip but doesn't come across as aloof or a know-it-all. Ron is a self-proclaimed ladies' man and not shy about telling you this. He refers to himself as tall, dark, and handsome. He's always goofing around and never stops trying to get me hooked up with someone. One day he threw a quote at me: "You know, Mark, it's better to wear out than rust out." He was referring to the fact that I was single and that I should get back in the game.

I replied, "Hey, Romeo, I'll make a move when I'm ready. Who said that anyway—it's better to wear out than rust out?"

"Pretty sure it was Millard Fillmore." Then he added that time waits for no man.

I smiled as I thought about the time machine—maybe, but maybe not.

So I texted Ron, asking him if he could stop by the lab in the afternoon to help me with the math that I was stumped on. His return text went: "Can't, swamped, how 'bout tonight at the cave I'll bring Chinese." *The Cave* was my apartment. Because of its small size, Ron referred to it as the Cave.

"Okay, seven work for you?" I asked.

"Yup, see you then, ol' buddy."

I decided to end for the day, so I began cleaning up the lab. The lab I was working in today was my private lab, the one where all the time travel work was done. Being the ranking professor in the physics department, I had a private lab as well as the one I used with my students. No one could enter this lab without my permission; even plant maintenance and the janitorial service could gain entrance only after clearing it with me.

As private as it was, I still left as little as possible of the signs of my work around when I closed shop for the day. It was a tedious process but something that had to be done before I left. On the outside chance that someone gained entry, they would not know exactly what I was working on. The university was privy to my work but had no idea I was taking it to a much higher level—no idea at all that I was building a time machine! Some limited findings would be released here and there, but they would never see me achieve success with the real thing—meaning animal then human time travel!

I locked up the lab then went upstairs to my office and proceeded to secure my laptop and all the written research in the safe. I was old-school. A lot of my research was jotted down in notepads. I kept the notebook with the equations Ron would help me with tonight.

# Chapter Eleven

At a little past seven, my friend arrived.

"How's it hanging, old man?"

"It's still there, baby face," I replied. "I see you've got the goods."

"Of course, the usual."

"Come on in, bring it out to the kitchen."

And as expected, Ron's facetious reply was, "Well, I wasn't gonna stand in the doorway all night."

"Come on in, smart-ass, have a seat."

So we chowed down on the Chinese food and cracked open a few cold ones to wash it all down. That place in Winthrop where Ron gets it is definitely the best—man it's good! After eating, we retired to my rather small living room off the kitchen and got down to business.

"So what-a-ya got for me, Pilgrim?" Ron asked in his awesome John Wayne voice.

"Well, there-ya-go," I said as I handed him the notebook—my impersonation still needed a bit of work—pointing to the page in question. "I need a little help with that left page. It's a bit beyond my ability. I think I have the sequencing screwed up too."

Ron looked surprised. "These aren't the numbers you usually work with. Look at the energy needed to generate these results!"

Ignoring Ron's curiosity, I continued, "I need help with the complex derivatives mostly. Should I expect logical results with these constructs?"

"Yeah, everything looks good. Let me work out these two problems though. Give me a few minutes," Ron said, looking up at me briefly then back down at the notebook.

"I'll grab us a couple more beers," I said.

"Sounds good."

A moment later I returned with Ron's beer then slowly wandered the apartment as I sipped on mine. I had made a promise to myself long ago that I was going this alone. No one would ever know about my work until I thought it was practical to tell them. Honestly, I doubted that I would ever reveal my secret—that is of course if I actually did achieve human time travel, although by all indications, I now firmly believed I could do it. Even my good friend Ron could not be privy to it. As I mentioned before, the world wasn't ready for this. Even the scientists or governments with good intentions could create a chain of events too crazy to even think about, never mind the nuts of this world getting their hands on it. It would all lead down the road to greed, corruption, and most likely world domination by some evil, power-hungry faction. No—it will never happen. The secret will be mine and mine alone. This is why I knew that I was taking a chance showing Ron the mathematical theory. The dots really didn't connect yet, but he was smart enough to know that this was something different, something big.

Ron looked up as I was returning to the living room. "Okay, ol' buddy, all set. That'll be five big ones for my services."

"Sure," I said, "but you'll have to wait till Friday when I get paid off by my bookie."

He laughed and then explained his computations. I looked down at what he had done and said, "All right, I see—I did have the sequencing screwed up, what's this...oh, okay, I got it. Nice job, Ron, thanks."

"Yeah, yeah, yeah, I know you physics guys can't handle the math," Ron said, smiling, then added, "I'm always here for you, buddy."

"You know I don't take you for granted, I really don't. I appreciate your help with the math I can't grasp."

"No problem, I like doing this stuff—that's why I teach it, but grab me one more beer and we'll call it even."

Ron was wearing a sly smile when I came back with the beer. "Sit down here and tell me what you're doing."

"What I'm doing is sitting here with you having a beer, what do you mean what am I doing?"

"You know what I mean, Mark. That math, those equations—what are you working on?"

Without hesitating, I said, "Well, you've seen my old research, this is just beefed up for larger bodies."

"Yeah, and those are some mean numbers and energy levels… you're not up to real time travel yet, are you?"

"Come on, be serious, Ron, of course not. When I say larger bodies, I don't mean humans, just larger quantum particles. This is all theory anyway, just mathematical theory. I don't think time travel will ever be possible for humans…well, not in our lifetime anyway. There are too many obstacles that prevent it. But I'll keep hammering away, clearing some of the hurdles on the way to that end—that will be the thrust of my research."

"Well, anyway, if you figure out a way, I want to be the first to know. We could go together—wouldn't that be something, you and I witnessing the construction of the pyramids or maybe even walking with Jesus," Ron said with a boyish enthusiasm.

"Yeah, that would definitely be a trip, but seriously, Ron, like I said, you won't see it in our lifetime." Inside, I breathed a sigh of relief, believing that I had successfully navigated around the truth with my friend.

Ron stayed a while longer. We watched a little TV and talked about our plans for golf over the weekend. At about eleven, we called it a night.

Back in the lab on Monday morning, I went over the calculations that Ron had helped me with and began applying them to the final developmental stages of the time machine. I didn't have any classes till later that afternoon, so I had plenty of time for my work. As I progressed along, I sang out loud to Jim Croce's *His Greatest Hits* album. I loved his songs—it always brought me back when I listened to them. It was an unbelievable tragedy when he died in 1973 at the young age of thirty, in full stride and hugely popular. I felt like a kid again, singing along, full of energy and impatient excitement. The day flew by as did the successive days and weeks.

# Chapter Twelve

In the months ahead, I plodded on, working tirelessly until one day, that glorious day, I had finally finished what I had set out to do years ago. I had accomplished what millions of others could only dream of. I had constructed a fully functioning, working time machine! It was January 11, 2013. I was extremely proud of myself and felt like shouting it out to the world: "Look what I have done, look what I have fucking accomplished. I have made history!" But of course, I couldn't tell a soul. I had to keep this excitement, this grand sense of achievement, bottled up inside. I had to simply keep a lid on it.

Anyway, I wish old Einstein could see me now—shit, even he'd be impressed.

In the early testing stages, mice were used because of the obvious hazards, and after many trips without harm to them, I decided it was time for me to give it a whirl. I would activate the time machine in the lab for my departures, and I had created a handheld device that signaled the machine for my return trips.

Let me restate how time travel works with humans. Traveling to a time period before you were born or after you died is very straightforward. Although, as mentioned previously, traveling to a time period where you already exist is a different matter. Two of the same person cannot exist at the same time in the same universe. This is common sense but also the physics that keeps the universe in sync. So I can't go back to an earlier time or ahead into the future and coexist with myself. This would be impossible. I can't go walk around my own past or future and see myself because there is not and never will be two of me—except in a parallel universe, but I'll talk about that later.

So once again, the way it works—if I attempt to go to a time location where I already exist, I supplant my past or future self. In other words, if traveling to my past, my present-day self basically takes up residence in my former body while my former self goes into a limbo state. So I would not change at all except in outward appearance. In every way I am the same person, but I would be living in my younger body. When I return to the present, I will return to exactly how I left: in my original body, thinking and feeling as I did when I left. My former self will return to its original state also, to equalize the equation, if you will.

I began to shy away from trips into my future. I did not want to find out when I would die.

So I began to make small leaps into my past, gradually traveling further and further back. Much was learned in these early trips, and I felt fine on my return with no unpleasant side effects except for an occasional mild headache. But, and this was a very important *but*, after several longer duration trips, I discovered that I did change… gradually. Let me explain. As I spent time in the past, my former self would gradually reclaim its body! This realization terrified me. As the days went by living in my past, I began feeling and behaving like my younger self again but at the same time having the presence of mind that I had come back from the future. My past and future selves were linked, allowing me to literally reexperience my past life in this duality of selves. This was a gradual process, but the end result was undeniable. The obvious danger involved would be staying too long and not remembering I had come back in time at all. I essentially would be erased and become my former self without even realizing it.

I knew there must exist a point of no return (PONR), but I couldn't know exactly when this would take place. From my trips, I realized that it probably wasn't much longer than three weeks spent in the past. The PONR is just that. When this point is reached, there is no going back and my future world (the one I came back from) would be changed, no longer existing in the way I knew it. To what degree, I couldn't possibly know. If I got back earlier than the PONR, before the transformation was complete, I would return as I had left, with no traces of my former self remaining. However, as explained above, after the PONR, the future I knew and traveled back from would be gone forever. It would be there but would now be an altered future. I would slowly be creating this new future as I relived my past. You might ask why this would happen if my former self had reclaimed its body. It's because I stayed long enough in my past to leave residual traces of my future self behind, thus influencing the further development of my younger self.

Not that I would be traveling outside my universe, or in other words, to a parallel universe, it is worth mentioning just what is meant by one. The parallel universe theory posits that there are multiple, if not infinite, universes for each person. In our daily lives, millions of choices and decisions present themselves to us. For example, as you speed home from work, you approach a yellow traffic light about to turn red. You then proceed to slow down and stop. In another universe, just as real as the first universe, you run the light and arrive home one minute and twenty seconds earlier. In another, you run the light and are involved in a serious car accident, and on and on. These universes are branches or parallel universes that exist separately from each other—but do indeed exist! So yes, there are multiple, or to be more accurate, an infinite number of *you* existing simultaneously but in separate universes.

To make sure everyone is on the same page, when I travel back to my past, I am not creating or traveling to a parallel universe. I am staying within my original universe. I am simply taking up residence in the body of my former self until I return to the present, or God forbid, my former self reclaims its body.

So as mentioned above, I discovered that as the days went by living in my past, I gradually changed. Before the first week was out, I would begin to feel and act the way I did back then but on the surface knew I was transforming. For the most part, I was completely aware that I was living in my past but began feeling and acting like my former self simultaneously. It's like getting drunk but not totally smashed: you are self-aware but allow yourself to be caught up in the moment. You somehow allow yourself to do and say things that you wouldn't normally do or say. Your inhibitions are down, and you *go with the flow.* So I was gradually being influenced or controlled by my former self but had not yet been taken over completely—these feelings were just *coming attractions.*

By the second week, I was well into the change, my mind waffling back and forth between past and future selves. I was still aware of my adult self, but now my former self was pretty much in control on the surface. So I wasn't as much concerned about getting back to my reality in the future but more preoccupied with the happenings I was experiencing in my past. Although, the *older* me knew to some degree just what was going on. This duality of selves would exist until my former self totally reclaimed its body.

By the third week, I was almost completely transformed into my former self. This is why I carried with me a note that I had written to myself, to remind me who I was and the importance of returning to my future before the past reclaimed me. In past trips, when I had stayed close to three weeks, the notes that I had written to myself were at times mysterious. I didn't always remember writing them. It took a concentrated effort to make sense of what they meant and where they came from. On more than one occasion, when I was nearing the three-week mark, I had come close to not coming back at all. If not for those notes, those reminders, I wouldn't have made it back. I never would have signaled the machine to bring me home. This is why I decided to keep all my future trips to no more than ten days. This would give me a cushion of over a week so that there would be no mishaps.

So I would have to be very careful and vigilant during my trips and get myself back before my past self reclaimed its body. If I stayed too long, my former self would take over and create a new future in the universe that I came from.

Against everything I knew was true, I decided to confide in Ron—I simply had to. He had to know about my travels because of the potential risks. I had already made multiple trips knowing that I could possibly be stranded in the past.

Of course he was over the top with excitement.

"I knew it, I knew it when I helped you with those computations, I knew it, you sly fox," he said, and of course, he wanted to travel right away. I told Ron that I was going on one more trip, and when I got back, he could go. We could also travel together eventually if I got my ex involved as a backup for us. This was a consideration, but I doubted that I'd actually go through with it. I also couldn't warn him enough to keep a lid on it. As I explained earlier, no one must know, and he was only privy because of the dangers involved. So Ron became well versed in the use of the machine in case I didn't get myself back. He was instructed to bring me back at twelve noon exactly ten days after I left if I hadn't returned on my own by then. He understood the implications of me staying too long in the past, so the ten-day rule was a hard and fast one that he must adhere to. We went through a few trial runs, and Ron got me back safely on every occasion without my use of the signaling device.

By the end of May 2014, all the experimental trips had been taken and all the research from those trips was complete. I had gathered and analyzed all the information I needed. I now wanted to take one special trip for myself before I let Ron travel. I planned to leave soon. I just wasn't sure what time period I wanted to visit.

# Chapter Thirteen

*Sunday, 8 June 2014*

Across the street from the Winthrop Golf Club, demolition was in full swing at the site of our old high school. As we waited to tee off at the first hole, Ron and I had front-row seats for the destruction of our alma mater. The school was built in 1966, and now nearing fifty years old, someone decided it had to be replaced. We both had graduated from Winthrop High, so we couldn't help but reminisce. Ron had graduated in 1993, many years after me, but we both had walked the same halls, had a few of the same teachers, and ate the same shitty food from the cafeteria.

The starter got our attention to get going as the group in front of us had already teed off and was out of the way well down the fairway. We both hit nice shots straight out, but Ron's ball had traveled a bit farther, as it invariably does. That was okay. I'd get him with my short game. I grabbed my pull cart, and off we went.

It was now just past eleven in the morning. With a temperature in the mid-seventies and a slight breeze, it was a perfect day for golf. My lower back had loosened up from the usual morning pain and stiffness. This pain and stiffness is caused by degenerative disc disease. I go through a morning routine of lying on a heating pad for fifteen minutes then do a series of stretches. As the day progresses, my back usually loosens up. Through the years, many of the doctors I had seen about my back suggested walking or swimming. Both these aerobic exercises help keep the weight off, which decreases the stress on the lower back, and increase blood flow and nutrients to the area that support healing. I've always enjoyed walking anyway, so I walk the course in good weather and swim in the not-so-nice weather.

Time seemed to pass quickly that day as it always does on the golf course. We soon caught up to the group in front of us as we made it to the sixth hole. It was a short par three leading back toward the clubhouse, and our high school was now in sight again. We sat on a bench behind the tee box, resting and chatting quietly so as not to bother the group on the tee.

"I can't believe it's been over twenty years since I got out of there," said Ron, pointing at the school.

"Lot longer for me, baby-face."

"Yeah, you graduated when Kennedy was still in office, right?"

"Real funny," I said, "but that's impossible. The school hadn't been built yet when JFK was president."

"Yeah, but you're still an old man," Ron continued.

"Let's see how old I look after eighteen holes. I believe I'm whipping your butt already."

"I'm right on your tail, and I should have you long before eighteen," Ron rebutted then changed the subject as he looked over at the high school. "That's where you met Lena, wasn't it?"

"No, we actually met in ninth grade, in junior high, but we were still going out when we entered sophomore year in high school," I said.

"Do you think you'll ever get over her?"

I paused briefly, thinking of that girl from long ago. "Well, I don't love her anymore, if that's what you mean. I'd be really messed up if I still did. But she'll always have a place in my heart though." Thinking back, I could see her photographically in my mind—like it was yesterday, forty-one years ago and so clear. Then I went on, "It was um…it was a special time for me, Ron. I was in love for the first time… I was just a kid, but I was really in love. Everything came together that summer, everything seemed perfect. I was so happy." I was staring straight ahead, but I wasn't seeing what was in front of me. My mind was back there, and I didn't realize that I had stopped talking.

"Hey, Mark, you all right?" Ron asked as he reached over and gently shook my shoulder.

"What...yeah, sorry," I said as I snapped back to the present. "Talking about her really sent me back."

"Yeah really, you were far away for a few minutes."

The group in front of us was just making it to the green. We wouldn't be able to hit for a few more minutes, so I continued on about Lena.

"You know, Ron, I've never met anyone who affected me the way that girl did back then. I have never in my life wanted to be with someone more than I had wanted to be with Lena. It sounds kinda corny, but she was the first thing I thought of when I woke up and my last thought before I fell asleep. I thought we would marry and spend the rest of our lives together. We were only fifteen, but we had actually talked about getting married in the future."

"Really...you guys talked about getting married—at fifteen you were planning your future together! Shit, Mark, I still don't think about getting married, and I'm how old?"

"Yeah, I know, my old friend, Ron—the man who will never tie the knot," I said, smiling.

"Well, never say never, but at fifteen...I think I was still playing with my GI Joes."

# Chapter Fourteen

Later that night, watching TV on the couch, I mulled over where and when I wanted to travel to. This would be the first trip I could just relax and take things in: no analysis, no self-monitoring, or otherwise researching any aspect of the trip. It would be like a vacation—no work. I turned over in my mind countless historical events that I'd like to witness but decided I'd have plenty of time for those types of trips later on. I just wanted to relax and get away.

My mind then drifted back to what Ron and I had talked about earlier today on the golf course—the time in 1973 when Lena and I were in love. I thought again of that innocent period of my life where happiness was the norm, a simple time without the complications of life as an adult. Maybe this is the time period I should go back to then, a time in my life where everything seemed perfect, everything fell into place. And I knew if I traveled back there, I would again have feelings for Lena as my former self began reclaiming its body. I could experience that happiness and intensity of being in love for the first time once again! I found myself saying it out loud, "Why not go back?" I let the idea linger for a while—and it felt good.

Lost in my thoughts, I began planning. By July of 1973, Lena and I were beyond those early, awkward moments of a typical teenage romance and enjoying the summer before our sophomore year in high school. No homework, no job, and we were spending the majority of our time together. I thought that if I were to go back to 1973, then July or maybe August would be a logical choice. As mentioned earlier, ten days and no longer, and I won't go back to try to alter the past, just visit it.

I became so engrossed with my plan that I decided I wanted to leave as soon as possible. One day of preparation and the following day I'd be off. There would be much to do tomorrow, but I should be able to get it all done so that I'd be ready the following day. Okay, I would leave for 1973 in less than two days—June 10!

I looked over at the clock on the cable box and was surprised to see that it was closing in on midnight. Jesus, time had flown by since I had lain down. I decided I'd better call it a night and start in tomorrow with the real planning for this trip. I got off the couch and went to bed.

# Chapter Fifteen

*Monday, 9 June 2014*

I rose early, and after making myself a big breakfast with plenty of coffee, I started in on my pretrip preparations. I didn't need much money for the trip—how much money does a fourteen-year-old boy living at home with his parent really need? I'd bring two hundred of the *old money* (printed by the treasury prior to 1973) with me—probably more than I needed but better to have a little extra. Not that I had any immediate commitments with the university, but I would notify the department head, Kevin Costigan, that I wouldn't be available for a couple of weeks. I also needed to call my ex-wife and daughter to let them know I'd be away for a while. Most importantly though, I'd tell Ron what I had planned and make sure he would be available should something go wrong. I didn't anticipate any problems, and I trusted the technology 100 percent. Redundant systems were built into the machine if one or more failed, but if I couldn't or didn't signal the time machine to retrieve me, then what good was all that technology. Therefore, as I mentioned earlier, Ron was my emergency backup—if I hadn't returned in ten days, he should bring me back.

I decided that I would set the machine for July 15, 1973, at 3:00 a.m. At this hour, I should be in my bed at home. This would make for the smoothest transition into the past that I could think of. I didn't want to arrive abruptly, finding myself thrust into some awkward situation.

The day flew by as I took care of all the pretrip tasks that had to be completed. I had talked to Ron, and he was on board, at the ready should I require his assistance. I made sure he still had his key to my lab if he needed it. He assured me that he had it. Ron really wanted to come by the lab tomorrow to see me off but was tied up with a must-go department meeting in the morning. He joked over the phone about traveling to Scotland before the game of golf was invented so that we could invent it ourselves.

Before long, I was eating supper and felt pretty worn out. This was good because I wanted to go to bed early to get a good night sleep prior to my trip. By 9:00 p.m., I was in bed. I turned out the lights expecting sleep to come quick—but it didn't. My mind was racing. Apprehensive thoughts and countless questions swirled in my head: *Had I done everything in preparation for this trip? Am I going to feel excessively awkward with my family and Lena? How will they react to me? Will I be able to pull it off? I might look the same, but can I come across as a teenager to everyone I interact with? Okay,* I thought, *just settle down. Remember, you're going back there to have fun, so relax and have a good time—think of it as a vacation,* I told myself so I'd calm down.

So I tried to get comfortable in bed once again, but it was useless. Over and over, it was the same routine—getting into a comfortable position only to move again five minutes later. I just couldn't seem to quiet my mind or still my body. I finally gave up and got out of bed. I needed to take a leak anyway.

I returned with a glass of water and sat on the edge of my bed—my mind alert and active, like a thousand bees working in a hive. I began to think about something that I had pondered before but never acted on—making a little money with my knowledge of the past. I know what you're thinking. I could easily buy a winning lottery ticket by looking at past winning numbers or place a sports bet on a known outcome, but I wanted to do something different, something fun. Then the thought occurred to me—what about the stock market. I could buy some stock real cheap in 1973 from a company, some big company that would do very well over the years—a company like Coca-Cola perhaps. I went over to my desk and fired up my MacBook. I researched Coke and found out that the market price in mid-July of 1973 was roughly $1.50 per share. If I invested one thousand dollars, that would buy me about six hundred shares allowing for commission taken out for the sale. Between 1973 and 2014, the stock would split six times, actually the amount of shares would triple in the 1986 split. So in 2014, I would be holding approximately fifty-seven thousand six hundred shares. At the average market price of forty-two dollars per share, the stock would then be worth an amazing 2.4 million dollars. This would be more than enough money to make life comfortable and to easily pay for my daughter's college tuition in a few years.

I returned the glass to the sink, and as I walked back over to my desk, I realized that I'd probably be too young to purchase stock in 1973. I could have my mother do it for me though. I'd have to convince her to let me withdraw one thousand dollars from my savings account for the purchase but actually leave the money in the account. I'd bring it back instead so as not to upset my 1973 finances—that would be tampering with the future.

I knew I had about two thousand dollars in my account in 1973. My mother or father had never touched that money, and I wouldn't either. Even through all those lean years, every cent that I had ever saved remained in that account, and that's where it would stay. It had been accumulated from delivering newspapers before school, cutting lawns in the summer, and shoveling snow as a kid during those snowy New England winters. It arrived in birthday cards, Christmas cards, and other cards for those special occasions. Any money that had found its way to me also found its way into that account. My parents wanted us all to go to college, so we were taught that saving our money along with keeping our nose to the grindstone at school would get us there, and it did.

So I'd need twelve hundred bucks of the *old money* for the stock and spending. I'd have to check my travel money in the safe to make sure I have that much, but I was pretty sure I did. By now it was already past midnight. I should have been asleep hours ago, so once again I returned to my bed to give it another shot. I picked up a novel from the nightstand that I'd been reading. I enjoyed reading, and reading in bed usually made me tired. Hopefully this would rest my mind and allow sleep to come. So I opened up *Around the World in Eighty Days* by the great Jules Verne. I had just started reading it yesterday, so I had plenty of pages ahead of me to make me sleepy—hopefully. The main character, a wealthy, eccentric Englishman named Phileas Fogg, had just bet half his fortune that he could travel around the world in eighty days. The wager with his fellow Reform Club members was twenty thousand English pounds, an astounding amount of money for 1872—the equivalent today of about five million US dollars.

So I read a few chapters and finally put the book down at about 12:45 a.m. I tossed and turned for a while, and the last time I looked over at the clock, it read 12:57. Shortly after that, I must have drifted off.

# Chapter Sixteen

*Tuesday, 10 June 2014*

I arrived at the lab at nine the next morning. I was somewhat tired from not getting the sleep I needed last night, but my excitement about leaving today perked me up. The two cups of coffee I had earlier at the house didn't hurt either.

I ran a systems check on the time machine, and everything was a go for my departure. I remained at the console a bit longer to write that all-important reminder note to myself that I would keep on my person at all times. As I mentioned earlier, the note would help me remember my mission through the ten-day period as my former self tried to regain control. Before writing the note, I had pushed some paperwork and notes aside to clear a little room on that rather small console surface. In doing so, the signaling device happened to get brushed off the back edge and down behind the console—unbeknownst to me!

I then went back out to my desk near the front of the lab where I tidied up then nuked and finished a cup of coffee I had made when I first arrived. After checking the front door, making sure it was locked, I proceeded again to the back of the lab and the time machine. I double-checked the loading dock door. It was secure. *Okay, I guess that's it,* I thought, so I went into the locker room and stripped down naked. There would be no reason to wear any clothes because I would just have to get rid of them anyway. I stowed my clothes and personal belongings, except the money and the note, in the locker, then returned to the machine.

Now standing inside the time machine in my birthday suit, I was ready to go. I had the twelve hundred dollars, the note in my hand, and nothing else. I had done this many times now, so I was anticipating the sensations on my body and the mild side effects I would experience after I had arrived. The computer was programmed, and the countdown had begun—the event was set in motion. Just as in my earlier trips, I experienced the sudden jolt of pressure on my entire body, the dizzying light-headedness, and then nothing—as if I had fallen asleep.

> *Take me back*
> *To the world gone away*
> *Memories*
> *Seem like yesterday*
> —Chicago, "Old Days"

# PART 2

# Chapter One

*Sunday, 15 July 1973*

I arrived as expected: groggy, the way you feel when you first wake up but with a mild headache, not bad for a leap of forty-one years through time. It took only a couple eye blinks to realize that I had made it. I was in my small twin bed in the old house. I sat up quietly and looked around. It took a little while. Then my eyes adjusted to the darkness. There was another twin bed next to mine. Of course—it was my younger brother Billy's bed, and he was in it.

After getting over the initial excitement of my arrival, I lay back down and attempted to go to sleep. It didn't come right away, but eventually I drifted off. It couldn't have taken very long because it seemed like just a few minutes later it was light outside—I must have slept three or four hours.

The covers of the bed next to mine were thrown back. Billy was young, and he was always up early in the morning. Today was no exception.

I quickly remembered that I had arrived sans clothing, so I made haste over to the dresser and found a pair of underpants in one of the top drawers. I put them on then went over to the dormer window, drew the curtain, and looked outside.

"I'm here. 1973," I said out loud as I stared in a kind of dreamy way, almost not believing it myself, then couldn't help the smile that came to my face. As I walked away from the window, I looked down at my new body. I was shocked to see how much thinner I was. I certainly must have weighed a lot less. My thoughts escaped my mouth as I said out loud, "Jesus, I'm so skinny—I feel so light." I then proceeded to jump around the room in my underwear in this light but firm and also tanned young body. I had none of the usual morning back pain or any stiffness for that matter in any part of my body.

"Shit, this feels good," I said. As I sprang up once again and then came down hard on the bare wooden floor, I heard a loud voice coming from downstairs. It sounded like my mother—shit, my mother! I ran over to the door, opened it a smidgen, and peeked out. I felt like an intruder in the very house I had grown up in. As I leaned out, my mother yelled, "Mark, what are you doing up there?" I quickly replied that I was sorry for the noise and that I'd be down in a minute. Shit, I thought, this was going to be awkward. Let me see, how old would my mother be now. With a quick calculation, I determined that she was thirty-six years old. I'm old enough to be her father for God's sake.

I found my old plaid bathrobe in the closet and put it on. As I made my way down the stairs, I wondered how I would react to seeing my family in these earlier years. I warned myself not to act too surprised because the changes would be dramatic. Then I stopped dead in my tracks on the fourth step as it came to me that I had not brought the signaling device with me! How could I be so fucking stupid. I had taken over twenty trips prior to this one, and I had never forgotten it. The device was my lifeline for God's sake, and I knew—even if I wanted to—I could not construct another signaling device here in 1973! The advanced electronic components that made up the device weren't even invented yet. There was no way I could get my hands on that stuff.

How could this have happened? It was on the console when I was doing my systems check; I'm sure of it. Why didn't I pick it up; why didn't I have it in my hand when I left? I then ran back upstairs to my room and tried to calm down. I went over to the bed and sat on the edge. With my knees supporting my elbows, I brought my face down into my cradled palms and began messaging my forehead with my fingertips. *Okay*, I thought, *it's not a disaster, you still have Ron as a backup, and thank God for that. I'll just have to bide my time and hope he comes through, he should, he knows the routine: If I'm not back by twelve noon exactly ten days after I leave, then he brings me back. So at twelve noon on the twenty-fifth, Ron should retrieve me. He brought me back three times when he was learning to use the machine. Yeah, everything should be fine, don't get all worked up over this, Ron will come through—he had better!*

*It's not so bad,* I thought as I made my way back down the stairs. After reaching the first floor, I headed for the bathroom down the hall. I closed the door and took a minute to prepare myself for the *new me* before looking in the mirror.

I slowly gazed in then jumped back immediately, covering my mouth to suppress a shriek that escaped me. As I took a second look, I hardly recognized myself. I now had a full head of wavy brown hair that sort of flipped up just below the ears. I couldn't find one wrinkle or furrow on my teenage face. Gone were the crow's feet around my eyes. No facial hair or any of that bothersome hair growing in the ears or nose. I bared my teeth, and again, the mirror was kind to me. My teeth were white, not as yet yellowed from years of smoking and drinking coffee, and by God, no double chin either. I had a touch of acne but nothing to write home about. *Damn, I was—no, I am a good-looking kid, what a fucking change, holy shit,* I thought, and then I laughed out loud.

As I backed away from the mirror, my right heel came down hard on the scale behind me, lifting the opposite end up. I lost my balance momentarily as I took my weight off the scale, which caused it to come crashing down loudly on the tile floor. This abrupt and startling misstep angered me, and I suppressed a few choice words as I gathered myself. *Settle down,* I told myself, *relax!* I took a few deep breaths and left the bathroom.

# Chapter Two

I made my way to the kitchen for some breakfast and a look at my family of the past.

As I entered the room and my gaze fell upon them, I was floored. The sight of my family thoroughly shocked me. I took a seat and averted my eyes, looking down at the table. It was overwhelming, too much to take in at once. They looked so different, so freaking young. It was affecting me more than I had anticipated.

I finally got ahold of myself and raised my head as I glanced around the table. Seated there for breakfast were my mother, who was at the opposite end of the table from me and my younger brother, Billy, and my older sister, Joanne, sitting next to each other, diagonally across from my mother and me.

My mother looked great. I'm used to seeing her in her debilitated state. She has a disease called polymyositis, a condition in which the muscles deteriorate, thus weakening parts of the body. It went undiagnosed for years till one of many doctors finally diagnosed it by way of biopsy. At first she lost strength in her thigh muscles as the disease took hold, and then eventually she required a walker because her core muscles were too weakened to support an upright posture.

Even the muscles in her esophagus had been affected, resulting in trouble swallowing. A medication called Imuran was taken initially to lessen the inflammation and keep the disease at bay. Presently, in 2014, she gets rituxan therapy by way of infusion twice a year. So my mother gets by, but not without difficulty. Right now, as I look at her, she's the picture of health—so young and strong. It wouldn't be until the late 1990s when she would start showing signs of this crippling disease.

My gaze turned to Billy. Let me see. He would be twelve years old now, close to three years my junior. Full of restless energy and raring to go, he couldn't eat quick enough to get outside and play with his friends.

Joanne is a year older than me, turning sixteen next month. She is pretty with black hair and a bit taller than the average girl her age.

"Good morning," I finally said. My mother and sister returned the greeting, but Billy was preoccupied with finding the prize at the bottom of the cereal box. He may have been in a rush to get outside, but the prize in the cereal was something that had to be found before his day commenced. I couldn't keep myself from blurting out, "Howya doin', Ma?" It was hard to believe what I was seeing, and I just wanted to hear her talk.

"I'm fine, Mark, did you sleep okay last night? And what was all that noise upstairs, and then just now in the bathroom?"

I hesitated while I stared at her for a moment. "Oh...fine, I slept well, thanks for asking. The noise...um, I guess I'm just being klutzy this morning, sorry."

"Okay, relax, Mark, just relax," I said under my breath.

Joanne then got my mother's attention. She asked if it would be all right to go into town (Boston) with Shawna to do some shopping. Shawna was Joanne's friend who lived in the neighborhood. They were both cashiers at a local supermarket in Revere, one of two towns that bordered Winthrop. Mom said it would be fine as long as she got home by six for supper.

"Billy, what are you doing today?" my mother asked.

"I'm going over Steven's house."

"Come home for lunch at noontime, and you can go back over if it's all right with Steven's parents, okay?"

"Oh, Ma, why can't I just eat over there?"

"Because we're not a charity case. You'll come home and eat here or you're not going at all, understand?"

Billy replied with a reluctant, "Okay, Ma."

My mother and father had separated in 1972, so Mom was the final word. We obeyed her for the most part, albeit not always so enthusiastically. She was tough but fair, and we all loved her.

"I know where you'll be today, Mark," my mother stated with a crooked smile on her face.

I didn't have to figure out what she meant by that. At this time in my life, I lived and breathed Lena. Trying to make myself sound a bit younger, I said, "Yeah, I'll give Lena a call soon and find out what's goin' on today."

"Well, you be home by suppertime too."

"No problem, Ma, I'll be home at six," I said.

Billy bolted from the table as soon he finished, making haste to begin his day, my mother yelling after him to be home at noon. Joanne left the table shortly after, telling my mother that she was leaving as soon as she took a shower and dressed.

That left my mother and me to share breakfast together. It was really nice just sitting there and talking to her. I grabbed a big bowl of cereal and some toast, which is still my morning staple.

"Looks like a nice day out there," I said as I sat back down.

"It's seventy already, and it's supposed to reach the mid-eighties according to the radio," my mother added.

I looked over at the counter near the refrigerator and noticed the radio playing softly. That old reliable thing, it always came in clear and crisp if you had it right on the station. It was a GE model from the 1960s. A rectangular white plastic box with that big dial on it, and it was now playing Bobby Goldsboro's hit song from 1968, "Honey."

My mother had a popular music station on, probably WRKO, an AM station that played a lot of top-forty hits. She liked some of those popular songs that this type of station played, but mostly the political folk music of the sixties that was sprinkled in: singers like Joan Baez, Carol King, Simon and Garfunkel, and others who wrote meaningful songs about the times. Their voices were soft, but their lyrics were powerful. My mother was progressive, not stuck in the 1950s like most mothers her age. This was due to the fact that she was back in school and also worked with many people younger than herself, people of the younger generation.

The younger generation of the 1960s and early 1970s had a new voice, a voice that questioned the status quo of the establishment.

They were against the Vietnam War and many of our government's policies. They separated themselves from the older generation, used drugs, and had slogans like "Make Peace, Not War." They were of a generation that witnessed the assassination of their president, his brother, and Martin Luther King Jr., all within a five-year period. They lived in the most revolutionary times since the Civil War. There were race riots and all types of Civil Rights issues to deal with. The Vietnam War raged on into the early seventies when this generation's distrust in the government was at an all-time high. The music that came out of this era, just like the times, was revolutionary and political. There were bloody protests in the streets and protest music being played on our radios. By late March of 1973, we ended our military involvement in Vietnam and music was beginning to change, but we weren't at the end of the problems with our government: the Watergate hearings were in full swing, which would lead to the disgraceful resignation of the president of the United States, Richard Nixon, the following year.

By this time, my mother was attending Boston State College full-time. She took courses right through the summer and worked part-time at the school in the athletic department. Our family received monetary aid from AFDC (Aid for Families with Dependent Children) to help make ends meet. I talked with her about school and what she thought of the courses she was taking, if she was tired from carrying this immense load of family, work, and school. This was something I had never considered the first time around—kids just don't get the sacrifices their parents make for them. My mother was a strong woman to be able to handle the load she carried day after day.

"Sure, I'm always tired and it's tough, but, Mark, you just have to deal with your responsibilities. We'll never get ahead if I just sit back. I don't want to ever see you struggle, but if you find yourself in a similar situation, I'd expect you to give it everything you've got also. No accomplishment is worth anything without hard work."

"I know, Ma, and I'm proud of you." Right after I said this, I realized that it probably came out a little too adult sounding, but what the hell, it needed to be said.

"Thanks, Mark, I love you too, and that was nice of you to say."

This one-on-one with my mother reinforced how I already felt about her. I admired as much as I loved her. Mom was a great role model for her kids, and she still had many years ahead of her where she would accomplish great things besides raising six children on her own. She would go on to earn her bachelor's degree then her master's, and eventually start up and operate her own successful business. Mom has an easy way about herself. She is comfortable around people, and they are comfortable with her. She genuinely cares for others, and the people she meets know this. They are drawn to her.

"I better get goin', Ma," I said, and then before I left the room, I went over and kissed my mother and told her that I loved her.

# Chapter Three

I was able to relax a bit while showering now that I had met most of my *early family* and not one of them detected anything unusual about me—I don't think. I was out of the shower quickly and looking for something to change into for a warm July day. I found a pair of plaid shorts and assorted short-sleeved shirts in my dresser. In my underwear drawer, there were some plain white T-shirts, so I decided to wear just a T-shirt with the shorts. The shorts were an astounding thirty-inch waist, and they didn't feel tight at all—a far cry from my normal thirty-eight-inch waist of the future. I had plenty of white socks to go with my old Keds sneakers, which I found at the foot of the bed. While looking through the rest of my clothes, I found my dungarees (what we called blue jeans in this part of the country) in the bottom drawer. I laughed when I pulled a pair out and the flared leg and wide-pant-leg bottoms were revealed. They were appropriately called bell-bottoms, and that's what all the young people wore. The clothing styles were all coming back to me now. When I entered my sophomore year in high school, which would be in less than two months from now, I would be clad in, get this, a wide-collared polyester dress shirt, cuffed bell-bottom slacks with a wide belt, and two-inch platform shoes. Can you picture Elton John on the cover of his "Yellow Brick Road" album? I would be looking something like that—wow!

On my way back downstairs, I realized I didn't know Lena's phone number. I knew she had an unlisted number, and I believe I had it memorized back then. I didn't think I had it written down anywhere, but I wasn't really sure. I turned around on the landing and went back to my room to search. I found my old, thin wallet in my junk drawer, but her number wasn't in it. There wasn't much of anything in it for that matter: no license yet, no credit cards of course, no social security card—none of the adult things that over-stuffed a man's wallet. What I did find was a clipped photo of Lena and me, a ten-dollar bill, and a small piece of scrap paper with a series of numbers written on it: 10-24-26. I thought for a minute then realized this must be the combination to my bike lock.

Before I left the room, I suddenly remembered the twelve-hundred bucks and the note that I brought back with me. I pulled back the covers, and there were the bills, strewn about along with the note. I put two hundred dollars of the money and the note in my wallet, which wasn't so thin anymore. I hid the thousand for the stock under some things in my junk drawer, the top-left dresser drawer.

Since I forgot to bring back the signaling device, the note couldn't really help me now, although it would serve as a reminder of who I really was and that I should try to focus on this during the transformation while I waited for Ron to retrieve me. I tucked the wallet into the front-left pocket of my shorts and headed for the door.

So I went back downstairs with little hope of finding Lena's number there. I most likely would have kept it in a private place, but I decided to look around down here anyway. I checked our local phone book to see if I had written it in there, then the drawers of the hutch, but in both cases came up empty. Then it came to me that Alicia would most likely have it. Alicia Ferrier was a friend of Lena who also lived on my street. She didn't hang with our group, but she would later in the fall. Alicia helped get Lena and me together. She had told me that Lena liked me and invited her to come down to our neighborhood on several occasions for a chance meeting. As a result of one of those visits, Lena and I became a couple. Anyway, I'll have to figure out some stupid excuse why I needed Lena's number, why I didn't know it by heart or have it written down somewhere. And that's not the hard part. I was beginning to think that the call to Lena would be.

I am a fifty-five-year-old professor, not a nervous fourteen-year-old kid, so you wouldn't think I'd be nervous about calling a fifteen-year-old girl, but I was. I came back to visit my teenage years and the happy time I had with my girlfriend and friends—this shouldn't make me uneasy. I guess it just felt awkward, and I wasn't sure what to expect. I probably had always called first anyway, but as awkward as that would be, it would be easier to call first and make some conversation before I actually saw Lena face-to-face.

"You leaving now?" my mother asked as I was heading out the door.

"I'll be back in a few minutes. I have to talk to Alicia before I leave for the day." I opened the front door and stepped outside, taking my first breath of the air I used to breathe so long ago. On the porch, one of my younger sisters, Ginny, was sitting there taking sticks of chalk out of the packaging.

"Morning, Gin."

"Hi, Mark."

"What are you gonna do with the chalk?"

"Maura's comin' over soon to play hopscotch, so I have to make a board on the sidewalk with the chalk."

Ginny, or Gin as we sometimes called her, was eight years old. She was a little sweetheart with blue eyes, curly blonde hair, and the cutest smile you could imagine. Besides Joanne and Ginny, I have one other sister, Barbie, who is six and lives with my aunt in Georgia temporarily while my mother gets her schooling done.

"Well, have fun with your game," I said and then leaned down and kissed the top of her head.

"That's gross, don't kiss my head, it's disgusting," Ginny said as she jerked her head away.

It was something that I don't remember doing the first time around, but kissing my little sister on the head now seemed normal—she was so cute.

"Oh, come on, Gin," I said, "you're too cute not to kiss."

"Go away, I need to do this before Maura comes over," she said.

"Okay, I'm leaving, have a good time."

I strolled down my street, lined with maple trees on both sides, in the warm morning air, looking around at the neighborhood of my youth. I couldn't get over how light I felt. It was like I had been transported to the moon where the effects of gravity are minimal.

Our neighborhood was a veterans housing development that consisted of single and duplex rental homes built in the late forties, modest homes but nice enough. The houses were well taken care of for the most part, and nearly every lawn was well groomed.

Most of our fathers were WWII and Korean War veterans. My father was a Korean War era veteran who enlisted after high school, shortly after the war ended. Tommy, one of my friends who also lived on my street, told me a horrific story told to him by his father who fought in North Africa in WWII. He said that his father witnessed another soldier trying to put his hand back on his arm after it had been blown off during combat. Others had seen their best friends die before their eyes. How could these men not be changed by the brutality of war? And in the latest war, the Vietnam War, veterans arrived home only to be spit on for what many Americans thought was an unjust and unnecessary war. They, too, would occupy these houses in our neighborhood. All these veterans had seen the worst of what men can do to each other and came home with the physical and mental injuries as a result of that horror. Some of them would never again speak of what they saw, what no person should ever have to see. They would lock away those memories in some dark recess of their mind hoping against hope that just maybe it would all fade away. Many of these men drank to ease their suffering and to dull the horror hidden within.

Ours was a working-class neighborhood of low-wage-earning, blue-collar families, and every one of the men had done service for his country—every single one of them.

Some of the younger neighborhood kids were out playing, but I didn't run into any of my friends on my way to Alicia's house at the bottom of the street on the opposite side.

"What's up, Mark?" were Alicia's words when she came to the door.

I hesitated momentarily. I wasn't prepared to see this *young* Alicia. Like seeing my family, it was a shock. Actually, I almost laughed. In what was probably a split second, I told myself to snap out of it and act like everything was normal even though this was so far from the truth. Suddenly I found the words, and they began to flow—but a little too fast.

"You're not gonna believe it, but I need Lena's number from you, I can't remember it and I don't have it written down anywhere." I spit out this line so fast in one breath that it probably sounded comical, but it must have made me sound more like a fourteen-year-old than the middle-aged man I really was.

"You can't remember your girlfriend's number! How could you forget it?" she said.

"I don't know, it'll come to me eventually, but I need it now, I wanted to call Lena before I went down."

Alicia didn't have to go look it up. She shot it out like machine gun fire. "Let me write it down for you too." She left for a minute then returned with Lena's number on a piece of scrap paper.

"So you're goin' down The Point to see Lena today?" The Point was short for Point Shirley, the outermost section of Winthrop that jutted into Boston Harbor and where Lena lived.

"Yup, it's supposed to be hot today. I'll see if Lena wants to go to the beach."

Alicia is in our grade too, so she is around our age. She is a pretty girl, tall and slender, who happens to bear a slight resemblance to Cher, who was very popular in 1973 and amazingly still is. I told her not to mention to Lena that I forgot her number. It would be too embarrassing.

"I won't, don't worry. How's it going with you two anyway?"

"It's goin' great. I like her a lot." I didn't want to say too much as I was still unsure of how I was coming across. It felt very much like I was acting out a part. "I'd better get goin'," I said and then thanked her for the number.

"Well, have a good time today and tell Lena I said, hi," Alicia said as I was walking away.

"All right, I will."

"And write down that number, put it where you can find it," she shouted to me as I was almost to the street.

"Okay, I'll see you later, Alicia," I shouted back as I headed back up to the house.

# Chapter Four

I found the kitchen empty, where the phone was located. An old-style rotary phone attached to the wall, the only one in the house. It would have been nice to have my cell phone to ensure privacy, but people wouldn't be using those things for about another twenty-five years. I pulled Lena's number out of my pocket, took a deep breath, and then called the girl I hadn't talked to in over forty years.

"Hello," was the greeting on the other end, and it wasn't Lena. I froze momentarily, then realized it was her mother.

"Oh, hi, Mrs. Mendleson, is Lena there, please."

"Mark, is that you?"

"Yes, ma'am."

"Good morning, Mark, it didn't sound like you. I'll get Lena."

"Okay, thank you." *Starting off really smooth*, I thought, *Jesus*. I waited briefly. Then Lena came on the phone.

"Morning, Mark."

The following words came out hesitatingly slow and choppy. "Good-morning, Lena, how-are-you-doing?"

"I'm fine," she said. "What's the matter, you sound like a robot?"

"Oh, nothing, I was just distracted for a minute. I'm sorry," was all I could come up with.

"When are you comin' down?" Lena asked.

"Soon I guess. You wanna go to the beach today?"

"I thought we had already decided that yesterday?" she replied.

"Yeah, that's right, I forgot." If only Lena knew how long ago *her* yesterday was for me.

"Joan's babysitting today, and she told me Trisha's not around. I talked to Roy, and he can't make it either, so unless you're coming down with Jamie, then it'll be just me and you."

Joan Callum was Lena's best friend, and Trisha Minor was their mutual friend.

"Okay, yeah, I was planning on calling Jamie before I left."

Jamie Ballard was my best friend who lived near me, and we were all friends with Roy Compasse who lived next to Lena.

"No, wait a minute…just you, don't ask Jamie. Let's make it just me and you today. I want you all to myself."

"All…right," I said, drawing the two words out slowly, not anticipating Lena catching me off guard with her amorous feelings. "I'm gonna take my bike down, so it'll be about twenty minutes or so."

"Okay, I'll see you then," Lena replied, then added, "Be careful."

I said bye, hung up the phone, then exhaled a big breath of air. Well, I had made initial contact, and it didn't go too bad, I thought facetiously, except for freezing up with her mother and sounding like a robot to Lena.

I grabbed a towel from the linen closet and ran upstairs to look for something to wear at the beach. I found a pair of Winthrop High gym shorts in one of the dresser drawers. I took a pair of underpants out and rolled them and the shorts in the towel.

My ten-speed bike was down the cellar as expected. "Jeez, it's been a long time," I caught myself saying out loud. When I was young, before all the back pain set in, I thought it was the coolest thing. It got me where I wanted to go quickly. As I got older, it wasn't comfortable leaning over to grasp those curved-under handlebars. Anyway, I got my license a couple of years later, and my preferred mode of transportation became a car.

I wheeled it out of the cellar and around the house, passing my mother's 1962 Ford Falcon in the driveway. The car would become mine by 1976. That four-door sedan was in good shape for its age. It had a strong six-cylinder engine and a three-speed manual transmission with the shift lever on the steering wheel column. The position of the shift lever was why it was called a three-on-the-tree. It was the car that I learned how to drive in and the first car that I ever changed the oil on. I've changed my own oil ever since. I loved driving it and was sad when I finally had to let it go. I would love to have the old Falcon back again in 2014, fully restored and running like new.

I stowed my towel with the change of clothes on the metal rack on the back of the bike, and off I went. I anticipated trouble pedaling up the street as it was rather steep, but it was a breeze—I forgot that I had this strong young body now. I put it in a low gear and found myself at the top and crossing Main Street in no time at all.

# Chapter Five

The most obvious change I noticed on my way to The Point was the look of the vehicles. I passed a nice-looking Ford Mustang parked along Washington Avenue, probably a late sixties model. What kid wouldn't want that car. It was a dark-green Fastback, like the one in the movie *Bullitt*. I also saw a fair amount of station wagons. This was the family car that years later would be replaced by the minivan and SUV. It was strange seeing these boxy-looking cars before cars became more aerodynamically rounded in the future. The cars of this age just seemed to have so much more character. Their lines were totally different. It didn't cost much to fill one of them up either. The price of gas would rise dramatically in October as the Arab Oil Embargo went into effect, but in the summer of 1973, the price of gas was fairly cheap. I'll have to ride by a gas station to actually see what gas cost these days—just for a laugh.

As I breezed by the Winthrop Yacht Club, I began thinking of that night I asked Lena out. Let me tell you about it.

In late spring of 1973, Lena and a couple of her friends had come down to my neighborhood to hang with Alicia, who, as I mentioned earlier, conveniently lived on my street. A couple of weeks before this, Alicia had told me that Lena liked me and that I should ask her out. I had had my eye on her for some time, and now, knowing for certain that she liked me thrilled me beyond words. It also scared the hell out of me. So now, I had the perfect opportunity to ask her out, but I was so shy and self-conscious. I thought that I'd somehow screw it up. I'd fuck up and look stupid in front of all my friends and hers for that matter. Lena would think I'm a fool, and she'd never go out with me.

During the course of the night, my friends kept on me to go over and ask her out, but I couldn't summon the courage. How could I even approach her; Lena was so pretty and way out of my league. Time was flying by—as if someone had sped up the clock. I was losing my chance to make my move, and then it happened. They started making their way up the street to go home. *Shit*, I thought, *I've blown it, she's leaving!* But with my friends' urging, we followed Lena and her friends up the street—at a safe distance. They gathered by the bus stop across the street. We congregated on the opposite side of Main Street. My friend Tommy took me by the shoulder and told me that I was going to blow it if I didn't go talk to her before the bus came. I knew this, of course. I had to make a move. I had to overcome this fear inside that held me back, but it was much easier said than done.

With butterflies in my stomach and my friends exerting as much peer pressure as possible, I decided it was now or never. I made that slow, lonely walk across the street. With wobbly legs and as much teenage angst as one young boy could have, I approached the most beautiful girl I had ever seen. In my nervous state, I hadn't planned out what I would say to her, so I just blurted out, "Do you want to go out with me?" I don't remember her exact words that night, but she smiled and said something like it's a little late right now, which was totally obvious to me as soon as the words escaped my mouth. But then she gave me her phone number! I lit up inside, and I'm sure I was smiling ear to ear. I had done it! I had really done it! I actually had her phone number! I knew, as sure as I stood there, that I was the happiest person on earth. We said good night. Then I flew across the street to my friends. I was filled with an overload of nervous energy and felt fucking triumphant!

When I got back to the house that night, I went straight to the bathroom. Closing the door, I leaned in over the sink and stared into the mirror. "You did it, you got her number—you're really gonna be goin' out with her. You...how the hell is it possible that she would even go out with you?" I asked the face that stared back at me. It felt like a dream. This couldn't really be happening. How could I be this lucky? But I knew I was, I had her number now, and we would be together—holy shit! I still remember that day. It was May 27, 1973.

# Chapter Six

Turning left onto Lena's street, I slowed my bike and then stopped. I balanced the bike with my left foot on the pedal and right foot atop the low sea wall on my right side. I was close, only a few doors away from her house now. My heart was pounding, and I knew that it wasn't from the ride down.

Her street faced the airport and the Boston skyline beyond as you looked west. A channel of water that was fed by Boston Harbor separated Winthrop from Logan Airport at this location. It was less than a half mile across. Boats of all types were making their way up and down the channel as the gulls soared then dived on the wind. I could smell that refreshing salty air as I inhaled deeply through my nose.

I gathered myself and then pedaled the short distance to Lena's house. It would be the first time that I would be in Lena's presence in over forty years—of course, to her, it would be just like any other day.

I parked my bike in the driveway then returned to the front of the house. Lena appeared in the doorway as I was climbing the stairs. As I reached the landing, she pulled the sliding door open, abruptly leaned out, and gave me a quick peck on the lips. I couldn't speak. I just stood there in a stupor looking at her.

"What's the matter?" Lena said. "Come on in."

It was really her standing there in front of me. I had to stop myself from staring as I tried to fully comprehend just what I was seeing. I regained my composure, stepped through the doorway, and finally said, "Hi, Lena."

"What the heck's the matter with you, you were looking at me like…like you've never seen me before."

"I just can't help admiring a beautiful girl, that's all," was all I could think of saying.

"Yeah right," she said.

Seeing Lena standing there, so young, made me feel every bit as old as I really was. She had that youthful complexion. Her shoulder-length jet-black hair was silky smooth, and her brown eyes were clear and bright. Lena didn't have perfect features. Instead she had an overall cute appearance, the type of girl that I had always been attracted to.

Lena's mother said hello as I walked into the living room. She was tall and skinny, just as I had remembered her.

"I need to use the bathroom to change, Mrs. Mendleson, if it's okay."

"Of course, Mark, you know where it is."

When I returned to the living room, Lena and her mother were talking.

"So you two are headed to the beach today?"

"No, Mom, we're really going to Vegas to elope."

"Oh, that's real funny, Lena," her mother replied, "You'll be lucky if I let you out of the house today." Mrs. Mendleson smiled as she replied, but her underlying tone said "Don't even joke about such a thing." I couldn't help the smile that broke out on my face as I listened to this exchange between mother and daughter. It helped put me at ease.

"You know I'm kidding, Mom, relax. Do you have a couple dollars?"

"You're bringing your lunch to the beach, aren't you?"

"Yeah, but I'd like to get an ice cream afterward."

"Lena, I have some money, no worries," I said.

"All right, then I guess we're all set."

"No, here, take it anyway. Mark, shouldn't have to pay all the time."

Lena took the two one-dollar bills from her mother, and I thanked her for her consideration.

"Do you have suntan lotion in your bag, Lena?" her mother asked.

"Almost a full bottle."

"I don't know why you kids don't take that beach umbrella we have. There's no chance of burning when you're under it."

"Yeah, and no chance of a suntan either," Lena replied.

"All right, suit yourself, just make sure to keep a good coat of that lotion on. You don't want to burn."

"We gotta get going, Mom, we're gonna miss high tide," Lena said a bit impatiently.

"Okay, you two, be good. Be home by five thirty, Lena, supper's at six."

"Okay-sure," was Lena's reply as we headed out the door.

# Chapter Seven

We walked the three blocks to Yirrell Beach located on the eastern length of Point Shirley, facing Boston Harbor and the Atlantic Ocean. The tide was in, the sun was out, and the temperature was approaching eighty degrees. This would make for a nice day at the beach. After laying our towels down, we headed for the water. A chilly Atlantic awaited us as we stepped into its cold embrace.

"Oh my god, it's freezing, Lena!" I said as I made my way into the water.

"Tell me about it," she replied.

"Doesn't it ever get warm? Damn!"

"You know it never does, it just gets tolerable at best."

In this part of the country, you'd be lucky if the ocean temperature reached seventy degrees in the heat of the summer. Lips turned blue, and your shins would often ache from the cold water. We both dived in but surfaced and got out quickly. It was refreshing though, and you would get used to it if you could just stay in long enough for your body to adjust. We didn't wait for this and made our way back to our towels on the hot sand. As Lena and I walked together, it occurred to me that the beach wasn't that crowded for a Sunday. Thinking back though, it never was crowded regardless of the day. Point Shirley was always its own little community within Winthrop. It's out of the way, and so is the beach, making it seem private. I always liked that about Yirrell Beach.

Lena turned the little transistor radio on that she pulled from her beach bag and set it down on her towel. "Alone Again (Naturally)" by Gilbert O'Sullivan crackled to life as she adjusted the antenna. I turned, looked at the radio, and smiled.

"Are you hungry, Mark? It's about noon."

"Yeah, actually I am. What did you bring?"

"The usual. Ham and cheese with relish for you and the same with mustard for me, and there's lemonade in the jug."

I couldn't remember ever putting relish on a ham and cheese sandwich, but I must have, if that was *my usual*.

"Oh, and there's also cookies, chips, and a couple apples in the bag."

So we ate our lunch as the sun dried us off, listening to music from a little transistor radio in the summer of 1973. It was all too surreal. Less than ten hours ago I was in my lab at Harvard University in the year 2014. Now I'm with my old girlfriend in Winthrop, Massachusetts, in the year 1973. The fact that I was actually sitting here, eating a picnic lunch on the beach with my former girlfriend, decades in my past, was completely blowing my mind. It was not unlike a dream. When I first arrived, I thought mostly of the people being younger, but now I'm realizing everything—everything around me that I could see, feel, touch, hear, and smell was forty-one years younger now. The actual sun itself that felt so good on this young body was over forty years older from whence I came.

After eating, we put the Coppertone suntan lotion on. I applied some to Lena's back and she to mine. It wasn't called sunscreen yet, and there were no SPF numbers on the bottle. This would come later when people realized ultraviolet radiation from the sun caused skin cancer, not just a bothersome burn. Later in life, my uncle would die of skin cancer. I loved him like a second father, and it seemed cancer swept him away as quickly as the tide washes away a kid's sandcastle. He died shortly before his retirement began, robbing him of those precious years when life can be enjoyed at your own pace. This affected me deeply and after that I was always careful out in the sun.

Lena shook out her towel then laid it down so that we were facing each other. We were lying on our stomachs with our faces almost touching. I felt like I was lying there with a young girl, certainly not my girlfriend. I had no desire to kiss Lena, but she had other ideas. Lena leaned in and kissed my lips. I responded in a way not unlike kissing my own mother—by smooching quickly then pulling back.

The surprise on Lena's face told me everything. She expected a longer kiss, a french kiss that she must have been accustomed to by now in our relationship. I had clearly disappointed her.

"What's the matter? Don't you want to kiss me, Mark? Usually, you're all over me."

"Yeah, of course I do. I'm just tired, that's all."

"All right, if you don't want to kiss me, then I'm just gonna put my head down and get some sun."

Trying to sound as convincing as possible, I said, "You know how I feel about you, Lena."

"I know, it's okay."

After a brief lapse in the conversation, Lena looked up and said, "Back at the house you used the term 'no worries.' I never heard you say that before. You sounded different."

"I said no worries…? Oh yeah—that. I recently saw a movie on TV that was set in England. One of the characters used that expression. I guess I just picked it up," I said.

"It just didn't sound like you. I like it though—no worries. I'll have to use that on my mother, it'll keep her off balance."

"Yeah, it does sound cool, doesn't it?"

There was a break in the music on the radio as the news came on. Among other stories, the newscaster talked about the ongoing Watergate hearings and how last night, at a concert in California, Phil Everly stormed off stage, declaring that The Everly Brothers were finished. In sports, he mentioned how the Red Sox hung on to beat the Texas Rangers 6–5 last night at Friendly Fenway, improving their record to 47–40.

We went back in the water several more times and didn't leave the beach till well after four. It was a relaxing first day for me with none of the typical adult worries. The only thing that concerned me was how I was coming across to Lena, but I think I was doing okay— for the most part.

We got that ice cream Lena wanted and walked slowly back to her house. Before we got there, she stopped abruptly and asked me how my ice cream was.

"Pretty good, not bad," I said.

"Oh yeah, let me see," Lena said as she quickly closed the space between us.

She seductively brushed her lips against mine then opened her mouth and gently licked off the traces of ice cream I had on my lips. I knew what she wanted, so I reluctantly opened my mouth and responded by allowing her to french kiss me. I pretended to enjoy it, but inside it felt so wrong. I was really just an old man that shouldn't be near a girl of Lena's age. Not only that, but I truly felt that I was deceiving her. I felt like an impostor in a place I shouldn't be. We reached Lena's house at about quarter past five. I went around back to grab my bike while Lena brought the beach stuff inside. She met me on the side of the house as I was pushing the bike out.

"You're coming back down tonight—right?"

"Sure, if you want me to."

"Of course I want you to," Lena said as she stepped in front of the bike, blocking my forward progress. While straddling the front wheel and with both of her hands on the handlebars of my bike, Lena leaned over and gave me a quick kiss on the lips.

"You know what?" she said with those bedroom eyes I've seen before on women much older than her.

"What?"

"I can't wait till you come back down."

This really made me feel awkward, so I decided to employ a little humor to the situation.

"Good night, good night! Parting is such sweet sorrow, that I should say good night till it be morrow"

With a puzzled look on her face, Lena simply said, "What?"

"It's Shakespeare, from *Romeo and Juliet*."

"I know what it is, Mark. Are you making fun of me?" Lena said with a peeved look on her face.

"No, no, no," I said, backpedaling. "I'm just joking around, Lena. I'm looking forward to coming back down tonight."

"Apology accepted. You know how I feel about you." She paused then added, "I just hope that you feel the same way about me."

"I do, Lena. That's one thing you don't have to worry about. Okay?"

"Okay, I know. I'm sorry I got all irritable."

I smiled and said, "No worries." This made Lena laugh, and it released the tension that had built up.

"No worries," she repeated with a smile.

I knew that we should kiss before I left, and just an ordinary kiss wouldn't suffice considering what had just transpired. I pulled Lena close, and we french-kissed there under the windows and out of sight. I felt as I did earlier—guilty.

"I'll call you after supper, okay?" I said.

"Okay. Be careful riding home."

"All right," I said as I pedaled away.

# Chapter Eight

As I pedaled home, I realized that I never got changed back into my shorts. It didn't really matter. I was dry anyway.

Then my thoughts turned back to Lena. It's nice being back, but I didn't realize how awkward the initial intimacy issues would be. I knew the change would begin soon and the old feelings would return, but would they really be my feelings anyway?

Before I knew it, I was pedaling down my street, approaching the house. When I got inside, it was close to six o'clock and most of my family was at the supper table.

As I passed the entrance to the kitchen, I saw my mother standing near the stove.

"Ma, I'll be right in, I just want to take a quick shower," I said.

"Don't take too long, supper's just about ready."

"I'll be quick, Ma." The shower felt good, and it gave me a little time to think.

When I returned to the kitchen for supper, I remembered that I needed to speak to my mother about purchasing the stock. I had no idea how long the whole process would take—from convincing her that it was a good investment to actually laying my hands on the stock certificates. So now that I was over the initial shock of seeing my mother at thirty-six years old, or should I say thirty-six years young, I decided I'd broach the subject with her. The only problem was that all my siblings were at the table vying for my mother's attention, including John, my older brother. John was out of the house earlier this morning, so this was the first time I'd seen him since I was back.

"Hey, Mapes, you been down Lena's all day?" he asked in his obnoxious, nosy way. John knew I didn't like that name but insisted on using it just to antagonize me.

"Well, that's my business, but yeah, I was."

"You're lucky, I wish I had a girlfriend."

"Well, clean up your act and maybe you'll get one," I said.

"What's wrong with me the way I am? Are you trying to say something's wrong with me?" John said in a threatening tone.

My mother stepped in at that point and told us both to stop it, and our conversation ceased. I realized I was reacting the way I would when I was young, so I told John that I was sorry and didn't think anything was wrong with him. I knew he had a lifetime of trouble ahead, and I felt sorry for belittling him.

"No problem, kid," he said, and I almost laughed at his choice of words. If only he knew.

Then Ginny chimed in, "Did you go to the beach with Lena today, Mark?"

"Yup, I did, Gin."

"Bet it was nice, huh. I wish Momma brought me today."

My mother looked up as Ginny said this, and she responded, "You know that I couldn't bring you today, hon." She said with that *I'm sorry* face. "We're all going to Horseneck next Sunday anyway. It'll be a lot of fun," my mother said with a reassuring smile.

"Yeah, Gin, we'll have a great time, I promise," I said.

"Will you go in the water with me, Mark?"

"Sure I will, and we can build sandcastles if you want to."

Ginny's eyes lit up, and a broad smile began forming on her face. "You promise, Mark?"

"I promise. And you know, the water will be a lot warmer down there. You know how it's always freezing in Winthrop."

"Okay, I guess I can wait till Sunday then," Ginny said as she brushed back the curls from her face.

As we all ate supper and chatted, my thoughts returned to John. He was two years older than me, about my height but a good deal heavier with messy straight brown hair. He was generally unkempt and didn't care very much about personal hygiene. He was plagued with emotional problems, later to be diagnosed as schizoaffective disorder, and signs of this were already evident. John was constantly upset with someone or something most all the time. He was immature, a loose cannon, and verbally abusive. In general, he was a problem for my mother and all of us. I had got into some shouting matches with him, but it had never gotten to fisticuffs. He was loud, bossy, and didn't like being told what to do. So for the most part I just steered clear. It was easier than trying to deal with him. Later in life, I would spend more time with him, helping him when I could. After being in and out of psychiatric hospitals his whole life, John died at the age of forty-one from heart failure. This was brought on by a reaction to a blood pressure medication he was taking. His was a very difficult life to say the least. A life fraught with frustration, anxiety, paranoia, and everything else that accompanies such illnesses.

When supper was over and everyone but Ginny was gone from the table, I brought up the stock purchase with Mom.

"Ma, I'd like to invest some of the money I have in my savings account."

My mother replied, "Your money is already invested, what do you mean?"

"I'd like to take a thousand dollars out of my savings account and buy Coca-Cola stock. Actually, I need you to purchase it for me."

She looked at me with a combination of shock and concern. "A thousand dollars, that's a lot of money! And what do you know about stock anyway."

"I've been reading about it in books and periodicals that I've checked out of the library. Coke's a solid company. It's been around for years, and most analysts think its future will remain bright. You know, Ty Cobb made a ton of money with Coke."

"Who's Ty Cobb?" she asked.

"A great baseball player who played the game years ago. He wasn't very well-liked, but he was a smart man."

"Mark, that money is for your college education," my mother replied.

"I know, Ma, I understand that, but the stock will be an investment. I won't touch it till I get to college, I promise. I'll bet it will make a lot more money than if it sat in the savings bank. It'll be just a portion of my savings anyway, and it's not like I'm spending it on something stupid." Then I added pleadingly, with the sweetest face I could muster, "Come on, Ma, please."

"It's not a portion of your savings, as you say, it's half of your savings." My mother hesitated—she was quite aware of how much money was in my savings account—then said she'd think about it. She always used to say that. "I'll think about it." That was my mom. It was a very diplomatic way to deal with children. I had used the same technique with my daughter at times. You're not saying no, but you're not saying yes either. You are leaving the door of hope open to the child. This would have to do for now, so I thanked my mother for taking the time to think about it. I'd check with her tomorrow to see if she had made up her mind.

Before I left the table, I told my mother that I was heading back down The Point tonight and I'd be home about ten thirty. She was fine with that, so I called Jamie to see if he wanted to take the bus down with me. Obviously, I had no idea whether or not he had plans with Trisha. Trisha, by the way, was Jamie's girlfriend. It would be another awkward first call, but not as awkward as my call to Lena. I just had to remember that I had probably talked to him as recently as yesterday—his yesterday. So I had to make it sound like that, not forty-one years ago, even though it had been that long for me.

"What's happenin', Mark?" Jamie said as he picked up the phone.

"Hey, Jamie, how are you doin?"

"Good, what's up?"

"Are you getting together with Trisha tonight? I'm gonna take the bus down in a few minutes if you want to come."

"No, Trish won't be home till late tonight. She's been out all day with her parents. I guess we're all going to the beach tomorrow though."

"Oh…okay, good. I'll give you a call tomorrow morning then. What's goin' on tonight?"

"Just hangin' out at home with the family. We have relatives over. You know, the usual thing—it's boring."

"Yup, I know what you mean. All right, I better go if I wanna catch that bus. I'll talk to you tomorrow."

"Okay, see ya," he said then hung up.

*That didn't go too bad*, I thought. Actually, it felt sort of natural.

# Chapter Nine

I got myself to the top of the street shortly before the bus arrived. You could catch either of two buses that travelled two different routes to Point Shirley from this location. The two buses would arrive at opposite corners of Herman and Main Streets at different times. The one that was routed through the center of town and, therefore, called the *Center Bus* pulled up at 6:55, and I jumped on. The fare was a whopping ten cents for a ride through Winthrop that ended at Delby's Corner, near Winthrop Beach. From there I caught a second bus that got me to The Point by 7:20 p.m.

I met Lena outside, on the steps of her house.

"Howya-doin', cutie?" I said as I sat down next to her and gave her a quick peck on the lips, trying to act as normal as possible.

"Not so great. It's my stomach, it feels queasy. I think I might have a touch of the stomach bug. Do you mind making it a short stay tonight?"

"I came all the way back down and you want me to go home?" I said.

"No, Mark, I just wanna make it an early night."

"I was just kidding, Lena. Seriously, if you don't feel well, I can—"

"How about if we just take a slow walk around the park then call it a night?"

"Yeah, that's fine, we'll take it easy."

Coughlin Park was just down the end of her street. We strolled along its perimeter, which was for the most part surrounded by water. Small boats moored in this picturesque inlet reflected the sun's slanting rays. It was the time of day that artists and photographers refer to as the golden hour: late afternoon or early morning when the sun is low in the sky and the surroundings are bathed in a golden light; when colors are deep and contrasts strong—my favorite time of day. With the temperature around seventy degrees and a slight breeze, the conditions couldn't have been more perfect for a walk.

"Jamie says that we're all going to the beach tomorrow?"

"Yeah, I talked to Joan tonight. I guess everybody will be around tomorrow. I just hope my stomach's okay by then. It should be a lot of fun with all of us there."

"Yeah, it'll be fun. How's your stomach right now?" I asked.

"So-so. I'll just have to be careful what I eat for a while. I had chicken soup tonight."

"Yeah, they say a bland diet is best for stomach problems. You know, it might just be a twenty-four-hour bug and be gone by tomorrow," I said.

"Hopefully."

We stopped about halfway around to look for an area to sit down on the shoreline. The shells crunched underneath us as we cleared a little spot. We were looking east toward the big water tower perched on Cottage Hill. Two beacons constantly flashed on and off atop the rim of the tower to warn incoming aircraft. Not only was it rusty, but also it was painted a rusty-orange-like color. In three years' time, in 1976, the town would paint it red, white, and blue in three horizontal sections to honor the Bicentennial. I remember the talk about it being painted to resemble a giant Budweiser can. Supposedly, the beer company would paint it free of charge, saving the town the expense and providing advertising for Bud. I don't know how true this was, but either way, it's a great story. Just for fun I said, "Can you picture the water tower painted to look like a giant Budweiser can?"

"Yeah, I can, but I doubt the town would go for it."

"No, I guess not." She was right. They never did.

Then I decided to go a little deeper, to find out more about this girl who blew me away when I was just a boy. I really wanted to know more, delve a little deeper and discover something that I didn't know the first time around.

"Lena, tell me something that I don't know about you, something that you keep to yourself for one reason or another."

"There's nothing really," she said unconvincingly without looking at me.

"Come on, Lena, there's gotta be something," I said as I nudged her slightly.

"Well, there's one thing, but you'd think I'm crazy."

"No, I wouldn't, Lena, I promise."

"You sure?"

"I promise, I won't think you're crazy."

"Well, all right," she said then paused. "I um…I listen to classical music."

"Really," I said, surprised.

"See, I told you. You think I'm weird, right?"

"No, no, I just didn't know. Actually I think it's cool."

"My family knows, but I haven't told anyone else…well, except for you, now. Actually, I'm thinking about taking piano lessons."

"That's awesome. What got you into classical music?" I asked.

"My mother listens to it. She has a bunch of classical records and plays them a lot. I guess it just rubbed off on me. I love the piano stuff, mostly Chopin and Beethoven."

"I've heard some but never really got into it."

"There's this one piece called *Silence* by Beethoven that is the most beautiful thing I've ever heard. I'll have to play it for you one of these days."

"Yeah, sure, I'd like to hear it. And it's not weird to like classical or want to learn to play the piano, Lena. In fact, I encourage you to go for what's in your heart," I said then thought that I sounded too much like an adult and not like the fourteen-year-old she was used to.

"Wow, I didn't expect this type of response from you. Are you sure you're not just trying to be nice, Mark?"

"No, I um…" I paused, trying to sound more like her teenage boyfriend. "I really think it's cool."

I was just about to ask Lena about the piano lessons when she broke in.

"Mark, do you mind if we get going? My stomach's acting up again."

"Yeah, sure. Are you okay?" My paternal instincts began kicking in, and I felt the need to comfort her.

"Yeah, it's just getting queasy again."

"Let's get you home then," I said as I helped Lena to her feet. I walked alongside her with my left arm around her waist, holding Lena close and comforting her more as a father would than a boyfriend. At her front door we shared a brief kiss and said our good nights.

"Get a good night's sleep, that will help. I'll call you in the morning to see how you're feeling."

"All right, I'll talk to you then," she said while wincing. Lena then suddenly turned back around, gave me a kiss on the cheek, and said, "Thanks for being so caring."

"That's my job," I said, smiling, and she smiled back.

My early night with Lena got me home much earlier than expected, which was fine because I was exhausted from this first day. I went up to bed by ten and was asleep shortly thereafter.

# PART 3

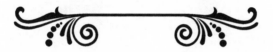

# Chapter One

*Monday, 16 July 1973*

I awoke early that second morning and caught my mother before she left for work.

"Ma, did you think about the stock purchase I talked to you about yesterday?"

"I'm going to talk to a friend that I work with that used to work in the Financial District downtown. He should be in today, so I'll let you know what I think tonight."

"Thanks, Mom, I'll see you tonight then. Have a good day at work, love you."

"I love you too, see you tonight."

After breakfast, I called Lena then Jamie. Lena told me that she was feeling much better this morning and asked if twelve thirty was a good time to meet at the beach. I told her it was fine then called Jamie and arranged to meet at my house at noon in order to catch the 12:05 for The Point. I had gotten a bus schedule from the driver last night, so I knew the 12:05 Highlands bus would get us to Point Shirley about twelve thirty.

I picked up the *Boston Globe* that was still on the table and started scanning through it. I quickly moved to the sports section to find out how the Sox did yesterday.

"Good," I said out loud, to which Ginny responded, "What's good?"

"Oh, nothing, Gin, I didn't realize I was talking out loud. I was just looking at the baseball standings."

They won again last night and were in second place in the American League Eastern Division with a record of 48–40. I've been an avid Red Sox fan since 1967 when they came within one game of defeating the St. Louis Cardinals in the World Series but fell short. It was a long, agonizing wait till 2004 when they finally broke *The Curse of the Bambino*. For those of you who have never heard of this dreaded curse, let me enlighten you.

George Herman Ruth, commonly known as Babe Ruth and by many other names, including the *Bambino*, was acquired by the Red Sox in 1914 when he first broke into the big leagues at nineteen years of age. He was an exceptional pitcher winning twenty-plus games twice with a sub-three ERA every year but one with the Red Sox. In fact, in 1916 he had the best ERA in the American League. Ruth was eventually converted to an outfielder because he wanted to play every day, and that's when his batting ability became evident. In his six years with the Red Sox, he helped them win the World Series three times. In 1918, he shared the record of eleven home runs in one year, and then in the following season, he dismantled the record by smashing twenty-nine home runs. Ruth showed unspeakable promise, but in 1920, the great Babe Ruth was sold to the New York Yankees for one hundred thousand dollars and a three hundred thousand dollar loan that would help owner Harry Frazee pay off his debts. Frazee definitely needed the money but also wanted to rid himself of the problems he faced with Ruth. The Bambino was a big drinker, oftentimes drunk before games. The last straw was when Ruth demanded twenty thousand dollars for the upcoming year, twice as much as he was paid in 1919. So on January 5, 1920, one of the greatest baseball players to ever play the game and certainly the most famous player ever, with years of playing time ahead of him, was gone, and the curse for trading away such a superstar had begun.

In the following year, his first with the New York Yankees, Ruth smashed an unbelievable fifty-four home runs, breaking his own record by an outstanding twenty-five homers. In 1927, he hit sixty, a record that would stand for thirty-four years! The Bambino brought attention to baseball and fans to the park, but no longer Fenway Park.

In the subsequent years, the lackluster Sox would never manage to capture that elusive prize until that glorious post-season that no Sox fan will ever forget. In 2004, the Boston Red Sox finished the season in second place in the Eastern Division of the American League, three games behind the New York Yankees, with a record of 98–64, capturing a wildcard berth. They began the playoffs by sweeping the Anaheim Angels 3–0 to win the Division series. In the American League Championship series, the Red Sox found themselves down 3–0 (facing elimination with another loss) against their arch rivals, the New York Yankees. In the greatest comeback in baseball history, the Red Sox won four straight games to win the series and get a chance to meet the St Louis Cardinals in the World Series. They went on to sweep the Cardinals four straight and to finally win that ultimate prize. On October 27, 2004, the Boston Red Sox won the World Series. To be a Red Sox fan at that time was like being in heaven. And for those older fans who waited so many seasons to see their team finally do it, well, even more satisfying and fulfilling for them. We were the world baseball champs, and no one could ever take that away—ever!

To put this in perspective, it had been eighty-six years since they had done it, the year 1918 when the great Babe Ruth still played on their team. Many an avid Red Sox fan had lived a long life and then died without seeing his beloved team win this ultimate prize.

They won the World Series again in 2007 and then again in 2013, but 2004 was the year that will forever stay in the hearts of Red Sox fans: the year that marked the end of a long drought and the year that "the Curse of the Bambino" was finally laid to rest.

# Chapter Two

Jamie and I grew up playing Little League together, and of course, we were both die-hard Red Sox fans. We had been with our parents and friends to Fenway many times and loved our home team. Like many kids, we collected baseball cards and always hoped to find a Red Sox card in every pack we opened. We cherished our collections, traded them to get our favorites, and also gambled with them by playing a game of tossing them toward a wall. Whoever could get theirs closest to the wall would win the other's card. I lost many a baseball card to the skill of Jamie's arm.

We are about the same height and build, and both have brown hair—his curly, mine wavy. As a matter of fact, people have said that we look alike. We became friends in fourth grade when our teacher called us Itch-One and Itch-Two. I can't remember who was One and who was Two. Of all my friends that I hung with in the neighborhood, Jamie was the only one to make the move to The Point with me in 1973 when we both began dating girls from there.

Just before noon, Jamie knocked on the door. I stuffed the last bit of ham and cheese sandwich in my mouth as I let him in.

"Hey, Mark, what's happenin'."

"Not much. You all set?" Jeez, he looked great—every bit the athlete I remembered him to be.

"Yup, ready to go."

"Let's get up the street then, before we miss that bus."

The bus arrived right after we crossed Main Street—just in time. We grabbed a couple of seats up front, plopping down with our beach stuff rolled up in towels as the bus pulled away.

"I talked to Roy, he won't be at the beach till two. He's gotta help his sister with something," Jamie said.

"How about Trisha, she's coming down, right?" I asked.

"She should be with Lena and Joan when we get there."

"Good," I replied then changed the subject. "How did it go last night?"

"Boring, boring, and boring. Glad it's only once in a while."

"I hear ya," I said, trying to sound like I might have sounded originally. I wasn't really sure if we were using that expression yet, but I felt like winging it—I was relaxed.

"I can't believe—"

"You keep it up back there, and I'm gonna stop this bus, and you two are gettin' out." The bus driver's booming voice stopped Jamie in midsentence. "Do you understand me?" Apparently two kids, a bit younger than us, were roughhousing in the back of the bus.

"Yes, sir," they replied in unison, and the ruckus ceased immediately.

I haven't seen that in a while, I thought. Kids in the future seem to get away with just about anything. Back in the 1970s, an adult could scold a minor that way and elicit a respectful response, not a lawsuit for upsetting their feelings. This is the way it should be. Kids had a great deal more respect for their elders when I was growing up. I looked at Jamie and said "Put them in their place—huh" and then "Oh, what were you saying?"

"I can't remember. All I know is—I don't wanna piss him off," Jamie replied in a hushed tone so the driver couldn't hear him.

I asked my friend how he was getting along with Trisha.

"Not bad. I like her, but not like how you like Lena."

"You can tell?"

"Are you kiddin', Mark, everybody can see that. I know how you feel about her. And those *kitchen eyes* she looks at you with," Jamie said, smiling.

"What do you mean—kitchen eyes?" I said with a puzzled look.

"You know, *come and get it.*"

"Oh," I said and started laughing. "Yeah, well, I'm glad she looks at me like that, I really like her a lot."

Jamie then turned his head, looked me in the eye, and said in a serious tone, "I'm glad you found someone you like." He really meant it, and it made me feel good.

"Thanks, I appreciate that." Our conversation was smooth and natural. I felt comfortable with Jamie as I did before. Being with him, sitting there talking with my best friend, made me feel like a kid again, in spite of my true age.

# Chapter Three

We got off the bus across the street from Pulsifers Market, a small mom-and-pop convenience store one block from the beach. It was a short walk from there to meet the girls.

"Glad you guys could make it," Lena said, trying to sound like Mae West.

I responded by saying, "It's our pleasure," then wanted to take it back—it didn't sound right.

We went over and gave our obligatory kisses to the girls, laid our towels down near them, and settled in for a day at the beach. Trisha was all over Jamie immediately, and the look on his face spoke volumes. He obviously wanted some space. In ten minutes' time they would be arguing.

Trisha was Lena's height. She was an attractive girl with almost perfect features. Her body was filling out as was Lena's. Trisha could have had just about any boy in our class but only wanted one in a bad way. This of course was my best friend, Jamie. She was friendly enough but somewhat aloof.

Lena was asking me something that I didn't quite hear as I watched Jamie and Trisha interact.

"What was that, Lena?"

"I was asking you whether or not you ate lunch because I only packed snacks."

"Yeah, I did eat lunch, snacks are fine."

"Do you want anything now?"

I turned and asked, "Do you have any cookies?"

"I have Nilla Wafers."

"Oooh, let me have some of those." I've always loved Nilla Wafers or just about any cookie for that matter.

While I ate the cookies, Lena and Joan began talking. Being best friends, they were always talking. They kept each other up to date with their lives and talked about everything else that could possibly be talked about. By the fall, Joan would be complaining to Lena that she was going off alone with me too much, that she never seemed to be around anymore. This rift would be mended with no small help from yours truly. Not that I'm an angel, but I couldn't see that long-standing friendship come to an end. Perhaps if Lena and I had kept our distance we would have stayed together…perhaps.

Anyway, let me describe Joan. She is a bit taller than Lena and Trisha but not quite as filled out as them. She's not a bad-looking girl, but she's flat-chested and is plagued with facial acne. She is more conservative than her friends, but you couldn't call her a prude. Maybe *reserved* would be a better word. You could say that she stays pretty much within the box of her parents' wishes.

I managed to get Jamie to break away from Trisha so we could throw around the tennis ball he brought down. I wanted to test this new and improved fourteen-year-old arm. So we found a good stretch of sand and began tossing it around for a while. My arm felt great—man could I chuck that sucker. It wasn't long before we ended up in the water, but we didn't stay in too long—it was cold as usual.

"You know, Mark, she's a pain in the ass," Jamie said as we walked back up.

"Who's a pain in the ass?"

"Trisha. Ever since we got here, she's been on me about spending more time together."

"That's not so bad, is it?"

"She's like this every day. Always complaining. I should just break up with her. I really should."

As we headed back up, we saw Roy walking our way. "Hey guys," he said as he got into speaking range. Roy is close to six feet tall, at least two inches taller than Jamie and me. He is somewhat of a smart-ass and an independent type who usually says what's on his mind.

"Thought you weren't gonna be here till later, Roy," said Jamie.

"It didn't take as long as we thought it would. We moved all my sister's furniture in one trip." Roy looked down and noticed the tennis ball in Jamie's hand. "Hey, let's throw that thing around."

"We just got finished," I said.

"Yeah, we were just going back up," Jamie added.

"Come on, I just got here, let's throw it around for a few minutes anyway."

"All right, Roy, let's go," I said. Then Jamie turned and said, "Why not."

We went back down to the hard-packed sand close to the water and formed a triangle about seventy feet from each other. Roy lobbed a high fly to Jamie beyond his reach, but he tracked it down and made a nice stab over his right shoulder. Jamie returned the favor, but Roy couldn't get to it and swore, "What the fuck!" Jamie started laughing, and so did I. Roy looked over at Jamie and said, "Screw you," then laughed at himself. We would all make the junior varsity baseball team in our upcoming sophomore year—Jamie as a pitcher, Roy as a catcher, and me as a left fielder. It was fun throwing the ball around, especially with all that speed and agility back.

The girls eventually joined us. It was great, not a care in the world as they say—just having a good time at the beach as a teenager once again. Trisha threw a wild toss to Lena. Lena scrambled hard to her left and dived right in front of a mother and her toddler son, spraying them with sand.

"Will you please keep your distance, I have a baby here!" The baby just giggled as his mother brushed sand from his face.

"Sorry, ma'am," was Lena's embarrassed reply, "it won't happen again." Lena came running back to us all red-faced. "Thanks, Trish, I just got chewed out over there."

"Screw her if she can't take a joke," Trisha replied, trying to contain her laughter.

"I'm going in the water. I'm covered with sand thanks to you," Lena said as she glared over at Trisha, then couldn't help the smile that broke out on her face. Trisha couldn't hold it in any longer and burst out laughing.

"Come on, I'll go with you," Trisha said, and we all followed suit. Before long, six teenagers were splashing, yelling, and generally having a grand old time in that cold summer water.

After twenty minutes or so, I had had enough. I couldn't get used to the frigid water, and the splashing and dunking of each other got old quick. I might have looked fourteen, but I was far too old for those kids' games. I just wanted to relax back up on the towel. I asked Lena if she wanted to get out.

"Sure, let's go," she said, and we made our way back to the towels alone. Then we heard Roy yell, "Pussies!" Lena turned and flipped him the bird. I just smiled and kept walking.

# Chapter Four

Lena turned the radio on, and we lay down next to each other. She grabbed a book from her beach bag and began reading. I was happy just lying there soaking up the sun. With my head on the towel and facing the shore, I could see the rest of the gang still messing around in the water. Lena looked up from her book and said, "Did you talk to your mother?"

Of course, I had no idea what she was talking about, so my ignorant reply was, "About what?"

"You know, Horseneck Beach. I asked you a couple days ago to ask her if it would be all right if I came along too."

I must have looked totally dumbstruck for a few seconds until I put it together. We had gone to Horseneck Beach in Westport, Massachusetts, together that summer. Of course, I wasn't sure if I had asked my mother at this point the first time around, so I said, "No, I had forgotten about it. I'll talk to her tonight at supper. Anyway, she likes you, she's gonna say yes."

"Okay, good, but don't forget," Lena said.

About a half hour later, our friends returned; and ten minutes after that, Lena decided she wanted to go back in the water. She jumped up from her beach towel.

"Come on, let's go in the water, Mark." Looking around, she asked, "Anyone else wanna go back in?"

"I'm comfortable right here," Joan replied. "The sun feels so good on my back right now. Besides, we just got out." Jamie and Trisha were lying on their towels making out about ten feet away from us and didn't hear Lena's question at all.

I looked at Lena while pointing to the two lovebirds and said, "Why don't we just leave those two alone."

Lena agreed, "They're obviously happy right where they are."

Roy opted out, "No, I'm gonna hang here and listen to the tunes." Just then, Dobie Gray's "Drift Away" came on the radio.

Lena tightened her grip on my hand and pulled slightly. "Come on, let's go."

"Hold on, I love that song," I said, and then realized I was singing along.

*Oh give me the beat boys*
*And free my soul*
*I want to get lost in your rock and roll*
*And drift away*

Roy looked over and said that he had never heard it before. I knew it came out in 1973, but it might have been a summer release—it might have just come out. It would hit number five on the Billboard Hot 100, one of my favorite songs of that summer. It was still being played forty-one years later, and whenever I heard it, it took me back. The ironic thing was that I am back, listening to the song when it first came out once again.

Lena got my attention again, and we made our way down to the water. As we walked hand in hand, a plane roared overhead on its approach to Logan Airport. I'd forgotten how close they came over Yirrell Beach and how loud they actually were. Planes take off and land into the wind. Yesterday, the wind was blowing more or less from the south, but today it was coming from the west, blowing offshore. This resulted in the planes coming in right overhead on their way to runway 27, which faced due west.

Just like yesterday, it felt weird holding Lena's hand, never mind actually kissing her. Little did she know that I was actually an older man in a younger man's body. No changes were taking place yet, and I still felt like any normal adult would around a teenager. Lena was a vibrant young girl, full of life, and me, just an old man looking in from the outside. But it was nice being back in the Winthrop of my youth, revisiting my past and seeing once again the girl who had once made me so happy.

After returning from the water, Jamie asked me if I wanted to take a walk to Pulsifers to get a Coke.

"Sure," I said, "why not, let's take a walk."

Roy didn't want to go, and Lena said she wanted to stay and talk to the girls, so we took off together. Lena joined Trisha and Joan in what appeared to be a girls-only conversation.

"I forgot the butts," Jamie said as we walked toward the store.

"The what," I said.

"The pack of Winstons," he said.

Then it came back to me. We were smoking at this age. We split packs of cigarettes, and one of us would hold on to them. Since we didn't smoke much, the pack would last awhile. Jamie apparently was the one holding on to them but forgot to take them with him when he left this morning.

Coming out of the store, Jamie noticed a couple of his brother's friends, and we began talking. He bummed a cigarette from them, and we all went around the side of the store out of view. Jamie lit it, took a drag, and offered it to me, which seemed weird, but I guess sharing a cigarette was common practice in our youth. I hesitated then took a drag, expecting it to taste disgusting, but I was pleasantly surprised—my younger body was used to cigarettes, and it actually felt good, normal you know. We ended up talking for a while and didn't get back to the beach for almost an hour.

# Chapter Five

"You guys get lost?" Lena asked when we returned.

"We ran into a couple of Jamie's brother's friends at Pulsifers," I said.

"Oh, really."

"Yeah, they were down here partying at someone's house."

I lay down, and Lena rubbed some lotion on my back. The sun was warm, and I felt tired. Soon I drifted off to sleep and began to dream: I was a young boy. The carnival was due in town any day now, so I got up early and made my way down to Ingleside Park to see if it had arrived. It was a bright, sunny morning, and I had the whole day ahead of me. These summer days awaited my exploring them, like Christmas presents waiting to be opened—fresh, new experiences lie ahead. As I got toward the end of Walden Street, I saw it. It was here. Construction had begun! I could see the framework of the Ferris wheel looming high above the park and the platform or track for what would become the Tilta-Whirl. The white tents were also visible where carnival goers would soon be playing the Quarter Game or throwing darts at balloons to win a prize. How exciting it all was. It was summertime, the carnival was here, and I was on my way down to see it come to life. Then suddenly, the carnival disappeared. I was now sitting in a not-so-comfortable easy-chair in Albert Einstein's study, waiting for the *Great One* to appear. I had been invited to sit with him and discuss my time travel work. Hours passed, and Einstein never showed. Instead, from a secret door in the wall across from me, in walked my friend, Ron. He began talking about golf and a tee time he had set up for us. I was trying to tell him that I needed his help, that he would have to bring me back. I couldn't seem to make him understand that I didn't have the signaling device, that I wasn't able to bring myself back. "Ron, Ron," I screamed as he faded out of view.

Now someone new was calling my name. Whose voice is that? It's so familiar, so sweet. It was Lena who was trying to rouse me. Then I awoke. I blinked a couple of times, and her face came into focus.

"You've been asleep for over an hour now. Everyone left a while ago."

"Really, that long," I said as I tried to shake off the cobwebs.

"Yup, you were out cold. Who's Ron by the way?" Lena asked.

"Ron, I don't know." I suddenly realized that I must have been talking in my sleep.

"You were talking to someone named Ron in your dream."

"I don't know any Ron. I don't even remember the dream." Certainly I knew who Ron was, and I remembered the dream lucidly, but this of course would be kept from Lena. Then it came to me how ironic it was—that instead of falling asleep and dreaming of the unreal as most people do, from what I could remember, I dreamt of my real life then awoke to what could certainly be considered the unreal: back in time, living in my past.

"I forgot to tell you that I'm going out to eat with my family tonight."

"Which restaurant?" I asked as I got up from the towel and brushed sand from body.

"The Hilltop Steakhouse."

"Oh, I love a good steak, wish I were going."

"I don't really like steak, I'll probably just get a burger," Lena said.

"Oooh, I'd get a steak! I'd get a rib eye, now that's a good steak."

"I didn't know you liked steak that much, Mark."

"Yup," I said. "Steak with fries, coleslaw, and a cold—" I almost said beer then added "Coke" to the end of the sentence. After I said this, I realized that we didn't eat much steak growing up. At fourteen, I wouldn't have been able to tell a rib eye steak from filet mignon. It took a little growing up and ordering a number of steaks before I found out that the rib eye or sometimes called the Delmonico cut was my favorite. It's a tender and tasty cut of meat that has a good amount of marbling or fat in it. It's a fairly expensive steak but worth every penny.

"I'd rather not go," Lena said. "I'd rather hang out with our friends and be with you than go out to eat."

"No, go ahead, have a good time," I said.

"Then why don't you see what Jamie and Roy are doing tonight?" Lena asked.

"No, I think I'm gonna spend some time with my family. I haven't seen them in—I mean, I haven't done anything with them in a while."

"You, and hopefully I, will be with your family at the beach all day Sunday," Lena added.

"Yeah, that's true, and I will ask my mother tonight about you going with us."

"Good, I really want to go, Mark."

"Don't worry, you're definitely going," I said.

We held hands as we walked the short distance to the bus stop. I didn't realize it on a conscious level, but it felt natural to be holding Lena's hand.

"I had a great day today, Mark. It was fun...even though you fell asleep on me."

"I'm sorry, I just got so tired after I came back from Pulsifers."

"I'm just kidding. You know, you looked so peaceful when you were sleeping. But when you were dreaming...you looked troubled. You were actually moving about on the towel. You don't remember that dream, huh?"

"Nope, I can't remember any of it. I don't remember dreaming at all," I said, lying once again. The bus pulled up before we could talk much more. Lena leaned in and gave me a quick goodbye kiss. As I turned to get on, she said, "Call me tomorrow, and have a good time with your family tonight."

I looked back at this young girl who showed me so much affection and said, "All right, you too." Then I winked at Lena before stepping aboard the bus—again something I never would have done at fourteen.

# Chapter Six

At supper, I asked my mother if she had talked to her friend about the stock purchase.

"Jerry seems to think that it would be a good investment. He called it a safe long-term strategy. As a matter of fact, he has stock in Coca-Cola himself. So yes, I'll let you do it. Withdraw the money from your account and I'll take care of it."

"Thanks, Ma," I said and then remembered to ask her about Horseneck. "Do you mind if Lena goes with us to the beach on Sunday?"

"You asked me that a few days ago—remember?"

"No, I don't recall asking you."

"You don't recall?" my mother said with a smile on her face. I suddenly realized that she was questioning my choice of words rather than my memory. *Jeez, be careful,* I thought. *You're still sounding older than you look.*

"Well, anyway, I said yes. Of course, she can come."

"Thanks, I'll let her know."

After supper, I went out to the living room and plopped down on the couch. I was about to get up again to turn the TV on when I noticed a *TV Guide* magazine on the coffee table. Sonny and Cher were on the cover. I leafed through it looking for the night's lineup. Compared to 2014, there wasn't much available to watch: no movie channels, no twenty-four-hour news channels, no sports networks, and no Weather Channel. What was available were the three major networks and a couple of channels on the UHF frequency. There was no remote to turn the TV on or switch the channels, no cable box, and no special equipment like a DVD player or a DVR. But there were two antennas affixed to the back of the TV! These, of course, enabled you to manually adjust the picture reception—if you wanted to call that grainy black-and-white picture you got reception. I saw that *Gunsmoke* was coming on at seven, that classic Western series, and ironically *The Birds* was slotted into the nine-o'clock spot on ABC. This just happened to be my all-time favorite movie: a Hitchcock thriller about a small town in California that's attacked by birds.

I called out to the kitchen, "Ma, you wanna watch a movie tonight with me?"

"Which one?"

"*The Birds*," I said. "It comes on at nine."

"That one's kinda creepy," my mother said as she appeared in the doorway between the kitchen and living room. "You know, I saw that with your father when it first came out."

"I didn't know that."

"I think it was about ten years ago now. I have some homework to get done for school tomorrow, but I can probably get most of it done before nine. I'll finish whatever I have left during the movie," my mother said.

"You sure, Ma. I don't want to keep you from concentrating on your homework."

"I shouldn't have much left by nine. All the reading will be done by then, so what I'll have left won't require any deep concentration—answering questions and maybe writing a short essay."

"Ma, you were always good at multitasking, that's for sure," I said.

"Multitasking...huh, I like that term. Is that a common expression with the kids now?"

*Ah shit*, I thought. There I go again, either sounding too adult or using words or terms not currently being used.

"Yeah, something like that, Ma."

I turned the TV on, and with a little adjustment of the antenna, I had *Gunsmoke* coming in fairly clearly. *Gunsmoke* had been around since 1955 and still had three seasons of life left, an amazing run for this popular TV Western.

Ginny came in around seven thirty and asked me if I wanted to play Crazy Eights.

"Sure, sit down. We'll play while we watch TV," I said.

So I sat there playing cards with my little sister on the floor of the old house while Festus locked up the bad guys in the Dodge City jail. Billy came in a little while later and joined us. We all laughed when I ended up with a slew of cards in my hand at the end of the first game. I was really enjoying myself!

I was back to watching TV alone when Billy and Ginny decided that two games were enough. Billy headed outside and Ginny to her room while my mother quietly worked on her homework out in the kitchen.

# Chapter Seven

Billy walked into the room shortly before nine and asked what I was watching.

"There's a movie coming on in about five minutes called *The Birds*." I was telling him what it was about when my mother interrupted me.

"That movie is too grown-up for you, Billy, and besides, it's time for you to go to bed." She then asked, "Where's your sister?"

"She's upstairs playing with her dolls, I think."

"Tell her to brush her teeth and get ready for bed, and you do the same," she said in her motherly way, not mean, just firmly.

"Can I watch a little of the movie, it sounds real good?"

"No, you cannot. Now go get ready for bed."

"Ah, Mom," Billy said then turned and trudged off. Joanne was still over at her friend Shawna's house, and John was God knew where, so my mother and I would be watching the Hitchcock thriller by ourselves.

My mother surprised me by making popcorn for the show. No microwave yet, it was made the old-fashioned way: on the stove-top in a saucepan with oil. With a little bit of salt, it tasted great. She handed me a bowl full and set another on the coffee table for herself.

"I'll be right down, I'm gonna go say good night to your brother and sister."

As I adjusted the TV, I heard laughter coming from upstairs. My mother got back downstairs right as the movie was starting.

So we enjoyed the popcorn together in the quiet of the living room while birds noisily ravaged that small seaside town, killing many of its residents. The beautiful young actress, Tippi Hedren, did a great job in her debut role under the guidance of the master, Mr. Hitchcock. The crazed bird attacks seemed to coincide with her arrival in town, setting the stage for this interesting movie based on Daphne du Maurier's short story. With Hitchcock at the helm and a cast of veteran actors including Jessica Tandy, how could this not be a great movie. I love my mother, and this was special for me. I would have taken this for granted the first time, but now I understood that times like these are fleeting.

Joanne came home shortly before the movie was over.

"What's on?"

"*The Birds*," I said, then added, "Why don't you sit down and watch the ending with us?"

"No, I've seen it before—no reason to see it again."

"Suit yourself, but this end part is *killer*."

"No thanks, I'm tired, and as I said, I've seen it before. Hey, make sure you pick up when you're done. I'm the one who does most of the cleaning around here."

"And I appreciate that, Joanne," my mother interjected, looking up from the notebook in her lap. Joanne did take care of the majority of the house cleaning since my mother had gone back to school. I don't really remember how much I pitched in, but apparently it wasn't enough.

"I'll help you with the cleaning tomorrow, if you like," I said.

"Yeah, sure you will."

"No really, I will, I'm serious."

"Seeing is believing," Joanne replied with a smirk and then said good night.

While the young woman crept up the stairs to investigate the noise she heard, my mother closed her notebook.

"Oh, I hate this part," she said.

Little did she know that the birds had made their way into one of the upper rooms and were awaiting an opportunity to strike. After opening the door, her flashlight attracted hundreds of those killers, and one after another, she was pecked almost to death. She is rescued from this avian assault, but by then the young woman is in rough shape. The movie ends when it's decided that she needs to be brought to a hospital. They have to leave the relative safety of their board-ed-up house where they've been hunkered down all night. The final scene is typical Hitchcockian. They drive away from the house with birds eerily perched in every possible nook and cranny and ready to strike, but they don't. They seem content to have taken over the town and driven out, what appears to be, its last inhabitants.

"That's a great ending, huh, Ma?"

"Yeah, except for the part where the birds almost kill that poor girl," my mother said with a look of disgust on her face. "It's a little too much for me."

"Yeah, I know, but I mean the way the birds are everywhere in the very end. On the porch, all over the yard, in the trees and the telephone wires. That last shot is fantastic! It just sums up the whole movie visually."

"You sound like a real movie critic, Mark. That's an astute observation."

*Remember, Mark, you're fourteen*—silently scolding myself again. "Thanks, Ma, I just love that movie."

"Well, I better get to bed, and so should you," my mother said, getting up from the couch.

"All right, Ma, I'm exhausted anyway." I went over and kissed my mother's cheek and wished her good night.

"I hope John gets home soon, he worries me sick sometimes."

"He'll be home soon," I said, trying to reassure my mother as I made my way to the bathroom. He'd most likely be home soon and things would be all right tonight, but I knew things would only get worse with him and us.

John came in about a half hour later. I heard him just as I was drifting off to sleep. I just hope my mother knew that he came home so she could sleep peacefully.

# PART 4

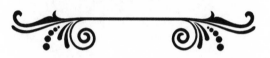

# Chapter One

*Tuesday, 17 July 1973*

I woke up the next day to the sound of pouring rain on the roof and at the windows. The weathermen got it wrong this time. Yesterday they said the storm racing up from the south would be blocked by a high-pressure system parked off the coast, but apparently this wasn't the case. Most people are hard on meteorologists, complaining about how seldom the weather reports are accurate. Being a scientist myself, I'm not one of those people. Although meteorology is a science, it's not an exact one. There are way too many variables that are juggled to form a weather forecast. Even with the computer models used today, it's still imperfect. The complexity that goes into developing a forecast is actually mind-boggling and the simple-minded people who complain could not even begin to comprehend the scientific computations that are involved.

Lena called me not long after I finished breakfast. She asked if I wanted to play board games at her house since it was such a crummy day.

"Yeah, sure, sounds like a good plan. What time should I be over?"

"Come over before noon and I'll make you some lunch. How-bout-that?"

"How about you make me supper too then I sleep over?" I said jokingly.

"That would be great if my parents weren't home," she whispered into the phone. "It's funny you say that though, because they won't be home Saturday night. They're goin' down The Cape and staying over my father's friend's house."

"Oh really," I said as a lump began to form in my throat.

"Yeah really. And after my brothers go to bed, we'll have the house to ourselves," she said in a very hushed tone.

*Here we go again*, I thought. *I'll just have to dance around the inevitable intimacy issues when they come up.* "Good, we'll have some alone time together," I said, trying to sound like I couldn't wait for Saturday night to come.

"Yeah, just me and you, Mark."

"Can't wait. Anyway, I'll be down about eleven thirty today."

"Okay, see you then."

"All right, Lena, bye."

# Chapter Two

Jamie called a half hour later and asked if I wanted to go to the Sox game. He had tickets from a game that was rained-out earlier in the year. It was a one o'clock start, the first game of a day-night double header at Fenway.

"Nah, I can't. I just made plans with Lena."

"Shit, I can't even give these tickets away! Roy can't go either, and my brother's out with his girlfriend."

"You asked Roy first, huh."

"Hey, don't bust my balls. You're always with Lena, so I figured you'd be with her today."

"Just kidding, Jamie. You figured right—I'm gonna be with her today." Then I added, "You can't get anyone else to go? I take it Trisha's not around."

"Trish is with her mother in town today—clothes shopping I think. She really doesn't like baseball anyway. I'm not even sure if the game's gonna be played, with all this rain we're gettin'. Imagine if it gets rained out again—a rainout of a rainout. Maybe I'll call my cousin if the game's still on, see if he wants to go."

"Well, I hope you find someone. I'm gonna get goin', so I'll talk to you later."

"All right, I'll see ya later."

# Chapter Three

By the time I got off the bus the rain had started up again, so I ran the two blocks to Lena's house. The weight I now carried made running seem effortless. I glided along like a well-oiled machine with no pain and plenty of wind. Just a few days ago I was experiencing my usual right knee pain as I carried groceries up the stairs to my second-floor apartment, slightly out of breath. It would be an understatement to say that it's nice to be young again—it's great; it feels unbelievable!

Lena was in the front room when I arrived.

"It's coming down hard again, huh," she said rhetorically while handing me a towel as I stepped into the house.

"Yup. It wasn't raining while I was on the bus, but as soon as I got off, right on cue it started pouring."

While I began drying my hair, Lena leaned in and kissed me quickly. We never dared to kiss in front of her parents, so this was always done quickly and on the sly. Lena's father was at work, but her mother was in the kitchen, so I went out and said hello while Lena set up a folding card table in the front room. She was busy, working away on what to me was an archaic, obsolete relic of the past—a typewriter. Mrs. Mendleson made a little extra money by typing college students' papers that were written out longhand. She banged away at the keys, smiling as she returned my greeting. Mrs. Mendleson once told me that her work was therapeutic—she could get lost in it. It sure as hell looked like she was enjoying herself.

Lena was holding up two games when I returned to the front room.

"Monopoly or Scrabble?" she asked.

"Monopoly I guess."

"Here, you set it up while I get the sandwiches and drinks. What would you like to drink, Mark?"

"Do you have any ginger ale?"

"I think so, let me check," she said.

It was then I realized that I hadn't had any coffee since I had left the present. I guess my younger body had no use for it and wasn't craving something that I wouldn't be addicted to for years to come.

"Water's fine if you don't have ginger ale," I called after her.

I set up the game on the card table in that entrance room. You could call it a sunroom really. Once a porch but now enclosed, it provided an open, airy feel. The large sliding door and expansive windows on either side created a warm, well-illuminated room. With built-in bench seats and comfy chairs, it was a nice place to sit and read, play a game, or just relax while looking out at the water and skyline.

Most people will tell you, and I am one of them, that time passes a lot quicker when you get older. Of course, this is an illusion. Our worlds are filled up with so many things that we have to do, the precious little time that remains seems to fly by. As a kid with not near as many responsibilities and commitments, you have more time for yourself; thus your life in general seems to move at a much more leisurely pace. So on this rainy day in July of 1973, two teenagers enjoyed each other's company, playing a game of monopoly as the afternoon slowly ticked by.

# Chapter Four

At five o'clock, Lena's mother came in to see if I wanted to stay for supper. "Spaghetti and meatballs," she said, coaxing me to stay.

"That would be nice, Mrs. Mendleson, let me call my mother to see if it's okay with her." Just then I smelled the marinara sauce coming from the kitchen—it smelled great.

"Sure go ahead, Mark. Supper's at six, so you guys should start wrapping it up in about a half hour or so."

"I think we'll be done before that. If Lena lands on Boardwalk or Park Place again, she won't have any more money to play the game."

"Hey, don't count your chickens before they're hatched," Lena said as she reached over and nudged my shoulder. "I still have a few things up my sleeve."

I made the call to my mother and got the okay to eat over and then returned to the front room where we finished the game. Lena never did land on Boardwalk or Park Place, but she lost regardless when we ended at five thirty. As we were putting things away, her father came in from work. A tall, imposing man who never said more than a few words to me. As far as I can remember, I never heard him say much at all. He greeted us with a deep-toned hello as he made his way to the kitchen. Her younger brothers came in a few minutes later, playfully teasing each other. They came across to me like good friends, not just brothers. They were two years apart but hung out together along with their friends in the neighborhood.

Lena's mother made her own sauce and meatballs, and it was always delicious. Tonight was no exception. We started with a salad then feasted on the main course with some fresh Italian bread. As usual, Mr. Mendleson was for the most part quiet during the meal, adding only a few words here and there to the conversation. Mrs. Mendleson was talkative as usual, keeping the conversation entertaining. The subjects varied, from the weather to the Red Sox to the Watergate hearings in Washington. I couldn't help myself when I said, "I think the president's got himself into a bit of hot water."

"You think so, Mark. I think it's just the press blowing it all out of proportion," Mrs. Mendleson replied.

I backed off with, "Yeah, you're probably right, Mrs. Mendleson, maybe there's nothing really there." But little did she know that old *Tricky Dick* would be history in a little over a year.

After dinner, we all went out to the living room and watched television except for Lena's father who went upstairs to get work done that he had brought home.

At nine thirty Lena walked me outside. It was time to get going.

"That was really nice eating together. You know, someday we'll be married, and I'll be the one making supper for you in our own house," Lena said.

"Let's not rush things, we're still young."

"I know, but I just like to look ahead. To imagine things the way they could be someday for me and you."

I couldn't help feel the pain thinking how the whole thing would unravel in less than six months' time.

"What's the matter, you have a strange look on your face, Mark?"

"Do I?" I never did have a poker face, and Lena could read my expression.

"I know we're young, but we've talked about this before. You still think about marrying me someday, don't you?"

"Yeah, of course, that's exactly the way I'd like it to work out, Lena," I said, but knew it wouldn't. "Listen, I better get goin', I gotta get my bus." I gave Lena a closed-mouth kiss on the lips, said bye, then turned and walked away. I left her standing there with a kind of sad, puzzled look on her face.

I just had to get out of there, I felt the pain of the impending loss, and surprisingly I also felt anger below the surface. Why would I feel this way? I had been over her for years. I'm an adult now.

But then I realized the transition must have begun and I was feeling things as the boy would, knowing what the man knows. My two selves are now linked. My knowledge of the breakup must be known and felt by my former self as well. Either way, I felt like shit and wanted to get the hell out of Dodge as quickly as possible. I walked along briskly then began to run. Maybe by tiring myself out I'd rid myself of these feelings.

When I got home, my mother was in the living room.

"Hi, Ma," I said.

"Hi, Mark, everything okay?"

"Yeah, sure," I said unconvincingly, then remembered that I needed to give her the money for the stock. "Let me go get the money for the Coca-Cola stock before I forget." I ran upstairs and retrieved it from my dresser drawer. When I came back down stairs and gave it to her, she looked shocked.

"The bank gave you a thousand dollars in cash. I assumed they'd give you a check."

My mind was still on Lena, and my mother caught me off guard with her questioning. I wasn't sure either way since I never really did visit the bank.

"I don't know, Ma, that's what they gave me," I said, lying as I handed her the money.

"Are you all right, Mark, you don't sound yourself—you sound down."

"Yeah, the night just didn't end right," I replied.

"You'll have days like that, but you guys will work it out. I know how much you like each other. Get a good night sleep and start fresh tomorrow. Tomorrow's a whole new day."

My mother had a knack for making me feel better. I felt guilty that I had to lie about the money. She always looked out for me, and as I stood there, I realized once again how much I really loved my mother.

"Thanks, Ma," I said, then kissed her on the cheek before I went up to bed.

*Friday, 13 June 2014*

Ronald Joseph Sarno's morning routine never varied. He arrived one hour before his day began at Harvard and ran his route around the Charles River. Today was no exception. An accomplished runner in high school, Ron held the one-mile record at Winthrop High for several months before it was broken by a fellow classmate. At Boston College he ran all four years, keeping pace with some of the best milers in the state.

Ron once told me that he ran to stay young for the girls. He also knew that with age, weight gain and general deterioration of the body were inevitable. To stave this off, he ran, keeping himself in top physical condition.

Coming down Kirkland Street, Ron was two minutes from the Science Center where his office in the math department was located. He was on autopilot, thinking of last night with Jessica, a graduate student he had recently met on campus. Ron had had many women over the years, but she was different. Something he couldn't put his finger on, something in his gut, seemed to be telling him that she might just be the one. He couldn't believe it. He finally might be settling down, he thought to himself, then laughed out loud. He wanted to tell me, but of course, that was impossible. In spite of the heavy rain and his soaked running shoes, Ron couldn't keep himself from smiling. Just as he was wondering how I was doing back in 1973, a cargo van slammed into him as it backed out of an alley-way and onto Kirkland. Ron was thrown to the ground and rendered unconscious when his head slammed against the pavement. Blood began to pool under his head by the time the driver of the van reached him. He kneeled down next to Ron and reached for his head to somehow comfort him but then pulled away quickly, not sure of what to do. The driver looked up at the growing crowd surrounding the scene and said to no one in particular, "I didn't see him. I looked in my mirror and no one was there...then...Christ, oh fuck, what have I done!" Someone in the crowd had called 911, and sirens could be heard in the distance screaming to the scene.

Ron was taken to Massachusetts General Hospital in a coma where he was listed in serious but stable condition. He had suffered a severe concussion with lacerations to the head, a ruptured spleen, two broken ribs, and a broken right wrist. He had lacerations to his face and left arm that required stitches to control the bleeding.

Harvard University was notified regarding the accident, but no next of kin was contacted. Ron was one of those rare people who have no next of kin. He was an only child whose parents were both killed in a car accident during his first year of college. His father was also an only child whose parents were now deceased, and Ron's mother was an immigrant with no relatives living in the United States. His new girlfriend, Jessica Valjean, wouldn't find out about the accident for two days, so no one came rushing to Mass General to see this young college professor lying unconscious with severe trauma to his body. Once Jessica did discover what had happened, it was obvious how much she cared for him because she stayed at his bedside every day, long into the night. Jessica talked to him because she knew that's what you do—she would have anyway. She cried when she told him how much she loved him even though they had only known each other for a few weeks. She said she'd stay with him even though the doctors said that he might never wake up.

"I'm not leaving you, Ronald Sarno, I'm not leaving," she said as she tried to hold back the tears, but they came anyway.

On that first evening when the night nurse came in telling her that it was time to leave, she momentarily regained her composure, looked up, and in a quiet voice said, "He's got no one, only me... can't you—" Then she dropped her head and began sobbing. Ron's night nurse, Trivia, worked nights because it was quieter, not because she had to. She'd been a nurse for close to forty years and had seen just about everything including what she was witnessing now. She stood in the doorway for a minute fumbling with keys in her hand then walked over to Jessica.

"Come here, hon."

She helped Jessica to her feet then held her as Jessica released all the emotion bound up inside. When Jessica had stopped crying, she said, "You stay as long as you want, honey. I'm the charge nurse here, and no one's gonna make you leave if I have anything to say about it—okay." Jessica lifted her head and blinked back tears as she pulled herself together. "Thank you," she said.

Trivia pulled a couple of tissues from the box on the nightstand, handed them to Jessica, and said, "You stay as long as you need to. It's Jessica, right?"

"Yes, Jessica," she said as a smile formed on her moist face. Then she added, "I'm sorry."

"No need to be sorry, hon. And when your man wakes up, I'm gonna tell him straight out what kind of a woman he has here. And he better stick with you, or I'll whip his sorry butt," Trivia said, smiling. This made Jessica burst out laughing, releasing any remaining tension that she had felt earlier. When she regained control, Jessica said, "I've only known him for a few weeks, but I know I love him, I just know."

"I know you do, Jessica, it shows. And my name's Trivia—if you need anything just give ol Triv a holler."

"Thanks, Trivia, I appreciate that."

Twenty minutes later, Jessica bent down and kissed Ron on the forehead. "I'll be back tomorrow, Ron, I promise. I love you, I want you to know that."

# PART 5

# Chapter One

*Wednesday, 18 July 1973*

L ying on the beach the next day, the thought occurred to me to get some pictures to bring back. I don't remember owning a camera in 1973, so I asked Lena, "You have a camera, right?"

"Yeah, remember I got one for my birthday."

"You did show that to me, didn't you?"

"You're definitely having a problem with your memory, Mark. I not only showed it to you, you took some pictures with it—it was just last week."

I feigned remembering then asked Lena if she would bring it to the beach tomorrow.

"They'll make great souvenirs for when we get old and gray," I said. How true this really was. I had not one picture of us or any of our friends, and I definitely wanted to take some back.

"I'll throw it in my beach bag tomorrow."

It was getting late in the afternoon, and Roy told us he was heading home. Everyone else had already left.

"You guys wanna leave now with me, or you gonna stay a little longer?"

"Yeah, a little bit longer," Lena said.

"The movie should be good tonight," Roy added.

Lena and I agreed (even though I had no idea what movie we were seeing) as he turned and took off for home. I wasn't going to dig for more information now, making Lena more suspicious of my behavior. I'd just *go with the flow.*

Twenty minutes later, as I walked Lena back to her house, she stopped suddenly and turned to face me. We were standing on the sidewalk in the shade of a big maple tree.

"You know, you're acting kinda strange."

I knew this would come up soon. Lena would sense the change in me and get curious, so I was prepared with my *book* story.

"What do you mean?"

"For one," Lena said, "you forgot all about Horseneck Beach. When I asked you about it the other day, you looked at me like you had no idea what I was talking about. Secondly, you didn't remember the camera. That was a birthday present from my aunt. I told you that it meant a lot to me 'cause I really love my aunt. And thirdly, I don't know, but you seem to be looking at me differently, acting kind of strange. You know, you don't seem to want to french kiss me anymore either. Last night you seemed angry before you left and again not the type of kiss I've come to expect from you. Is everything okay?" Lena hesitated, looked away, then turned her gaze back on me and asked, "Do you still like me, I mean enough to go steady?"

"Of course I like you enough to be going steady with you." I hesitated for a bit then said, "I'm sorry, I've been distracted lately, thinking about things. This might sound crazy, but…well, I'm reading this book called *Man's Search for Meaning* by a guy named Frankl. It's really deep. Mrs. Rowe suggested it to me."

"Mrs. Rowe, our ninth-grade English teacher?" Lena asked.

"Yeah, Mrs. Rowe. At the end of the year, I asked her if she could recommend some good summer reading, and she suggested the book I just mentioned. She said that it would make me think and possibly reexamine my life. It's doing just that, it really is."

"Reexamine your life?" Lena interrupted, looking puzzled.

"Yeah, exactly—how short it is and how no one really knows when theirs is gonna end. The author tells a story about his time in a Nazi concentration camp. The odds of getting out alive were astronomical, but he made it. He held on to hope and found a meaning for his life in such brutal and dire conditions. It's a beautiful story about how the human spirit can triumph even in the depths of despair. Lena, after reading it, I made up my mind not to take anything for granted anymore, especially us. I'm happier now than I've ever been, and it's because of you. I don't want to lose you."

As I was saying these words, I realized I was being completely honest. They were coming from my heart. I was beginning to feel the way I felt the first time; the change was taking place. I knew it. I really had read Frankl's book but concocted my feelings of distract-edness to explain away the changes and awkwardness that Lena saw through. How I felt about her right at this moment, what I had just told Lena, was sincere. I once again felt that longing, that need to be with her. Lena came closer. She put her arms around my waist and pulled us together, our bodies now joined. She drew her face to mine, and my body, no my whole being, tingled. I wrapped my arms around her back and held her soft body. Our lips touched. Then they slowly parted—finding each other's tongues. I then slid my arms up her back to her head, which I then cradled softly with both hands. I tilted my head, pressing my mouth tight against hers, and we kissed long and deep while my eyes stayed closed. It seemed we were one, lost in each other as the world disappeared around us. The sensa-tion was overwhelming. It was erotic but almost spiritual, and it felt right—it felt so right. At that moment, I didn't feel my true age. I was taken away with that kiss to a place I hadn't been to in over four decades.

Lena broke the embrace by pulling her head back and looking into my eyes.

"Do you really feel that way about me—what you just said?" she asked.

"Yes, I do. I don't want to ever lose you."

"Don't worry, I'm not going anywhere." She paused and then said, "Because I love you. Have I ever told you that?"

I told her I wasn't sure as I stood there in a dreamlike trance. I reached out with my right hand, caressing and studying her face as if she might suddenly disappear. My next words came out without really thinking.

"I love you, Lena. I couldn't love you any more than I do right now." I just wanted to stay there with her, right there, holding her forever. We kissed again and, eventually after several minutes, said our goodbyes.

As I walked away, Lena turned and said, "Seven fifteen in front of the Winthrop Theater, right?"

I looked back and said, "Wouldn't miss it for the world."

# Chapter Two

I decided to walk home. This new body felt great. Fifty-five pounds lighter and no body aches yet. Later in life I would be plagued with chronic back pain and other assorted ailments, but right now I was 100 percent. Besides that, my general mood was euphoric, and I wanted time to think about all the things that had transpired in the three short days I'd been back, especially those last few moments. Wow, I'd forgotten how good it could feel! Then lyrics from a song I hadn't heard in years came to mind.

> *We kissed under the maple*
> *As rain poured down*
> *There was no doubting now*
> *What I had found*

I now knew for sure that I was making the change. I was experiencing the feelings I had for Lena when I was young but at the same time feeling pretty much as I always do as an adult. This duality of selves (past and present) would last a while, but eventually, at some point, my past self would take control, and my present-day self would be eliminated. That was a scary thought to consider, but if everything proceeds as it should, Ron would bring me back well before that ever took place.

I started walking and thinking about this movie we were going to see tonight. It obviously was planned prior to Sunday when I arrived, so I had no idea of the name of the movie, just that we were going to see it at the Winthrop Theater sometime after seven fifteen tonight. I assumed Jamie would be going, but I'd call him to make sure. The theater is in the Center, so just a walk from our houses. The rest of the gang would most likely take the bus from The Point.

# Chapter Three

When Jamie and I arrived at the theater, Lena and our friends were there waiting for us. They were in a small line that was forming outside. It was about 7:20 p.m. at that point. I joined Lena, and Jamie went over to Trisha. Joan and Roy were there also. They both would be hooked up with someone before the summer was out, but tonight they were there as friends.

"Wow, that's cool," Roy said as he stepped into the lobby. It was then I discovered what movie we'd be seeing tonight. What got Roy's attention was the movie poster inside the large metal and glass *Now Showing* display case for *The Poseidon Adventure*. Now it came back to me. I could even remember where we sat in the theater that night. It would begin at 7:40 p.m.

The 1970s was the decade of the disaster movie like *Earthquake*, *The Towering Inferno*, *The Swarm*, and many others. *The Poseidon Adventure* was another of these blockbuster disaster movies. After being struck by a tidal wave on New Year's Eve, the ocean liner SS *Poseidon* capsizes. A group of passengers, against the advice of one of the ship's officers, decides to work their way up to the overturned bottom of the ship where they believe rescue would arrive. It was built up heavily with advertising and promised to be a thrilling story with an all-star cast. It didn't disappoint.

We settled in with our popcorn and drinks as the movie unfolded. Lena was moved by a scene in which Earnest Borgnine's (Rogo's) wife died. When he cried out "Linnnnda," Lena let out a low shrill and grabbed on to me. She held close to me through the rest of the movie just like the first time, but this time it seemed to feel better. I put my mouth close to her ear and whispered "I love you," and she held me tighter. We enjoyed the rest of the movie in each other's arms. It was a great movie to see with Lena and my friends once again, and when it ended, most in attendance cheered.

I held Lena's hand as we waited for the bus that would bring the majority of our group back to The Point. We goofed around as young kids do, probably making too much noise, but we were having too much fun to realize it. There were the typical adolescent jokes including Lena getting ribbed for the aforementioned scene in the movie—it didn't go unnoticed. She said, "It bothered me, it sounded like Lena when he cried out her name."

Roy came back with, "Jesus, Lena, we're just kiddin'."

"Screw you, Roy," Lena said then smiled, letting him know she wasn't really offended.

The bus eventually pulled up. We stole our private kisses and said our goodbyes. Lena was gone, but just for a day.

# Chapter Four

Jamie and I set off for home but not before lighting up a couple of Winstons. We held them low, sneaking drags when we dared.

"Roy was talkin' about havin' some beers Friday night down at The Weeds." The Weeds was the name we gave the place in Coughlin Park where we drank. Actually it was a misnomer. Along the shoreline during low tide, eelgrass could be seen in the water from our little hideaway. We referred to it as weeds, thus the inappropriate name. Down below the grassy level of the park, dipping down along the dark shoreline at night, this was our drinking spot. The guys drank beer, the girls wine, and some of us smoked pot.

"He said he was bringing a few joints down too," Jamie added. I had smoked pot occasionally but didn't really care for it. It was too harsh on my throat, and the high I got left me too paranoid. "Are you gonna have some, Mark?"

"I don't think so," I said.

"I thought you liked it?"

"Not really. It makes me too paranoid. Beer mellows me out, but pot, it makes me paranoid." And as I said this I was thinking of a time down there at The Weeds where I worried all night about the cops catching us drinking and smoking. "If I'm gonna get buzzed, I don't wanna be paranoid too."

"More for me and Roy then," Jamie added. "Trish said she might try it the last time I mentioned it to her, so maybe she'll have a few tokes. It actually might be funny to see what it does to her."

We were at the top of my street now, and I felt relaxed, so I asked my friend a question that I already knew the answer to. I just wanted to see what he'd say.

"Hey, Jamie, do you think you'll ever get married?"

"I dunno. Why are you asking me that?"

"Just wondering if you ever think about it, that's all."

"Well, you know, I never really think about it. I can't picture myself married—tied down to some girl. I guess I'm too young to even think about being married in the future. I know I like my freedom, and I like to know I can break up with a girl and date another if I want to. Eventually, yeah, I'll probably end up married just like most older guys, but shit, not for a long, long time."

I was looking at Jamie with a smile on my face knowing full well that he'd be the first of my childhood friends married. In fact, it would be in less than ten years. He would end up marrying a distant cousin of mine who lived only one street away from where we were now standing.

"Why are you looking at me like that, and what's with the smile?"

Shit, I wasn't just smiling; I was almost laughing and could hardly contain myself.

"Oh, nothin', I just…I'm just in a good mood—you know, good time tonight with you and the gang." I regained control as we neared my house.

"Yeah, I had a good time tonight too. Good movie, huh?"

"Yeah, it was good, pretty exciting too. I'll see you tomorrow," I said as I started up the walkway.

"See you later, Mark." Then Jamie turned back abruptly in the street and called after me, "Hey, Mark…do think about gettin' married?"

"Yup," I said, and then added, "Every day."

"Yeah, that figures." My friend wasn't too far away for me to see that the smile was now on his face. "See ya tomorrow."

"Sure, I'll see you tomorrow."

# Chapter Five

*Friday, 20 July 1973*

The day began the way most of these summer days did: no alarm clock to wake up to, no important tasks waiting to be completed, and no job to hurry to get ready for. I was slipping right back into the casual routine of that youthful summer. When I lived through this period of my life the first time, I was of course happy, but I guess I was too young to realize the degree of happiness and contentment I was experiencing with Lena. It was like standing on top of Mt. Everest and not knowing it, realizing only that I was on a lofty peak, but not grasping that I was on the highest one. In the years to come, I would never achieve the heights of happiness that I experienced in 1973 but could only look back with fond memories knowing that I once stood on top of the world.

Lena wouldn't be around until late this afternoon. She and Joan were going into Boston to do some shopping. I called Jamie to see if he wanted to play Wiffle ball again down at the high school. We had played yesterday in the late afternoon with a couple of the kids from our neighborhood and Roy, who biked it down from The Point.

"Yeah, sure, sounds good. I can't get outa the house till after lunch though. I'm helpin' my father with some stuff in the yard.

"Okay, good, I'll call around and see who I can round up," I said. "Just come up when you're ready."

"All right, should be around noontime—see ya then."

"Okay, I'll see ya."

Tommy, my friend who lived next to Alicia, was the only one of the neighborhood kids around.

"Yeah, sure, I'll play—even though you guys ditched us a couple of months back to go out with your girls down The Point."

"Hey, come on, Tom, we still hang with you guys when we're not down there. We were around yesterday, but you weren't. We got John and Louis to go down to the school and play ball."

"Relax, I'm just kiddin'. If I had the chance to score a girl like your girlfriends, I'd definitely go for it."

"Yeah, we lucked out. We got some cool girls."

# Chapter Six

We walked down to the high school where we met Roy at twelve thirty. There were only four of us, so we played with just a pitcher and a fielder on each team. We were in the parking lot behind the school. The school itself was used as a backstop. The high chain-link fence that separated the parking lot from the baseball field about seventy feet away was the outfield wall. We played automatics where nobody ran out their hits. A grounder that got by the two players was a single, and a shot against the fence was a home run.

Like yesterday, we had a blast slamming the Wiffle ball around. We played nine inning games, two outs per inning for each team. They were quick paced, about forty-five minutes per game. We switched up the teams after each game. In the first game, Tommy and I faced Jamie and Roy. They killed us with the home run ball. The final score was 20–9. The second game was more evenly matched with Jamie and I facing Roy and Tommy. That game actually went into extra innings where we won in the tenth.

We took a break after the second game. We walked down to the White Hen, a convenience store a block away on Revere Street where we filled up on junk food and soft drinks.

"What are you guys doin' tonight?" Tommy asked on the way back to the school.

With a mouthful of Twinkies, Roy said drinking, but it sounded more like drinnin' with all the food in his mouth.

"Yeah, we are too," Tommy replied.

Jamie let out an enormously loud belch, and we all started laughing. Roy almost lost his Twinkies trying to contain himself.

I looked over at Tommy and said, "Why don't you guys come down tonight?"

"Nah, I think we'll just hang in the hood like we usually do," Tommy replied.

"Well, if you decide to come down, you know where we drink, right? In the park, down near the water facing the airport," I said, answering my own question.

"Yeah, I know where it is, but we'll probably just stick around," he said then asked, "Hey, we gonna play one more game?"

Then Jamie chimed in, "Yeah, at least one more, but I wanna have a cig first. You want one, Mark?" he asked.

"No, not right now."

While Jamie smoked, we sat finishing our food and drinks and talked. It was fun and very relaxing sitting there idling away the time on that warm summer afternoon in July. I wondered how many other young kids in this country were playing ball like we were this afternoon, enjoying themselves like young kids do—must be thousands, maybe tens of thousands. But how many have travelled back in time to do it, returning to their past to once again play ball with their friends. I felt so lucky to be sitting there with them, so grateful to be here once again.

We got one more game in. Then Roy took off, and the rest of us walked back home.

# Chapter Seven

I called Lena after supper to let her know Jamie and I would be down around seven o'clock. Roy's sister and boyfriend would get us our booze as usual. They'd meet us down at the park right after it got dark out.

We made our way into the park clutching our precious cargo: two six-packs of beer and a couple of bottles of wine. Thinking back, it's amazing we never got caught entering the park on our way to The Weeds, although it was usually dark and we tried always to be as inconspicuous as possible. We were careful tonight, too, not to draw attention to ourselves.

We found our spot. The girls all sat together on a large piece of driftwood. Roy and Jamie just sat down on the seashells while I perched myself atop a rather large flat rock firmly packed down into the shells.

Before long we were all feeling the effects of the alcohol. Jamie, Roy, and I had finished off the first six-pack in nearly a half hour while the girls had their first bottle of wine nearly consumed. It was then Roy decided to fire up a joint.

Jamie handed the joint to Trisha after taking a toke, looking at her expectantly. "I guess I'll try it," she said and took the joint from Jamie's hand. She took a long pull then immediately coughed violently. We all laughed as Trisha reeled from her first experience with marijuana. Jamie went over to Trisha and tried to comfort her while also trying to contain his laughter. Lena leaned over and rubbed her back while Trisha wiped tears from her watery eyes.

"Jesus, that stuff's harsh," she said as she coughed once more.

"Trisha, take smaller hits," Roy instructed, "and try to hold it in so you get a buzz."

"Yeah, just a little at a time, Trish. You won't cough if you just take a little in," Jamie said as he gave her a reassuring hug.

The joint was passed around again, and Trisha took a smaller hit this time. She was able to hold it in for a bit without coughing. Lena, Joan, and I all declined the offer to smoke, and Roy called us pussies. We knew of course that he was just busting balls, but we told him to fuck off anyway and then laughed.

By ten o'clock all the alcohol had been consumed and Roy and Jamie were working on the last joint. Trisha was way beyond smashed as her body was dealing with the effects of both the alcohol and the pot. She was now seated next to Jamie on the seashells, leaning into him and whispering into his ear. They eventually got up and took a walk farther down the shoreline to be alone. After a while, Lena and I followed suit. We left Roy and Joan back at The Weeds talking.

# Chapter Eight

Lena and I passed Jamie and Trisha on our way farther down. They were lying there making out as we went by. We found a spot about fifty feet away from them around the bend in the shoreline. I brushed away the seashells, stones, and other debris from an area and replaced it with straw—the dead, dried-up eel grass.

Lena looked at her watch and said that we had about forty minutes before she had to be home.

"Good, we can be all alone for a little while then," I said as we lay down on the straw. We positioned ourselves on our sides, spooning up to each other, and began kissing. I was so at home with Lena. It felt so natural to be holding her and kissing her. I could do this forever, I thought. I had been back six days now and felt completely comfortable here. I was still very much aware of my adult self and the fact that I had returned from my future but at the same time felt it slowly slipping away. That boy of fourteen was gaining a foothold now, and I knew it. I was spending less time thinking about my old self and the possibility of being stranded here. It seemed to have lost some of its significance. Lena was my focus now—even more so tonight.

As we kissed, I cautiously moved my right hand to Lena's waist and used my fingers to slowly pull up her blouse, untucking it from her pants. At first, Lena fended off my advances by restraining my hand but then released her grip. After getting the blouse free, I slid my hand slowly up under, reaching her right breast covered only by her bra. As I caressed her breast through the fabric, Lena let out a soft moan. I gently kissed her neck, and she responded by rolling her head back, exposing more of the soft flesh to my lips and tongue.

Lena didn't protest when I slid both hands under her back, searching for the hooks to release her bra. Just as I had finally managed to unclasp the bra, Trisha came out of nowhere and tripped over our legs. She fell flat on her face. Lena let out a startled shriek and quickly turned her body so as to hide anything that might be exposed. The intrusion startled me also. I sat up so fast that I felt my back spasm. "What the fuck!" I said as Trisha tumbled to the ground. I think she said "Oh shit" as she was falling, but I wasn't sure because of her slurred speech.

"Jesus, Trish," Jamie said, appearing suddenly out of the darkness. "She's really fucked up." Jamie went over to help Trisha. "Sorry to bother you guys."

"No, no problem," I said as I got up on my feet, wincing from the pain in my back.

"I'll be right back," Lena said as she briskly walked away. I assumed to find a concealed area to refasten her bra and straighten her clothes. On her return, she went right over to Trisha who was now sitting on the ground trying to get her bearings. Jamie was kneeling next to her, holding on to Trisha so she didn't keel over.

"I don't feel so…" And before she could finish the sentence, Trisha puked between her own legs. Lena rubbed her back while handing her a couple of tissues. "Thanks, Linna," she said drunkenly and then added, "I'm a mess."

Lena and Jamie steadied her as she got to her feet. Jamie asked me if I could go get Roy. "I wanna see if we can bring Trisha over to his house for a while before she goes back home. I don't think his mother's home, and she needs to sober up."

"Yeah, I'll go take a look for him." I found Roy and Joan where we had left them, explained the situation, and led them back over.

"Hey, Trisha, you okay?" Roy asked as he walked over to her.

"No, feel like shit," Trisha said. Then she lost her balance. If Jamie and Lena had not had a good hold on her, she would have toppled over. "Dizzy too," she said.

"We're gonna bring you over my house for a while, Trisha. You can't go home like this."

"Okay," was all Trisha said as we made our way out of the park. Roy took the lead, Jamie and Joan next with Trisha between them so they could steady her if needed. Lena and I walked along holding hands as we brought up the rear.

I felt more amorous than buzzed. I leaned over as we walked and kissed Lena. It startled her but in a good way as she smiled and then returned the favor. I was still all revved up from our literal roll in the hay.

"Hey, I can't wait till tomorrow night, wish it were tonight," I said as I squeezed Lena's hand tighter.

"Yeah, me too. Just one more day though, actually less. I don't wanna leave now, but it's just about eleven. I gotta go," she said as we approached her house.

"You okay, I mean, not too buzzed, Lena?"

"Yeah, I'm fine, I didn't drink near as much as Trisha did, and no pot."

We all stopped before Lena's house as she said her goodbyes to everyone.

"You're not coming over Roy's with us?" Trisha asked Lena. She sounded like a child in her inebriated state.

"No, I can't. It's eleven now, and I gotta get in the house, or else my parents will kill me. You know how they are."

"All right, Lena, I'll see you tomorrow," Trisha said and then added, "Hope my parents don't kill me."

"You stay over Roy's for a while and sober up, then Jamie will get you home," Lena said as she looked over at Jamie. She then told Joan that she'd call her tomorrow.

"Hey guys, I'll be over in a minute," I said, so as to give everyone a clue that I wanted to say goodbye to Lena privately.

They took the hint and walked next door to Roy's house. Lena and I walked over to the side of her house where in the shadows we french-kissed for a few minutes then said good night to each other. God, I didn't want to leave her! As I was walking away, I said, "I guess I don't have to tell you that I'll call you tomorrow morning, but it makes me feel so good to say it."

"Come here you," Lena said.

I smiled and walked back over to her. We embraced and began kissing again, neither one of us wanting to let go. And once more, the world disappeared around me as I fell under her spell. How could one person, one girl, make me feel like this? I thought, *This is how I want to die—in Lena's arms, holding her, kissing her, feeling her body against mine as I take my last breath.*

We said our goodbyes once again. Then I went next door to Roy's.

# Chapter Nine

Jamie and I got Trisha home by eleven thirty. She seemed a little less wobbly but was definitely still messed up.

"I told her to go right to bed so her parents wouldn't suspect anything. And for what it's worth, we got her home on time, so that should help," Jamie said as we made our way to the bus stop.

"Yeah, hope she doesn't get caught," I said.

We got the Center bus and were home shortly after midnight.

"How's your buzz?" I asked as we walked down the street.

"Not bad, I'm more tired than buzzed."

"Yeah, me too. I'm looking forward to hittin' the bed," I said then said good night to my friend as we approached my house.

"All right, see ya tomorrow, Mark."

"Yeah, I'll see ya, Jamie."

As I lay in bed, I couldn't get over the fact that I'd been back for almost a week now. Things were moving quickly, and I was having a hell of a time. Then my mind drifted back to home—my real world in the future. I wondered what was going on in that world of 2014—at Harvard, with Ron, and how my daughter was doing. The last few days I'd been pretty much focused here in the past. I'd been feeling like a kid again, comfortable with my friends and once again head over heels for Lena. This was great, but I knew it meant that my former self was controlling things now, and this kind of scared me. Then I thought nothing to really worry about—I'd ride out the remaining days here, enjoying myself, knowing Ron would retrieve me before the transformation could ever take place. I turned over, got comfortable, and slowly drifted off to sleep. And as I did, my mind went back to Lena.

# Chapter Ten

*Saturday, 21 July 1973*

I was dreaming when my mother called up to me at nine. At first, I assimilated her voice into a weird dream I was having then realized that it was my mother calling my name from downstairs. I jumped out of bed, ran over, and opened the door.

I called down, "Ma, were you calling me?"

She came to the hallway below and, while looking up, said, "Yeah, Lena was on the phone for you. I told her you were still sleeping."

"Okay, thanks, I'll be down in a minute."

I pulled my bathrobe on and went downstairs, a little groggy. I had slept more than eight hours and knew I'd feel fine after some breakfast despite last night's drinking. This younger body was much more resilient and snapped back a lot quicker than my adult body would. When I drank with Ron, the following day I always paid the price, a hangover and then that lethargic feeling all day.

I paid a quick visit to the bathroom then out to the kitchen.

"Morning, Ma," I said as I entered the room.

"Good morning, Mark. What time did you get home last night?" my mother asked while she poured hot water into a mug of instant coffee.

"Just after midnight," I said.

"That's cutting it close. You know I want you home by midnight."

My mother never kept a tight leash on us older kids as long as we respected and obeyed her, so she was pretty liberal about us staying out a little later, especially since it was summertime and we didn't have to wake up for school. Actually, I had forgotten about the midnight curfew, so I apologized.

"Sorry, Ma, we should have gotten an earlier bus—won't happen again."

"Also, you missed trash day. You forgot to take out the buckets yesterday morning…I took care of it," she said with a frown.

It was my job to take out the trash on Friday mornings. I had completely forgotten about it.

"Sorry about that too, I won't miss it next week, Ma."

My mother looked over at me and said, "I don't expect a lot, Mark, but I do expect you to come home on time and to do your chores." She paused then said, "All right, enough said, it's water under the bridge." My mother took a sip of her coffee then asked, "What are you doing today?"

"I don't know exactly. I'll call Lena back soon to see what's goin' on."

"You want some pancakes?" my mother asked. "There's a lot of batter left." I found out that while I was snoozing the morning away, my mother had made pancakes for the rest of the family. There was no trace of them, but there was enough batter left over for a few pancakes for me.

"Yeah, sure, sounds good, Ma."

As my mother got up from her chair, I noticed in the center of the table, next to the napkin holder, a bottle of Aunt Jemima syrup. Shit, I thought, that stuff's disgusting. As I got older, I discovered what real maple syrup tasted like, and I never went back. Oh well, go with the flow. "Take what you get and don't get upset," a simple but important adage that my daughter learned from one of her elementary school teachers. I smiled as I thought of her while my mother poured pancake batter into the frying pan.

# Chapter Eleven

After eating, I called Lena to make plans for the day. I found out that Trisha didn't get caught by her parents in her drunken state last night, but she was staying in today because she felt like crap.

"I feel like just takin' it easy today, just hangin' out, kind of a lazy day," Lena said into the phone.

"Yeah, that sounds okay. Don't think it's much of a beach day anyway, looks kinda cloudy out there," I said as I peered out the window.

"And it's not supposed to clear till tonight," Lena said, then added, "I have to be home kinda early. My parents want to eat supper at five so they can get on the road for the Cape before six."

"Oh yeah, that's today isn't it—why don't they leave earlier in the day?" I asked.

"My father's friend and wife have something goin' on during the day, so my parents will stay over tonight and then spend most of tomorrow with them. They won't be home till after supper tomorrow night." Then Lena's voice lowered to a whisper when she said, "So tonight, you can come over after my brothers go to bed, like we planned."

"Can't wait, Lena," I said as I thought about how much I wanted to spend time alone with her.

"Anyway, what time do you wanna come down?"

"Well it's just after ten now, so…how-bout I meet you at your house at around eleven? We could get a hot dog for lunch at Surfside."

"Yeah, we haven't done that in a while"

"All right then. I'll see ya about eleven."

"Okay, Mark, see ya then," Lena said then hung up.

# Chapter Twelve

Jamie was going to spend time with his older brother today since Trisha was staying in, so I went down to The Point on my bike alone.

On the way down, I was thinking about how I'd be leaving here soon and how much I'd miss it. I thought about the day I arrived, last Sunday. I had taken my bike down to The Point that day too and remembered I was wondering what the current price of gas was here in 1973. I never did check, so today I decided to stop by the gas station at Delby's Corner to take a look. Turned out it was just under forty cents a gallon, a far cry from close to three dollars per gallon in 2014. Then I noticed one of those old metal and glass-cased cigarette machines outside the station (you don't see those anymore), with the price set at seventy cents per pack. I knew the machine prices were generally higher than the price in the stores, so packs must have been running around a half a buck or a bit more. If they only knew that cigarettes would cost over six dollars a pack in the future, I think... well, frankly, I think smokers would just about shit themselves.

I was amazed at these low prices but knew that it was somewhat relative economically; people earned a lot less, so these prices were reasonable for them. But I also knew for a fact that it was easier for the average person to make a living back here. Not that I ever struggled financially, but in 2014, in the average household, both parents worked to make ends meet. In 1973, only the father worked in most cases. Our house being an exception with my parents being separated.

Lena and Joan were on the front steps when I pulled up.

"Hey, handsome," Lena said as I got off my bike. They were both looking over and smiling at me.

"Hey, girls, what's up?"

"Hi, Mark," Joan said.

"Hey, Joan."

"Roy said he'd be over in a couple minutes," Lena said. "I mentioned getting lunch at Surfside to him, and he said he'd go."

"Okay, cool."

"You guys wanna eat inside or get it to go?" Joan asked.

"Why don't we do takeout and go down the park and eat?" I suggested, and Joan and Lena both liked the idea.

Roy joined us within a few minutes. We sat there talking for a while then made our way to Surfside. The restaurant was located right around the corner from Pulsifers Market on Shirley Street. They had a takeout window in the summer months, which was great for beachgoers and hungry kids like us that didn't care to sit down inside.

# Chapter Thirteen

Lena and I sat on the swings as we finished our lunch. Joan and Roy were messing around on the seesaw.

"So what's everyone doin' tonight?" Roy asked.

"I have to babysit," Lena said.

"You gonna sneak Mark over?" Roy asked as he looked over at me smiling.

"Yup, just as soon as I get my brothers to go to sleep," Lena said.

"Yeah, you know, Roy, when the cats away, the mice will play," I said, looking over at Roy with a mischievous grin.

"Don't get yourself caught, Lena, you know how your parents are," Joan warned.

"I'll be careful. I'll make sure those two little devils are asleep before I let Mark in."

"I don't think they'd say anything anyway. I don't think they'd tell your parents, Lena," I said.

"You don't know 'em like I do. They'd rat me out just to get a laugh."

"Well, be careful, you don't wanna mess up your summer," Joan said.

"Yeah, we'll be careful," Lena said as she looked over at me smiling.

I returned the smile then let my cup drop to the ground beneath me so I could get the swing going. Pumping my legs hard, I got myself moving fast and high. Lena jumped off to get rid of her trash then returned quickly to the swing. She got herself going and had matched my speed and rhythm in a matter of seconds. It felt exhilarating, with the breeze in my face, pumping away and moving so fast. We were looking over at each other smiling then began laughing as we got caught up in the moment. On an impulse, I reached over and grabbed one of the chains that held Lena's swing to the metal bar above and jerked it toward me.

"Nooo," she said as her laughing ceased abruptly, and a sort of terrified look came over her now unsmiling face. "Mark, let go!" Lena shrieked as her swing became a wild pendulum out of control, nearly crashing into mine.

"All right, all right," I said as I let go of the chain.

Turning to me as her swing began slowing and returning to a more natural rhythm, she said, "You scared the hell outa me."

I stopped pumping my legs, slowing myself down to match Lena's slower speed. "I'm sorry, Lena, I was just foolin around—didn't mean to scare you."

Lena let her feet drag on the sand underneath to stop herself completely, and then I did the same.

I could tell she wasn't really mad at me, just freaked out a bit. When she was completely stopped, Lena grabbed the closer of the two chains holding my swing and abruptly jerked it toward herself, saying, "Don't do that again!" With her teeth clenched, it came out like a grunt as she scolded me. "Really—it was scary you know."

"Sorry, I won't do it again, I promise," I said sheepishly.

"No, do it again, Mark. I wanna see that look on Lena's face again," Roy said.

"Screw you, Roy, don't give him any ideas," Lena said with a half smile as I suppressed a laugh.

I got off my swing and went over behind Lena. Holding the chains above her hands, I bent my head down and gently kissed the top of Lena's head while whispering, "Sorry." She then bent her head back so she was looking up into my face and kissed me.

"Oh, that's so cute," Roy said.

"Leave them alone, Roy, they're in love," Joan said matter-of-factly.

I wasn't offended. I was smiling, knowing what Joan said was true. Lena blushed a bit, but I knew Roy's remark didn't bother her either. Lena leaned back and kissed me again. It felt great.

Lena got off the swing, and we both walked over to Joan and Roy. It had become overcast and breezy. I could tell the temperature had dropped a good deal since I had left my house earlier today.

"You guys mind walkin' back to Lena's house so I can grab my sweatshirt?" I asked.

"No, let's head back, I think I'll grab something warmer too," Roy said. "What's with this weather anyway—it feels like October, not July?"

"I know, really," said Joan. Both of the girls had put their sweaters on earlier. "Hope it's not like this tomorrow for you guys at that beach you're going to."

"What beach?" Roy asked.

"Horseneck Beach. Lena and I are going with my family. It's in southern Massachusetts near Rhode Island. It's pretty cool, bigger waves than around here, and the water is usually warmer. My family goes there a few times every summer," I said.

"Sounds cool," Roy said.

"Yeah, I hope the weather's better than it is right now. It's supposed to be anyway," I said as we began to walk back.

# Chapter Fourteen

We got ourselves situated on the low beach wall directly across the street from Roy's house, looking out at the water and talking. I had gotten my sweatshirt from my bike rack, and Roy grabbed a dungaree jacket from his house. It was warmer where we were now anyway because the houses across the street blocked the easterly breeze we felt earlier in the park.

"Hey, Roy, what do you wanna do when you grow up, what do you wanna take up in college?" Lena asked.

"I wanna be a fuckin astronaut," he said, and we all laughed. I was drinking a Coke, and some of it shot out of my nose as I was trying to swallow while laughing.

"Jesus, Roy, don't make me laugh like that. This Coke's all over me," I said as I began wiping my face with my hand. Lena handed me a couple tissues from her pocket, and I cleaned myself up while Roy looked over at me laughing. "So," I said, "not just an astronaut, but a fucking astronaut, huh?"

"Yeah, I wanna be high all the time." We all laughed again.

"I get it, Roy, but seriously, what do you wanna do?" Lena asked.

"Shit, I dunno. I'm gonna go to college, but I'm not sure for what yet. Why, what are you gonna do?"

"Still undecided, like you, I'm not sure either. We all know Joan wants to go into nursing, right, Joan?"

"Yup, that's what I want to do."

"How do ya know for sure, Joan?" Roy asked.

"I dunno. I've just known for a long time."

"Wish I were that certain about what I wanna do. I guess for now I'll just plan on being a fuckin astronaut."

We all started laughing again, including Roy, who barely got the remark out before he, too, was cracking up. When we all settled down again, Roy asked me what my plans were.

My reply was almost instantaneous. I didn't feel like the boy right then. I guess the conversation pushed my adult self back to the surface. Of course, I knew exactly what I'd be doing in the future. I'd just come back from it six days ago. I couldn't believe I said it, but what came out was this: "I'm gonna study physics, invent a time machine, and come visit you guys in the past when I get old and gray."

"Now that sounds better than my astronaut idea," Roy said.

"Yeah, that sounds cool. I think I'd travel to the future though," Joan said. "I'd like to see how everything turned out—who I'm married to, if I have kids, things like that."

Then Lena chimed in, "I don't know about that, Joan, you might find out something that you'd rather not know."

"Yeah, maybe, but I think it would be a lot more interesting than revisiting the past—I already know what happened there."

Lena was on my left side, nestled in close with her right arm wrapped around my waist. She gently pressed her fingers into my side and asked, "What do you really wanna do, Mark?"

I was oblivious to the conversation after I had made my remark and never heard Lena ask her question or feel her fingers pressing into my flesh.

"Mark," Lena said, trying to get my attention. She craned her neck around so she was looking straight into my face. "You okay?" she said softly.

"Huh—whaja say?" I replied, snapping out of it.

"I was asking what you really wanted to do when you get older, but you didn't hear me. It was like you were in a trance or something."

"Oh, sorry, I was just zoning, kinda driftin' off," I said as I regained my focus on Lena. "Um, I think I want to teach science, maybe physics."

"Really," Lena said, "you never mentioned that before."

"Yeah, I really like science," I said, but I think I had told Lena (the first time around) that I wanted to be a pilot.

"You really wanna study physics?" Roy said. "We don't even take that till our senior year."

"Yeah, I know, but I've been reading a lot about Einstein and how he turned the world upside down with his revolutionary theories. He crushed Newton's belief in absolute time and came up with his famous equation: $E = mc^2$. I think all that stuff is amazing, and it's got me really interested in the subject."

"You sound like a scientist already," Roy said. I smiled and said it was interesting stuff.

"Well, if that's what you wanna do, Mark, then you should do it," said Lena as she pulled me a little closer. "I wanna go to the same college as you though. We'll go together, okay?"

"That would be cool, Lena, hope we can do that," I said as I leaned in and kissed her.

"There they go again, the lovebirds," Roy said.

"You're just jealous, Roy," I said lightly.

"You know what, you're right, and I'm gonna start workin' on that real soon…I'm gonna get myself a girlfriend. A good-lookin' one with big titties."

Joan protested immediately by drawing out his name, "*Roy!*"

Lena laughed heartily and said, "Don't hold anything back now, Roy."

"Well, you certainly say what's on your mind, huh, Roy?" I said as I laughed.

"Sorry, girls, I shouldn't have said that."

"Hey, you callin' me a girl, Roy," I said, smiling.

"No, asshole, I meant them. I knew you wouldn't be offended."

"I know, Roy," I said, chuckling. I got off the wall and looked over at Roy, saying, "Hey, Roy, why don't you go get your football. We can throw it around out here in the street. It'll keep you out of trouble with the girls."

"Yeah…better keep my mouth shut for a while," Roy said as he glanced over at Joan and Lena. They didn't hear him though as they had become engrossed in a private conversation.

I turned back around to face the water as Roy crossed the street to his house. Tilting my head back as I raised my arms to stretch, I noticed a seagull swoop up into the air, evading other gulls nearby, then drop a clam or a mussel from its beak to the rocks below. The gulls did this to break open the shell and expose the inner, softer body of the mollusk that would be their meal.

The tide was out, exposing the rocky, muddy shoreline, and the air was ripe with that pungent, earthy smell of sea life at low tide. Some people, even some locals, find the odor offensive, but others like myself associate that strong, low-tide smell with home. It always brings me back to my youth and days at the beach.

Roy and I casually threw the football back and forth in the street while Lena and Joan gabbed away on the wall. At four o'clock, we all walked Joan home. We were back just before four thirty when Lena had to be in.

"I'll see you guys later," Roy said, leaving Lena and me alone for a few minutes before she went in.

Lena reached down, interlocking her hands in mine as she moved closer to me.

"All right, so be back here at nine thirty. I'm gonna send my brothers up to bed at nine, so they should be asleep by the time you get here, okay?"

"Sounds like a plan," I said. Then we kissed briefly. I told Lena to wait there while I went around back to get my bike. On my return, I kissed her again. "I needed another one of those before I left," I said. Her face lit up in a radiant smile, and she said that she loved me. "I love you too," I said then took off for home.

# Chapter Fifteen

After supper, Jamie and I played basketball with some of our friends from the neighborhood. We played a few pickup games till it was just about dark then headed down the end of the street to an area we called The Marsh to have a cigarette where no one could see us. After that we headed home. I needed to take a shower before going down The Point.

"I'll see ya tomorrow, Mark."

"No, I'm goin' to Horseneck beach with Lena and my family tomorrow," I said.

"That's right, you told me already—forgot. So I guess Monday then?" he said.

"Yeah, I'll call you Monday, see what's goin' on."

"All right, talk to you then," Jamie said as he turned to go, and I made my way up the street to my house.

I got the nine-o-five Center bus to The Point and was at Lena's house just before nine thirty.

"Come on in, I think they're asleep, but be quiet just in case." As I stepped inside, I pulled Lena close, and we kissed.

"Let me just run upstairs. I'll be right down. Make yourself comfortable."

I took off my sweatshirt, draped it over the couch, then wandered the living room looking at the photos on the walls.

"Okay, they're both asleep, but let's keep it quiet," Lena said on her return. "Do you want something to drink or eat, Mark?"

"Coke or ginger ale if you have it. I'm not really hungry though," I said.

"Okay, let me go see what we have," Lena said as she walked out into the kitchen. She returned a few minutes later with our drinks, a bowl of chips, and some coffee cake on a tray, setting it down on the coffee table in front of the couch. "No ginger ale, we had Coke though and some munchies, too, if you get hungry. I'm a bit hungry after eating so early tonight. Hey, I'm gonna put that Beethoven piece on that we talked about the other day. I've been waiting to have you listen to it. I think you'll really like it."

I didn't know what Lena was talking about immediately. Then it came to me that we had talked about her secret love of classical music. It was hard to believe that I never knew of Lena's passion for this type of music. We went steady for over seven months and I never knew—what else escaped me, I wondered.

"Sure, okay, I'd like to hear it, just hope it doesn't wake up your brothers."

"It won't. I'm gonna keep it low. I'll play the whole record for you some other time. I just want you to hear *Silence.*" Lena had the album set to go on the record player.

I walked over and kissed the side of her face as she turned it on. She lowered the tone arm onto the record, and that familiar crackling sound came from the speakers as Lena adjusted the volume. "We'll have to stay here and listen to it so I don't have to turn it up too loud."

The music began to play as I held Lena's hand. It was hauntingly beautiful. The piece had a rhythmic simplicity and an elegance to it that seemed to envelop you, pulling you into its contemplative and meditative strains. I, of course, had listened to some classical music before, but it seemed to all sound the same. This piece was different though. I was taken by it immediately.

"It's beautiful," I said to Lena. "I really like it. You were right."

"It is beautiful. I knew you'd like it. I'm glad you do," she said then kissed me. Lena was obviously happy that she could share this with me and very pleased that I enjoyed it too.

"And I do want to hear the whole album some other time, Lena. What you said about taking piano lessons, definitely take them. I'd love to hear you play this on a piano." I was saying this as the boy, not even thinking that I'd probably be back in my future within a few days' time. I'd never get to see Lena play the piano, but right now, that didn't matter.

We went over to the couch after Beethoven's *Silence* ended where we stayed until I left, close to two hours later.

# Chapter Sixteen

M y mother called up to me to get out of bed at 7:00 a.m. I remembered immediately that today we were going to Horseneck Beach. I knew the weather was supposed to get better today, but I wanted reassurance and asked my mother when I got downstairs.

"I just heard the weather report on the radio, and they said it would be beautiful—sunny and in the eighties down that way."

"That's great, Ma," I said, relieved that the original weather forecast was holding. It wouldn't be worth going all the way to Horseneck for a less than perfect beach day, so my mother would always wait to hear that morning forecast and then make a final decision. I found out that my brother John wouldn't be going with us today. He wanted to hang out with his friends in Winthrop. Joanne had already opted out so as to give us more room in the car knowing I was bringing Lena.

I called Lena after breakfast and reminded her that we would be at her house at eight thirty to pick her up.

"Okay, I'll be ready. I'll see you in a little while, Mark—oh, I had a very nice time last night."

"Yeah, me too, it was nice—just me and you."

"We'll have to arrange more time alone like that," Lena added.

"Yeah, definitely," I said then told her it was supposed to be a beautiful beach day.

"Great, can't wait to get there. I better get goin', I'm not quite ready, and my aunt will be here soon to watch the boys."

"Okay, we'll see you in a little while then."
"All right, bye, Mark."
"Bye, Lena."

# Chapter Seventeen

We were on the road shortly after picking up Lena at eight thirty. We paid a toll of twenty-five cents and entered the Sumner Tunnel, which took us under Boston Harbor and into the city. By the way, the cost to travel the same tunnel in 2014 is three dollars.

We then made our way down the Southeast Expressway heading out of Boston, eventually picking up route 24, which would take us into southern Massachusetts. With a couple more route changes, we would arrive at Horseneck Beach in Westport, Massachusetts, in a total trip time of about one and a half hours.

Billy rode up front with my mother in that old but reliable Ford Falcon sedan. Ginny, Lena, and I sat in the back. We talked and had fun on the way down. Billy and Ginny were fascinated with their big brother's girlfriend and asked Lena countless questions. Ginny made sure to find out what Lena's favorite ice cream flavor was because "we always stop at Howard Johnsons on the way home."

We had some of our personal belongings up front with us to keep us occupied for the long drive, but most everything else was packed away in the Falcon's trunk. It was loaded with beach chairs, clothes to change into at the end of the day (there are showers at the beach), towels, reading materials, a full cooler of food and drinks, a hibachi with charcoal to cook on, and many other beach-related items that we would need to spend an entire day there. We usually stayed till 5:00 p.m. when most other beachgoers had already gone home. It was a great feeling to stay all day and then have the beach almost to yourself in the late afternoon.

Horseneck Beach is a state reservation that charges a relatively small entrance fee. The beach is a six-hundred-acre property and has two miles of shoreline. Away from the shoreline, sand dunes run the length of the beach. Between those hilly dunes are areas not unlike troughs between waves in the ocean that provide private areas to encamp for the day. So we'd set up between the dunes well away from the shore and use that area as a sort of base camp where we would return to and relax when not in the water.

# Chapter Eighteen

We arrived shortly after ten and found a good spot between some high dunes. It was a hell of a lot of work as usual lugging all the beach stuff, especially that heavy cooler from the parking lot to the dunes but well worth it after finding a nice area to settle in for the day. We unpacked, put our suntan lotion on, and all went right down to the water except my mother who wanted to stretch out on her chaise lounge and read the newspaper. We always brought the *Boston Globe* with us, and the Sunday edition, which we had with us today, was over two inches thick—typical for a Sunday. My mother was just beginning to open it up when we turned to go.

"Keep an eye on your sister and brother, Mark," she said without looking up.

"All right, Ma, I will," I said as we started down to the water.

"Let's make sandcastles, Mark," Ginny said while she happily skipped along ahead of us.

"Why don't we go in the water for a little while first, Gin, then we'll build sandcastles," I said.

Lena caught up to Ginny and took her hand, telling her that she'd help with the sandcastles after we got out of the water. Ginny's face lit up now that she knew Lena would be playing with her too.

"I'm learning how to swim, Lena. I take lessons at Winthrop Beach. I know how to tread water, you know, and float on my back."

"That's great, Ginny, you can show me, okay."

Billy was walking ahead us now, and when he heard Ginny talking about her swimming abilities, he turned and said he could swim a hundred times better. I told him not to be fresh and that his sister was doing really well with her lessons.

The water was cool but not near as cold as back home. I think this is due to Horseneck's south-facing location. The waves were breaking farther out, but we stayed fairly close to shore as Ginny showed Lena how she could float and tread water.

I was watching Billy as he began swimming out a little farther.

"Not too far, Billy," I said.

"I know. I just want to get a little over my head."

Billy was a good swimmer for his age, but I swam out to where he was to keep things safe. Horseneck was known for its rip currents. These are localized narrow currents of water flowing offshore, back out to sea. They can catch you unaware and sweep you out before you realize it's happening. Over the years, lifeguards at Horseneck have had to rescue many people who were swept out in the rip currents, and some didn't make it. You'd hear the lifeguards blowing their whistles all day long, trying to keep swimmers from going out too far.

I noticed Lena and Ginny had gotten out of the water and were already working on the sandcastles. I got Billy to come in, and we all joined in on the construction. I whispered in his ear to let Ginny be the boss because of her age and the fact that she'd been looking forward to this all week. He agreed, and we all dug in. Billy and I worked together and eventually connected our castles and moat to their series of castles, forming a rather large castle-city in the sand as the tide receded.

We were working at it for a while when I realized that it had to be close to noon.

"I think it's about lunchtime, guys. Mom should have the burgers goin' by now, so why don't we start headin' back up."

"Oh, Mark, I don't want to leave now. It seems like we just got started," Ginny complained.

"We can come back down, we're gonna be here all day, Gin."

# Chapter Nineteen

Lunch was good. We had cheeseburgers with coleslaw, potato salad, and chips. We also had lemonade from the big jug we always took to the beach. My mother packed brownies and ginger snaps for snacks and also plenty of fruit. On the outside chance that we ran out of food or drink, we could always buy more at the snack shop located close to where the bath houses are.

Lena and I decided to relax up in the dunes while the rest of my family went down to the water after lunch.

"You know we can't go in the water for about a half hour," I heard my mother say as they walked away.

It was that old myth that our mothers believed was true about getting cramps and then drowning while swimming after eating. It is true that you can get a minor cramp, but the notion that a large amount of the blood supply goes to the digestive system after eating, thus taking it away from the arms and legs needed to swim is a myth. She was enforcing it once again at the beach as all mothers did these days. There were all kinds of variations to the rule depending on what you ate. For a large meal, your mother might keep you out of the water for as much as forty-five minutes and as little as fifteen minutes for a snack. And yes, there were incremental amounts that each mother figured out in her own *scientific* way like twenty-two minutes for a peanut butter and jelly sandwich but thirty-two if you had chips and a drink with it. Professional comedians have gotten a lot of laughs over the years from this whole thing of staying out of the water after eating and the way mothers determined the exact amount of time necessary.

"That's okay, Mom, we can finish our sandcastles," I heard Ginny say as their voices drifted off.

I picked up the *Globe* and stretched out on a chaise lounge. Lena grabbed a book she had brought with her and sat next to me in a folding beach chair. I went through the sports section pretty quickly then opened up the entertainment section of the paper. As I leafed through it, I noticed a small ad for a Jim Croce concert.

"Oh my god," I said, and Lena quickly turned her head.

"What's the matter, Mark?"

I held up my hand, gesturing to Lena to wait a minute as I continued reading. The concert would be held (of all places) at Sanders Theatre at Harvard University. To say that this was a coincidence would be an understatement. I'm a professor at Harvard University who has traveled back in time forty-one years to possibly see a concert at Harvard at age fourteen. Of all the venues he played during his relatively short career, he was playing at Harvard University during the week that I had travelled back in time.

I've been in the theatre on several occasions. It's a beautiful three-tiered amphitheater with all wood paneling known for its exceptional acoustics. It's relatively small, and if I recall correctly, holds a little over one thousand people. It was inspired by the architecture of the famous Christopher Wren. Sanders Theatre is one section of a three-part building called Memorial Hall, completed in 1878 to honor the Harvard men who fought and died in the Civil War.

I showed the ad to Lena, saying, "Lena, we could go see him—right in Cambridge, it'd be great!"

"Jim Croce, in concert—wow!" she said as her face lit up. "We've always wanted to see him, and I'd really like to go, Mark." Then she paused. "But I wonder if my mother will let me. Last year, Joan and I wanted to see Elton John in concert, and she said no to that without batting an eyelash. I'll ask her tonight when I get back home, see what she says. Hopefully she'll say yes this time."

"Yeah, I hope so. We gotta go to this concert, Lena. It'll be great!"

This was one concert I'd really like to see. We both liked Jim Croce's folk music, but we had never taken the time to see him in concert. One night back then, after listening to one of his songs, Lena said that we should go see him in concert, then remembered immediately after she uttered the words that he had just recently died in a plane crash. We stood there staring at each other in the sad, eerie silence. We had taken it for granted that he'd always be around, and of course, he wouldn't be. His life was cut short just as he was reaching his prime. The string of hits that he wrote in the last couple of years of his life was amazing. His songs told stories of his experiences—catchy tunes about ordinary people, love songs, upbeat tunes, and melancholy ballads about lost love. You could identify with some of the characters in the songs and the situations he sang about, making his music personal to many of his fans. In the end, his music would always stay with me. Now I have an unbelievable second chance to see one of the greatest singer/songwriters of his time. Somehow Lena and I would go to that concert. There wasn't a doubt in my mind!

"I'll ask my mother as soon as she comes back up. We just gotta go, Lena," I said emphatically. "We just gotta."

Lena turned the radio on, and Seals and Croft's "Summer Breeze" came to life.

"I love this song," I said then closed my eyes, enjoying the way it conjured up the feel of an early evening in the summer.

*See the curtains hangin' in the window*
*In the evenin' on a Friday night*
*A little light a-shinin' through the window*
*Let's me know everything is all right*

I reached over and found Lena's hand while the music played. Ironically, there was a slight breeze blowing to accompany those lyrics. With eyes closed, I held Lena's hand, feeling that gentle breeze cool my warm body, and enjoyed the various scents of suntan lotion, salt air, and the smell of food cooking on the beach. I suppose if I tried hard enough, I would smell the scent of jasmine wafting through the air. How relaxing it all was. It wasn't long before I dozed off.

# Chapter Twenty

I came to when I heard my mother talking on her return from the water with my brother and sister.

"Mark, you better get some more lotion on, your shoulders are getting red."

I looked up, blocking the sun with my right palm, and my mother's face came into view.

"I must have dozed off," I said then looked down at my shoulders. "Are they red, I can't tell?" Lena handed me the Coppertone, saying they did look a little red, and I applied a generous amount to my shoulders as well as the rest of my exposed skin.

"I didn't realize you were burning, Mark, I would have woken you up," Lena said.

"It's okay, it's not too bad yet," I said then remembered the concert. "Hey, Ma, would it be okay if I went to a Jim Croce concert at Harvard University?"

"When is it?"

"He's playing this Thursday, Friday, and Saturday night."

"I suppose. Which night would you be going?"

"Whatever night we can get a ticket for, I guess. I just found out about it in the newspaper."

"So I take it you and Lena are going," my mother asked, looking over at Lena, smiling.

"I'll have to ask my mother. I'm not sure yet, Mrs. Peterson."

"What time is the concert?" my mother asked.

"Eight till eleven."

"Sure, you can go as long as you get yourself home right after the concert, Mark."

"Yeah, we'll come home right after it ends. Thanks, Ma," I said.

I was hot and a bit groggy after falling asleep in the sun, so I asked Lena if she wanted to go swimming.

"Sure, let's go." Ginny wanted to go down with us, but my mother wanted her to stay up in the dunes with her for a little while.

"I'll go back down later on with you, Gin," I promised her as Lena and I turned to go.

The water was refreshing after lying in the hot sun. We dived in and swam out a little bit.

"Your mother's so nice, Mark. I wish my mother was so easygoing with me. She's just too protective, you know," Lena said rhetorically, then added, "I'm fifteen years old now, and she treats me like a baby sometimes."

"Well, hopefully she'll think you're grown up enough to go to the concert with me."

"I really wanna go, hope she says yes."

I dived under the water and quickly swam between Lena's legs. I resurfaced, blowing the water from my face and brushing the hair back off my forehead. Lena was laughing.

"You startled me. I didn't know where you went, then I felt something between my legs." She came over to me with a sexy smile on her face, putting her arms around my waist. Lena then leaned in and kissed me. I responded by opening my mouth, and we french-kissed there in the water.

"You taste salty," I said, licking my lips, "but I like it."

"You do too, and I like it—very much." I leaned back in, and we kissed again, more passionately this time, holding each other tight and close.

I pulled away then kissed Lena gently on the forehead. "I'm glad you could come with us today."

"Me too, I really like this beach. You were right, the water is warmer down here," Lena said.

We were in water above our waists, and the waves were rolling in past us, pushing us around a bit. The next wave in pushed us together, and we both laughed. Now tightly pressed against Lena's soft, young body, I let my hands slide down her upper arms to her waist, then under the water where I reached around, finding the soft, smooth flesh of her butt.

"Mark, careful, someone might see us," Lena said,

"Oh, nobody can see what we're doing—just kissing, that's all." Then I broke away and dived under an approaching wave, swimming out under the water. I resurfaced and motioned for Lena to come out to where I was, now over my head. She swam out, and we kissed again then began swimming around in the deep water.

We were treading water close together and talking when we heard a whistle blowing in the distance. It took a little while, but I realized the whistles were for us. The lifeguards were blowing their whistles and waving, motioning for us to come in. It was then I discovered that we had gone out farther than the other swimmers in the water, apparently beyond what the lifeguards considered safe.

"They want us to come in, Lena, I didn't realize we were out so far," I said.

"Yeah, me either. We better get in. I don't want to get in trouble with them."

We swam in till we were in water below our waist, stopping there momentarily before returning to the shore.

Once on shore, I couldn't keep my hands off Lena as we stood there talking and teasing each other in that flirtatious way teenagers do. I was lost again in that boy's body and mind, feeling young and full of life, forgetting once again that I had travelled back in time and all this would be gone in a few days.

Lena and I brought Ginny back down to the water with us later that day. Eventually, my mother and brother joined us. It stayed virtually sunny throughout the day with only an occasional fair weather cloud passing by. It was the most fun I had had since I had returned to my past. How could it not be: there with my family and the girl I was terribly in love with at the beach on a carefree and gorgeous summer day, reliving those happy moments of my youth.

In the late afternoon, we took showers and returned to the dunes for an early supper of cold-cut sandwiches and anything else we had left over from lunch. We relaxed for a while after supper, talking and enjoying the late-day sun.

By five o'clock, we were on the road, and yes, we did stop at Howard Johnsons to get ice cream, topping off a perfect day.

# Chapter Twenty-One

*Monday, 23 July 1973*

I awoke feeling melancholy. My adult self had resurfaced and was controlling my thoughts and feelings again, making me painfully aware that I would be leaving at noon on Wednesday.

I was lying there thinking how stupid I was to think that I'd get to go to the Jim Croce concert with Lena. Yesterday I never considered that I no longer would be here for even the earliest of the three concert dates on Thursday. If I were still here, something would be terribly wrong. The emergency protocol was clear-cut: at twelve noon, ten days after I had left, Ron would bring me back if I hadn't already returned. So Wednesday at noon I'd be back in the present, back to the reality of 2014.

I couldn't help feeling the pain that I would suffer from losing Lena again. If you have ever read Thomas Jefferson's letter "Dialogue Between My Head and My Heart," you might understand the tug of war that existed within me.

The widowed president was involved with a married French woman named Maria Cosway, and although they were deeply in love, he knew he had to end it. The struggle in his mind over what to do was described in his letter written to her.

The internal dialogue took place between his head and his heart. The head represented his intellectual side, the part of him that based his decisions on logic and that which would benefit him most in the long run. The heart represented his emotional side, which was governed by passion and love. These two forces are often at odds in human relationships and will affect most every man and woman. In

Jefferson's case, the head won out, and he regretfully broke off the relationship.

In my case, the head was telling me to do what was right and proper, that is to leave the past alone, let it play out as God had intended. And the heart longing to stay, wanting to manipulate events for the sake of my love for Lena. I knew that Ron would retrieve me, but I was beginning to toy with the idea of coming back again and staying for good. I knew that I should go back and stay put, but part of me wanted to remain, the part of me that was becoming that boy again. I didn't just want to stay either. I longed to stay. My body ached to stay with Lena—I needed her. If I did stay, might I be able to alter the future? Maybe, just maybe we wouldn't break up this time around. Perhaps our love would endure, and by some heavenly miracle, we would marry, living out our lives together in an altered future.

But this is not where I really belonged. My future had already played out. As devastating as it would be to lose Lena again, I didn't come back to alter my future, only to revisit the past. I mustn't attempt to play God and change what was meant to be. Events were meant to play out as they had: Lena would eventually fall out of love with me, and the relationship would end. As with Jefferson, the head would prevail.

# Chapter Twenty-Two

I pulled back the covers and got out of bed. *Fuck it*, I thought, *I'm getting those tickets anyway. If for nothing else, as a souvenir from my trip*. Who knows, maybe for some unexplained reason, I'd still be here and we'd get to go.

I caught my mother before she left for work.

"Mornin', Ma, do you know where the *Sunday Globe* is?"

"I think it's in the living room."

"Okay, you off to work?" I asked.

"Yup. I'll be home in the early afternoon. Joanne's gonna take care of lunch for Ginny and Billy, but I want you to start helping her out when you can."

"All right, Ma, I will," I said as my mother headed out the door.

I headed for the living room. I found the *Globe*. It was gritty with grains of sand from the beach yesterday. I leafed through it and found the ad for the concert. Tickets were on sale at a ticket agency in Harvard Square in Cambridge. I'd see if Lena could go over to Cambridge with me today to get tickets for the Thursday show. But first, I'd have some breakfast; then I'd give her a call. Then I remembered I had told Jamie that I'd call him on Monday. I guess I'd ask him if he wanted to come with us to Cambridge also.

# Chapter Twenty-Three

"Mornin', Lena."

"Morning, guess what?"

"What?"

"I can go. I can go to the concert!"

"That's great. I was thinking about going into Cambridge today to get the tickets, can you come?"

"Hold on, I'll ask." There was a brief pause. I could hear Lena talking to her mother, then returning to the phone. "Yup, I can go with you today. About the concert though, I can only go if my mother drives us in and picks us up. She doesn't want me *wandering around Boston at night*." Then another pause. "I know, Mom." Apparently, Lena's mother was lecturing her on the dangers of the city at night.

"Mark?"

"Yeah, I'm here. That's fine if she drives us in and picks us up. It'll be easier that way anyway. As far as today, when can you be ready to go?" I asked.

"I can leave in a few minutes if you wanna go right away."

"All right then—"

"Hold on a sec." And another pause. "Sorry to cut you off, my mother just said she'd give me a ride over to your house. She has some errands to do in the Center."

"Okay, good. I'll be ready when you get here."

It turned out that Jamie wasn't interested in going into town with us but he'd be going down The Point tonight so we'd hook up then.

Lena's mother ended up giving us a ride to Orient Heights in East Boston where we caught a train into Boston. After switching trains at Government Center, we were in Harvard Square, Cambridge by quarter of ten.

# Chapter Twenty-Four

Harvard Square, a plaza located at the intersections of Mass Ave (Massachusetts Avenue), Brattle Street, and JFK Street (John Fitzgerald Kennedy Street), is considered the historic center of Cambridge and actually very close to the geographic center. A bustling commercial area with the train and bus stations, the shops, stores, and cafés that serve the Harvard community and the many others who live nearby or are just passing through.

There were many people coming and going from Out of Town News, a longstanding business located smack in the middle of the square. It's been selling newspapers and magazines from around the world for many years. And across the street, I gazed upon my alma mater and place of employment, Harvard University, a beehive of activity even though it was the middle of summer.

The area has always been a melting pot of many types of people: the college crowd, local residents, shoppers passing through, street musicians, beggars, and eventually a United States Chess Federation Master chess player who would become a fixture beginning in 1982, a onetime student at Harvard University who would challenge all takers to beat him, posting a sign that read PLAY THE CHESS MASTER.

Through the years, many movies have been filmed in and around Harvard Square. Some of these include *Good Will Hunting*, *The Paper Chase*, and *Love Story*, the tearjerker that is still shown to incoming freshman at Harvard University.

# Chapter Twenty-Five

So old Harvard Square was busy as usual when we arrived at the kiosk to purchase our tickets. The Thursday show still had good seats available, scattered seats remained for Friday, and Saturday was sold out completely, so we bought two tickets for Thursday. The seats we got were in the lower mezzanine level just five rows up from the orchestra section or floor seating.

"That'll be eleven dollars and fifty cents with the tax," the woman behind the booth said.

"I'll get this, Lena. I haven't bought you anything in a while." Truth was, I had hardly touched the two hundred I brought back with me, and I wanted to be the one who paid for his girl to see the show. That's if I were still here to see the show.

As I handed the woman a twenty, Lena turned to me and said, "You don't have to do that. I brought money with me."

"Well, I just wanted to do something nice for you. You are my girlfriend. Besides, I haven't bought you anything for a while." I said this feeling kind of proud of myself, standing next to this young girl who I loved so much.

Lena smiled, and so did the woman in the booth.

"Yes, you have, you paid for the movies last week, remember?"

"That was only a few bucks," I said. Then Lena leaned in closer and kissed me on the cheek.

"Thanks, Mark."

"Well, either way, it should be a great show," the woman said. "Have you seen him before?"

"This will be our first time," Lena said. "We're really looking forward to it."

"If you like him as much as I do, you're gonna love the show. I've seen him twice before, and both times were unbelievable."

"Yeah, we can't wait to go," I said as the woman placed the two tickets in a small envelope and handed them to Lena.

We thanked the woman then turned to go. I hadn't taken more than two steps when Lena turned and pulled me close, saying she loved me and that we were going to have a great time at the concert. I pulled her even closer and brought my lips to hers. We stood there, a few steps from the kiosk, and made out amid the throngs of people coming and going in the square. It was innocent, and it was a totally uninhibited display of young love.

# Chapter Twenty-Six

We walked around Harvard Square for a while, browsing the shops while enjoying the sunshine and each other's company. Shortly before noon, I noticed a little curiosity shop wedged in between a sandwich shop and a bookstore. It was called Ella's Curiosities & More.

"Do you wanna go in here, it looks kind of interesting?"

"Yeah, let's take a look," Lena said, opening the door that jogged a little bell above our heads announcing our arrival.

"Hello," came a voice from the back of the shop. An older woman appeared from behind a rack of clothes. "Well hello dears," she said with a warm smile.

I looked around and didn't notice any other customers in the shop at the time.

"What is it you're looking for today?" She was probably in her sixties or maybe even early seventies and was dressed strangely to say the least. The look was a combination of someone's grandmother and a homeless person. She wore what looked like men's chinos and had sandals on her feet. The woman had a multicolored sweater on a few sizes too big for her and a tattered scarf wrapped around her neck. Her hair was done up in kind of a bun, but it was in the process of coming undone. It was going this way and that way all at the same time. She was a mess but somewhat charming.

We smiled and said hello. "Not looking for anything in particular, just browsing," I said.

"Well, I have a little of everything, as you can see."

I looked around the shop as she said this and noted her statement was quite accurate. Within the confines of this little place, there was quite an assorted collection of knickknacks, antiques, figurines, used clothing, and other items of all kinds crowded about the store and hanging from the ceiling. The smell in the air was mostly of lavender, probably due to the assorted soaps for sale not far from where the old lady stood.

"I read tea leaves too," she said, and this piqued Lena's interest. "Oh, really!"

"Yup, sure do. Been doin' it for close to fifty years. And I don't have to read your leaves to see that you two are in love," the old lady said with a twinkle in her eye. "I'm Ella, the owner, by the way."

"I'm Lena, and this is Mark, my boyfriend."

We shook hands. I was really beginning to like this old woman, this strange character we just happened upon.

"You're right, we're in love," Lena said proudly as she looked at Ella while nestling in close to me. "Mark, let's get our tea leaves read after we finish looking around."

"Yeah, sure, okay," I said.

"Well, you two go ahead and look around, I'll be out back— just give me a holler if you need me."

"Okay, thanks," I said as we proceeded to peruse the curiosities that filled the store.

"Hey, look at these," Lena called over to me.

She was looking at little crystal figurines arranged on glass shelving. The majority were animal figures. They were very elaborate, multifaceted pieces that refracted light in many beautiful colors.

"They're beautiful, they're like little prisms," I said. "Which one do you like?"

"They're all nice, but I like these," Lena said, pointing to a trio of elephants—mother and two small calves. "I bet they're expensive. I don't see any prices though, do you?"

"No, but I'll ask her if you want me to."

"I think I'm too afraid to find out, Mark. They are beautiful though."

"I'll go find out, be back in a minute," I said. I went back and got Ella. She took out an inventory sheet with corresponding pricing. The elephants were sixty dollars, the equivalent of three hundred in

2014. That was a little pricey, but what the hell, I had plenty of the two hundred left, and they would make a nice surprise gift for Lena. I told her I wanted them but wanted to surprise Lena.

"Tell you what, you go distract your girlfriend and I'll go scoop 'em up."

"Okay, sounds like a plan," I said.

Lena had already moved well away from the crystal figurines, so no distracting was necessary. She was looking at earrings in the front of the store. Lena spotted me returning as she held up a pair of earrings to her ears while looking in an antique Cheval floor mirror.

"How do you like these?"

"They're okay, I guess."

"You don't really like them, do you?"

"Not really," I said. They looked like rounded peacock feathers inside a metal loop, really strange-looking things.

"Did you get the price on the little elephants?"

"They were pretty expensive," I said, not revealing the price, making her believe they were much more expensive than I could afford.

We wandered around the store for a while checking out Ella's curiosities. I was trying on an old Fedora when Lena asked if I was ready to get our tea leaves read.

"Sure," I replied.

We started walking toward the back of the store just as Ella was returning from the back room. She gave me a wink when Lena wasn't looking to let me know she had the figurines ready for me.

"We're ready to get our tea leaves read," Lena said.

"Okay, I charge three dollars apiece or two for five dollars."

"We're both doing it, right, Mark," Lena said, looking at me expectantly.

"Fine, we'll do it together," I said.

"Okay then, let me go get my stuff. In the meantime, grab those two chairs from over near the wall and you can sit right here at the counter. I'll be right back."

We pulled the two folding chairs up to the counter, which was actually part of the wall that separated the back room from the store proper. Ella returned quickly with a hot plate and tea kettle. She placed the kettle, apparently already filled with water, on the burner then leaned down to plug the hot plate in near her feet, on her side of the counter. She then went out back to fetch the rest of her stuff. Ella reappeared with a full porcelain tea set and a tin of tea on an elegant wooden tray.

"So do you know how this works?" Ella asked, looking at Lena then me.

"I had my tea leaves read once before, and well…we just drank the tea then our leaves were read," Lena said.

"Exactly," said Ella. "We can chitchat while you enjoy the tea, then we'll get down to business."

She pinched a bit of tea from the tin and deposited it in our cups. A few minutes later Ella removed the kettle from the burner and tested the water by pouring a tiny bit onto her fingertips—the water was ready. Ella poured the boiling water into our tea cups, and we talked while it steeped.

"So you've been doin' this for almost fifty years, huh?" I said.

"Yep. I was taught by my mother. My mother read tea leaves before me and her mother before her and on and on. It goes pretty far back actually. My ancestors were gypsies—it's in my blood."

"Really?" Lena replied, intrigued.

"It's the truth, and I take tea leaf reading very seriously. I know a lot of people are skeptical about it, but it's as real as the rain," Ella said.

"Where do your ancestors come from, Ella?" I asked.

"Armenia. But we immigrated to England after the First World War." She paused. "You should start drinking your tea before it cools." She continued, "When I was eleven years old. About ten years later, I met an American while he was on vacation in England, and we fell in love. He took me back to the States, and we married shortly after. We settled here in Cambridge. Together we had a good life, we were so much in love…he passed away only a few years ago. I still miss him very much…Henry, his name was Henry," Ella said with a faraway look in her eyes.

"We are very sorry for your loss, Ella," Lena said for the both of us, and I acknowledged by nodding my head.

"How's the tea by the way," she said, snapping back to the present.

"I like it, it has a sweet taste to it, and you didn't put anything in it either—no milk, no sugar," Lena said.

Not that I drink much tea, I'm more of a coffee person, but I liked the taste of it too.

"That's an English tea. A good tea doesn't need anything added to it, and this particular tea has a natural and subtle sweetness to it. I just love it. Now don't quite finish it all, leave a little bit at the bottom. You'll swirl this around then tip the cup upside down on the saucer and let it drain."

I finished first and turned my cup over. Then Lena did the same a minute later.

"Okay, now turn your cups upright again with the handle facing you—because the handle represents you."

We did this. Then Ella asked who was first.

"You go first, Lena," I said.

"Okay, good, I'll be first," Lena replied, and the anticipation shone on her face.

"Before I start, I have to know that you're ready to hear this. What I mean is that I may read things that you're not gonna want to hear, you may not like them or believe them, but I always give an honest reading. I'm not going to butter it up. Now are you ready for an honest and forthright reading?"

We told her that we were, and the reading began.

# Chapter Twenty-Seven

"Okay, the rim of the cup represents the present, and I see obvious signs of love. These little heart shapes on the rim that fall away down the side of the cup represent your relationship with Mark advancing into the future. This verifies what I initially felt when I first saw you. There is a strong bond here." Ella then paused, looking up at Lena then over at me. "Unfortunately...I see a severing of this bond in the not so distant future—maybe in six or as much as twelve months' time."

"That can't be," Lena said emphatically, and her mouth hung open as she looked at me. "You're not gonna break up with me, are you, Mark?"

"Of course not," I said.

"Well, I'm not gonna break up with you," Lena said firmly. "It's gotta be some kind-a-mistake, that's all," she said, looking at Ella expectantly.

"I only interpret what I see in the leaves. There have been mis-interpretations in the past, but they are very infrequent—few and far between I should say," Ella replied.

"Well, this has to be one of those *few and far between* cases. We're strong—we're not gonna break up."

"Let's move on then, Lena," Ella said.

"All right, I'm sorry, please finish."

"Okay, I see flowers, actually, carnations here, can you see," she said, pointing to the scattered images about the cup.

"What do they mean?"

"This is a good sign. It indicates that happiness, friendship, and love are a big part of your life. If any of these are lacking, then they will come your way.

Ella went on to read the remaining symbols amid the leaves in Lena's teacup. The rest was all good news, a little consolation perhaps to what was stated previously.

"Could I use your restroom, Ella, if you have one?"

"Sure, child, it's out back here," Ella said as she lifted the hinged section of the counter up so Lena could get through.

"I'll just be gone a minute, Mark. Thanks, Ella," Lena said as she glided through the small opening.

"Before you read my leaves, here's the money for the elephants and the readings," I said after Lena was out of sight. I handed Ella three twenties and a five.

"Thank you honey," she said, slipping the money under the counter and retrieving the figurines packed in a plain white box and tied with ribbon. It was small enough for me to hide in another bag from a previous store we had gone in.

"Okay, let's see what your leaves have to say." She looked down into the teacup then back up quickly with bewilderment and shock on her face. Ella looked down again as she began to speak, "What's this, I've never…this can't be." Then she grabbed my arm and locked her eyes on mine. "Is there something you want to explain to me?" Her voice was a bit shaky. "Mark…clearly you are not my ordinary customer, in fact the leaves tell me you're not ordinary at all."

"What do you see?" I said coyly.

"Don't bullshit me, Mark. I've been doing this a long time, and I know something strange when I see it."

"Tell me what you see and then I'll tell you my story."

Just then Lena returned from the back room.

"Lena, on our way in I noticed a sandwich shop next door. Would you go get us some sandwiches for lunch?"

"I wanted to see what your tea leaves said. I wanted to watch your reading, Mark."

"Nothing really interesting so far anyway," I said. "Prosperity and happiness, no trouble or anything and our breakup doesn't show up in my leaves, so maybe yours was a mistake. I'm almost done, and I'm gettin' real hungry. I was thinking we could bring the sandwiches down to the Charles River and eat them there. Maybe you could give us a head start by grabbing them now before I finish up"

"Okay, if that's what you wanna do. What kind do you want?"

"See if they have egg salad. I have a craving for an egg-salad sandwich right now. Oh, and get some chips too. Do you need some money?"

"No, I have plenty. Ella, would you like anything?"

"No thank you, honey."

After Lena left, Ella went on to explain what she was reading in my leaves. "See this line that forms a closed loop?"

"Yes, I see it."

"Well, a line represents a journey. It appears, and I don't know how this could be possible, that your journey began in the future. I know the starting point because of the image of a house, right there"—Ella pointed to a small house-like image at the bottom of the teacup and next to the line—"represents your home and where you come from. This unbroken line works its way up to the rim, representing the present, then loops back down the side of the cup and continues back to the starting point, closing the loop. Now before you explain this to me, I want you to know that I have an open mind, I'm a mystic, and I've seen plenty in my life. I would appreciate you being straightforward with me. Your reading is strictly confidential and would never be revealed to anyone without your permission."

I hesitated a moment. Then I let her have it. Actually it was a relief revealing my story to someone.

"Ella…I'm a physicist, I'm a physicist who has traveled back in time by way of a time machine that I created. I come from the year 2014. The reason I came back was simply to revisit my teenage romance with Lena, my first love."

"How can this be, you look so young, you would be an older man if you travelled back from the future?" Her expression told me she had many more questions for me, but I knew I didn't have a lot of time to explain the whole story in detail. I went on to sum it up as briefly as possible and also mentioned how I neglected to bring the signaling device back with me and asked if this would pose any problems with my return.

"This is amazing! I believe you though, I honestly believe you," she said, and to my complete surprise, Ella then reached over and hugged me. We smiled, and no words were spoken for a moment. I felt a lot more relaxed now, and Ella continued, "Because the loop is closed, you will definitely be returning to the future, or should I say, to your present."

"That's such a relief, Ella. I know I have Ron as a backup, but anything could happen—I've been worried. This sets my mind at ease, thank you very much."

"It's my pleasure, I'm glad I could be of some help to you. I kind of feel like I'm part of it."

"You are in a way, Ella. You are one of only two people besides me who knows I am a time traveler.

"So you obviously know about the breakup?"

"Lena will break up with me in January of next year," I said.

"I thought so, it was pretty clear in her reading. I'm sorry, I know you two are so very much in love now."

"Ella, we don't have much time, and I'm not trying to rush you, but do you see anything else that looks important."

"Okay, let me look. The only things that stand out, are here, and here," Ella said, pointing to two series of images on opposite sides of the teacup.

"What do those dots mean?"

"The dots themselves represent money coming your way. I can't make out the image they are surrounding, which would indicate from where it would come. And on the other side, this looks like the number 11. Does the number mean anything specific to you?"

"No, I don't think so, I didn't even realize that that was an eleven," I said.

Ella then turned the cup, reorienting the two digits, and gradually the number appeared before my eyes.

"Oh, I see it now."

"The only other thing I see are some stars and other heavenly bodies scattered about. They indicate happiness, good luck, and some say success, which I tend to agree with."

"All right, thanks, Ella," I said then glanced toward the door.

"Tell me something, Mark, what's the future like, do you think it's a better place than now?"

"Well, it's hard to say. It's a double-edged sword. With all the advances in medicine and technology, you might say yes, life is better, people live longer, we have easy access to an unlimited amount of information and consumer goods. Yes, you could say that life is easier in general. But on the flip side, I'd say that it's become too fast-paced and too technologically oriented. I know that must be hard to understand coming from a scientist. I wouldn't be talking to you right now without all the advances in physics over the years, but that's the way I feel. I'm really a romantic," I said, and Ella smiled.

"I think I should have been born in the nineteenth century, a slower-paced time when people spent more time together. Maybe I could have worked with Albert Einstein and discovered time travel a hundred years ago. Of course, back then you'd be without modern medicine and the plethora of niceties that come with the modern age and all, but you'd be leaving behind the rat race that life in many ways has become. You know, there are twice as many automobiles on the road in 2014 than in 1973. And inside these cars, the individual family members are all on their own electronic devices, sometimes even the driver while he's driving. In fact, many people have died in car accidents because they were distracted when using these devices while driving. Communication has devolved over the years from personal visits to phone calls and now to e-mails and texts—that's modern-day computer messaging, Ella. In my time, when people ride the subway, instead of striking up a conversation or even saying hello to the person next to them, they bury their heads in their smartphones or tablets, detaching themselves from the world around them."

I suddenly realized I was ranting. "I'm sorry, Ella, I was getting a little carried away."

"No, not at all. Computers, smartphones, tablets—it all sounds so fascinating, but I think I understand your dissatisfaction. After all, we are people and we need each other. Tell me something, will you come back and visit me sometime, I'd really like it?"

"If I can, I will, Ella."

She then threw her arms around me, hugging me once again, and it brought back memories of my grandmother, Amy, whose love I felt in hugs like that. Just then Lena came through the door.

"I guess you're done, huh?"

"Yup, all done, did they have egg salad?"

"Yeah, and they had these giant chocolate chip cookies. I got one that we could share."

"Good. Well, I guess we're all set, thanks again, Ella," I said, standing up.

"Yeah, thanks, Ella," Lena added. "I hope you were wrong about us splittin' up though."

"You are both welcome. I enjoyed meeting you. It was my pleasure. About the reading, like I said, there has been an occasional misread. I hope I'm wrong, hon."

The little bell chimed above our heads as we exited Ella's curiosity shop.

# Chapter Twenty-Eight

We walked down JFK Street to the banks of the Charles River where we sat and ate lunch. The egg-salad sandwich was delicious, and so was my half of that giant chocolate chip cookie. There were many other people down there near the river enjoying the summer weather: couples of various ages stretched out on the grass, people with dogs, groups of kids throwing footballs and Frisbees around, and many others just walking about. Small sailboats and sculling craft glided along the Charles, and across *that dirty water* looking southeast, the tall buildings of Boston loomed in the cloudless sky.

"Mark, I really liked Ella, but that reading makes me nervous…I know I'm not gonna break up with you—"

"Lena, listen," I said, cutting her off, "I love you, don't worry. I liked Ella too, but nobody can really predict the future—they just can't."

What else could I tell her—I sure as hell wasn't going to tell her the truth: that the reading was highly accurate and that I knew for a fact that by the end of the year her love for me would be all drained away, and on the eleventh of January the following year she would sever the tie and our love would be a thing of the past. No, of course not. We'd enjoy what we have right now until I had to leave, and the future would take care of itself.

All day long, my older self seemed to be in control, and it made complete sense. I woke up this morning knowing that I'd be returning soon and probably wouldn't be here in time to see the concert with Lena. Then I meet a mysterious woman who knows my situation. Everything about my future self is in the forefront of all the thoughts passing through this body presently; my younger consciousness is being pushed back temporarily but inevitably will regain control.

I still felt young though in every physical way with a strong attraction to Lena—there was no doubting this as I leaned in to kiss her but then stopped myself when I remembered the elephant figurines. "I almost forgot," I said as I leaned to my left and extracted the small ribbon-tied box from the bag next to me and presented it to Lena.

"What's this—you got me something?"

"Yeah, open it up," I said, dying to see her reaction.

Lena untied the ribbon and opened the small box. Fishing through the tissue paper, she found one of the elephants and pulled it out. Her expression was priceless. Lena wouldn't have had to say a word to let me know how much she liked her gift.

"You didn't—you actually got them for me...oh my god, I love them—I thought they were too expensive though?" Lena removed the other two figurines and turned her gaze back on me. "You shouldn't have, they're beautiful, Mark."

"I wanted to get you something nice, and it was obvious how much you liked them," I said.

"I love them, Mark, thank you for getting them for me. I really do love them."

Lena carefully wrapped each figurine with the tissue paper then placed them back in the box. She put the small box into one of her bags at her side. She then leaned in close to me, whispering "I love you" and then our lips met.

"Hey, wait a minute," Lena said, pulling back as a smile formed on her face. With her right index finger, she wiped a bit of egg salad from the corner of my mouth and rubbed it off on the grass. "I thought I tasted a little egg salad." We both laughed then continued where we left off. We were sitting when we began kissing but then gradually reclined, lying together on the soft grass lost in our passion.

Later we walked along the Charles past MIT and down to the old Longfellow Bridge, named after the great Boston poet Henry Wadsworth Longfellow. The bridge connects Boston with Cambridge and is also referred to as the Salt-and-Pepper Bridge by locals because the center towers resemble salt-and-pepper shakers.

We walked hand in hand over the bridge, stopping to take pictures before we made it to the Boston side. We had an older couple take a picture of us there on the bridge with the Charles River and Boston as a backdrop. Around four fifteen we arrived at the Charles Street station just over the bridge and began our trek back home. At Orient Heights, we hopped on a Center bus that got me home a little before five. After changing buses at Delby's Corner, Lena was in her house by five thirty.

# Chapter Twenty-Nine

After supper, my mother surprised me with the Coca-Cola stock certificates.

"They called me at work and told me they were ready," she said. I reached out to take them from my mother's hand, but she pulled them back and said, "Hold on, not so fast. I believe these need to go in a safe-deposit box at the bank."

"That was my idea, Ma. I'll bring 'em down tomorrow," I said.

Actually I had thought about this, and it was a bit perplexing. If I did go ahead and put the certificates in a safe-deposit box, then they mostly likely would be redeemed when I went to college, not there waiting for me when I got back to 2014. My plans of making over two million with the stock would be history (if you will). Also, it would alter my future by changing my financial situation down the road. On the other hand, if I didn't deposit them and brought them back with me, my mother would find out (here in my past life) and all hell would break loose. I would have to show her the receipt for the rental of the safe-deposit box, and there would be monthly payments to keep it rented also.

So what I finally decided to do was this: I'd write a note to myself not to redeem the stock until June of 2014. The note would be placed in the safe-deposit box with the stock certificates. I would leave the key to the box here in the past expecting to locate it with my other valuables when I return to the future. Of course, there was no guarantee that I wouldn't redeem them earlier than 2014, but it was the only way I could think of to get them back to me in the future without upsetting the apple cart. If they weren't there when

I returned, then I could easily create another way to make a similar sum of money anyway.

"Okay then, first thing you do tomorrow morning is get down to the bank and get these in a safe-deposit box," my mother said as she handed me the certificates and the paperwork that went with them. There were seven certificates in all: six of one hundred shares apiece and one for fifty shares. "I want to see the receipt and your key when I get home from work tomorrow," she said. "Oh, there was a little money left over."

My mother then handed me eleven dollars and some change. I was surprised that I got this many shares and still got some money back. I glanced at the paperwork that provided details of the transaction and proof that I owned the stock. I discovered that the price per share was $1.45, and the brokerage fee was a mere $47.00.

"I'll take care of it, Ma, first thing tomorrow."

"Okay, good, make sure now," she said then returned to the kitchen.

"No problem, I will." I ran upstairs to put them away then returned downstairs to the bathroom for a shower before I went out for the night.

# Chapter Thirty

J amie and I were down The Point by seven thirty and hooked up with the girls and our friends shortly thereafter. We went down to The Weeds to hang out. Roy fired up a joint and jokingly asked Trisha if she wanted some, knowing full well what she'd probably say.

"Oh no, no way—I had my share the other night, and we all know how that turned out." Of course we all laughed at this.

"Just kiddin', Trisha, I really didn't think you'd have any tonight but give it a try again sometime—just a little though, when you're not drinking, you might like the buzz."

"Yeah, maybe next time," Trisha said as she looked at Jamie, and they both smiled.

We enjoyed ourselves down by the water—talking about nothing and about everything: about the weather, about our futures, about what we overheard our parents talking about. We discussed music and all the songs and groups we liked, about the trivial things and also about what we considered the important things. I didn't want to forget any of this, this second time with Lena and the friendships of my youth. I took it all in as I looked at her and around at my friends, and I smiled not only outwardly but also from within. Soon I'd be carrying these memories into the future.

It turned out that Lena and I would be the only ones around tomorrow. Everybody seemed to have something going on. It was supposed to be a hot one, so we made plans for a full day at the beach. This was good, my time was running out here, and I wanted to be alone with Lena now as much as possible. In fact, I wanted to be alone with her immediately, so we split from Jamie and Trisha at about nine, and I arranged to meet Jamie at the bus stop later that night.

My mind was on Lena now 100 percent. The boy was back with all his teenage needs—a narrowly focused, almost nervous-like desire for the girl who meant more than anything to him. We walked farther down the shoreline and found a spot to be alone where we made out and explored each other's bodies, going further than we had prior to this point. At about ten thirty, Lena insisted we stop before we went too far, so I sat up abruptly, slightly angered and breathing heavily, trying to shut down the powerful sexual drive within me. I sat there Indian style, head hanging low and catching my breath while Lena remained lying on her back buttoning her shirt and straightening her clothes.

"We just can't go all the way, Mark, we just can't right now—we have to wait, you know how I feel about this…I'm sorry."

"I know…I know that…it's just these feelings—I just want you so bad," I said. "You're all I ever wanted." I paused then added, "There'll never be anyone else—how could there ever be."

Lena then sat up, and I heard her sigh. I had my back to her. The air had turned cooler, and there was a slight breeze coming from the water in the channel, and I shivered. Lena wrapped her arms around me from behind and let her head rest on my shoulder, and I felt her warmth once again. I held her arms as she held me and waited for her to speak. And when she finally did, she said, "I know…I know how much you love me, and I love you for that. The day will come, Mark, when we finally do it…and it could only be with you—I love you very much too."

With these words, I turned to face Lena, and we embraced, my lips once again on hers, and once again the world melted away around me. I really had everything I needed on that little stretch of beach that night. I was feeling as the boy again, and I knew for sure that someday we would make love, and that was enough to know for now.

We held each other without speaking for several minutes then left the beach and the park, making our way back to Lena's house in a nondirect, circuitous route, stopping here and there in the darkness where we kissed, trying to delay our parting, which was fast approaching.

We embraced, saying our goodbyes on her doorstep, neither of us wanting to let go, neither wanting the night to end. But then, looking down at her watch, Lena said abruptly, "You better get goin', Mark, you're supposed to get the eleven o'clock bus with Jamie, right?"

"What time is it?"

"It's three minutes of!" she said.

"Shit! Yeah, I'm gonna have to run. I'll call you tomorrow," I said and quickly pulled Lena close, kissing her, then ran off yelling, "I love you!" I heard Lena's return "I love you" before I was out of earshot, and those words fortified me, giving me additional strength in my young legs and enough air in my lungs to sprint the two blocks to the bus stop where I met Jamie seconds before the bus arrived. We made it home well before midnight. I beat the curfew.

*Massachusetts General Hospital*
*Thursday, 19 June 2014*

In the early morning hours, just after three o'clock, Mass General Hospital was still and quiet. Jessica Valjean was dreaming as she slept in a chair beside the hospital bed that Ron Sarno occupied. Although asleep, she held Ron's hand in her own.

She was young, maybe two or three, and her mother was holding her hand as they walked to the beach. Jessica was smiling, looking up at her mother while trying to shade her face from the bright sun with her free hand. She could hear her mother talking to her, not fully understanding everything she said but knew from her mother's smile that everything was okay—of course it was, she was with her mother and knew, like the sun was shining, that her mommy loved her.

"Mommy, you're tickling me," Jessica said when she felt a finger softly scrape her palm. Then her eyes flew open, and she knew instantly that it wasn't her mother whose finger she just felt move against her palm. Still holding Ron's hand, she got to her feet, quickly flicked on the lamp on the nightstand, turned and looked into Ron's eyes. They were closed but moving about under the eyelids the way the eyes do when you dream. His fingers in both hands moving, his head gently rocking left and right on the pillow, and now lifting his right arm—the one in a cast and the one connected to the IV pole—as if reaching for something. Jessica was so startled and surprised by this that her mouth hung open as she tried to form words to express what she was feeling. Ron had not moved at all, not an inch since he was admitted to the hospital six days ago and now he was thrashing about, and this left Jessica speechless. Suddenly most of Ron's moving ceased, and his eyes opened. Ron's eyes were searching the room as if looking for something familiar. His head turned slowly, trying to keep up with his darting eyes, but his neck muscles were much too sore and stiff to accommodate him. But then his eyes found Jessica. It was then that Jessica regained her voice while tears formed in her eyes and she said simply, "Ron." He stared at her, but his eyes and mind saw nothing familiar. He had no idea who this woman was and for that matter where he was. As he tried to speak, a few words came out like a raspy whisper before he started coughing. The pain shone on his face as he winced, half closing his eyes and bringing his hand to his throat then up to the bandaging around his head.

Tears now rolled down Jessica's face as she sat down gently next to Ron on the bed. "Oh, Ron, Ron, you're awake," she managed to get out before Trivia entered the room. Trivia had been notified of Ron's new status by a telemetry nurse who monitored the vital signs remotely of every patient on the fifth floor.

"Okay, hon, let me get in there," Trivia said to Jessica.

Ron then began coughing again as Jessica got off the bed and let Trivia slide in to tend to him.

"Fill up that cup with water from the pitcher, Jessica." Then she turned her attention back to Ron. "Son, do you know what your name is?"

Ron reached for the cup of water that Jessica had just finished pouring. Trivia took it and handed it to Ron. "Easy now, you haven't had anything by mouth in almost a week."

Ron took a moderate sip from the cup, cleared his throat, and then focused on Trivia. "My name is Ron Sarno, where the hell am I?"

"Ron—" Jessica began to speak but was cut off by Trivia.

"Hold on, hon," she said to Jessica then answered Ron's question. "My name is Trivia, a nurse here at Mass General Hospital. You were in a serious accident six days ago and were brought here. Do you remember any of it?"

Ron tried pulling himself up a bit in bed but stopped immediately when excruciating pain shot up from somewhere, no, everywhere in his chest. He glanced down and saw the heavy bandaging around his ribs. Ron caught his breath when the pain finally subsided. He licked his lips and cleared his throat while trying not to move too much as he responded, "The last thing I remember is teaching one of my classes. I don't remember what day it was, but it seems like a long time ago."

Jessica sat patiently as Trivia continued the questioning.

"So you do know that you teach?"

"Yeah, of course, I hold a PhD in mathematics and teach at Harvard University."

"Good, that's good, Ron."

"What happened to me?"

"I was told that you were out jogging before your morning classes and were hit by a van backing out of an alleyway. Your head hit the pavement pretty hard, resulting in a concussion that put you into a coma that you just woke up from. The pain you just experienced is from the two broken ribs you received in the accident. Your spleen was ruptured also and had to be removed. And you must have noticed the cast on your lower right arm—your wrist is broken also."

"Jesus Christ, anything else?"

"Just a few stitches on your left arm there and a couple on your face."

Trivia paused a second as Ron glanced over at the cast on his right arm then brought his hand up to feel the stitches on his right cheek. She then continued, "That will all heal...what we'll all be concerned with is your head injury and the long-term effects of that."

"Like what," Ron asked.

"Memory of course, but because the brain controls the whole body, anything can be affected by a brain injury, and every patient responds and recovers differently. Anything that you have learned or attempt to learn in the future can be affected. All this will be explained to you by one of the neurologists tomorrow, and a full battery of tests will be scheduled." Trivia then pulled back the covers at the bottom of the bed and took hold of Ron's feet. "Can you feel this?" she asked as she squeezed the toes of each foot.

"Yeah, sure."

"That's good, Ron," Trivia replied, looking up at him with a reassuring smile. "Sometimes a head injury can cause paralysis. One more thing," Trivia said as she turned to look and point at Jessica. "Can you tell me who this is?"

Ron took a long look at Jessica, and again nothing registered. "I haven't a clue," he said. "I'm sorry, should I know you?" he asked.

Jessica began sobbing. "Oh, Ron." Trivia took Jessica by the shoulder while she regained her composure. "I'm your girlfriend Ron, I'm Jessica. We met about three weeks ago on campus," she said as she wiped tears from her eyes.

"This is normal, guys. Memory loss does occur, and it can also return," Trivia said, looking back and forth between Ron and Jessica, trying to reassure them. "There'll be other things you don't remember either, Ron, but that doesn't mean that they won't come back." Trivia paused then went on, "I do wanna make one thing clear, Ron." Trivia looked at Jessica and then back at Ron. "This girl has been at your bedside for most of the time you've been here. She's your girlfriend, she's devoted to you, Ron, and she loves you very much." She paused then added, "And that you can bet my hemorrhoids on."

"Whoa, that's way too much information about your bodily parts," he said, and they all laughed. Ron went on, "Well, she's pretty enough to be a girlfriend of mine." He smiled at Jessica. This made Jessica blush then laugh, and she smiled back at Ron.

"I was hurrying to a class when I dropped my books right in front of you in Harvard Yard. You were kind enough to pick them up for me." Jessica hesitated then went on, "You rescued a damsel in distress."

"I've been known to come to the rescue of many a fair lady, my lady," Ron replied, having fun now with his apparent girlfriend.

"Well, I thank you for that, kind gentleman," Jessica said, playing along.

"Always a service to the ladies."

Jessica hesitated and then said, while blushing once again, "I was hoping you'd be of service to just one lady."

"I think that can be arranged."

"All right, you two, this is getting way too personal for me, let me go check on the other patients who may really need my help. Oh, before I go, you must be hungry, Ron, do you want me to get you an early breakfast?"

"See if you can rustle me up some scrambled eggs and toast, oh, and a big glass of cold milk if you could," he said.

"I'll see what I can do, but you really don't want to eat too much. You've been on a liquid diet through your veins for a while now. You eat too much and you'll be barfin' it up and tearin' out your sutures, never mind the pain it'll cause you."

"Yeah, I get your point, Triv—can I call you Triv, I kinda like that. I know you don't want me to call you Aunt Jemima."

Trivia looked back frowning. "Triv's fine, you call me Aunt Jemima and I'll paddle your ass."

Ron laughed so hard that the pain erupted once again in his chest and head, causing the laughing to be short-lived. Jessica was back on the side of Ron's bed as Trivia left the room.

"Okay, catch me up, tell me all about yourself, Jessica, maybe something will jog my memory," Ron said as he interlocked the fingers of his left hand into those of Jessica's right hand. He would have taken hold of both of her hands, but the heavy cast and IV in his right arm prevented him from doing this.

And so it began. Jessica told Ron about her childhood and upbringing in a small farming town in Iowa. How her mother moved the family east after her father was killed in a fire. He was coming home from an appointment at the bank when he stopped to help a family get out of their burning house before the fire department arrived. She told him how much it hurt to lose her father at nine years old then move to Massachusetts and grow up in an alien environment so far from the place she loved and all the friends she knew. Her mother's sister's family lived there, and she needed help emotionally as well as financially. Jessica cried when she told Ron how her father used to sing "Puff the Magic Dragon" to her at bedtime but inserted her into the song—the little girl who became friends with Puff, rescuing him from his sadness when Jackie Paper grew up and no longer came to play.

She told Ron about her two older brothers who also lived through this tough transition, but with the help of a strong, loving mother, they all managed somehow. How protective her brothers were of their little sister, knowing how badly she missed her dad. About the new friends she slowly gained, about junior high then high school. About her earlier college years, then returning to school at Harvard after becoming disillusioned with her banking career. And once again telling Ron about their chance encounter when her books slipped from her hands right when he was passing by.

"Jessica! I know, it just came to me," Ron blurted out, interrupting Jessica in midsentence.

"What, Ron, what just came to you?"

"I remember the day, the last memory I have before I woke up here. It was May twenty-third—of this year! I was in class lecturing that day when I happened to glance at a calendar. It was May twenty-third, and that was the day both my parents were killed in a car crash in 1994."

"I'm sorry, Ron, I didn't know."

"Thank you, Jessica," he said, then began again. "I got distracted when I realized that it was exactly twenty years ago on that day. I kinda went off into my own world for a minute, then one of my students pulled me out of it by asking if I was all right. Jessica, what's today?"

"It's um," she hesitated while glancing down at her watch, "June nineteenth."

"That means I've only blocked out about a month. I mean, I can remember everything before that, I think...yeah, I know I can," Ron said, showing a boyish enthusiasm on his face. Then his expression changed. "I'm sorry, I'm so excited that I remember so much, but I...I don't remember you."

"That's okay, Ron, It'll come back, just like Trivia said." And then, without thinking about it, she leaned in to kiss Ron then stopped herself right before their lips met. She suddenly realized that Ron had never remembered kissing her and how awkward it would be for him, so she pulled back, slightly embarrassed. "I'm sorry...I... um—"

"No," Ron said in a whisper, "it's okay," and Jessica leaned back in gently. His kiss was warm, inviting and slow and passionate. He kissed her as if they had never been apart, like the accident had never happened—as if he remembered her. He then slowly pulled away while looking into Jessica's eyes as they opened. "I could get used to this, I really could," he said then smiled.

He was so handsome, Jessica thought, and he's back, thank God, he's back!

"Ron, we met on May thirtieth," Jessica said, squeezing Ron's hand a little tighter and looking deep into his eyes, "just a week after your last memory—it's so close, I know it will come back to you."

"I know it will too. How could I forget someone as pretty and as nice as you, Jessica?" Ron said, causing his girlfriend to blush once again. Jessica leaned in and kissed Ron tenderly. She had never felt quite this way with a man. She was at home in his arms, so comfortable that time seemed to stand still, and felt fairly certain that Ron was feeling the same way.

They talked through the early morning hours while Ron ate his breakfast and on into the daylight and didn't stop until the neurologist came in at ten.

# PART 6

# Chapter One

*Tuesday, 24 July 1973*

I knew it was warm already when I awoke Tuesday morning. I could feel it in the room. We didn't have air-conditioning in the house, and I should have reopened the windows after it stopped raining last night, but I was too lazy to get up out of bed to open them.

The forecast called for the three *Hs*—hazy, hot, and humid—with the high approaching the mid-nineties, slightly cooler along the coast.

As I headed downstairs, I was thinking how I had to go down to the bank before I left for The Point. My mother and Billy were at the table eating breakfast, and as soon as I entered the room, my mother reminded me (once again) to get to the bank today—first thing.

"I should be home in the early afternoon," my mother said, "and I was thinking about spaghetti for supper tonight. I'll pick up some fresh bread after work."

"Sounds good," I said. "Six o'clock, right?"

"Yup, six o'clock. And, Billy, you said Steven's coming over here today?"

"Yeah, Ma. Can he eat lunch over?"

"Sure, but let Joanne know so she can make lunch for Steven too. And, Billy, keep an eye on your sister. She's playing out front with Maura right now. Joanne will be back in a minute. She just went down the store for me."

"Okay, I'm goin' outside to wait for Steven anyway. I'll check on Ginny."

"Thanks, come here, give me a kiss first," my mother said to Billy, motioning him over.

Billy trudged over and kissed my mother's cheek. She kissed Billy on the forehead and then tousled his hair.

"You're growing up so fast and getting so tall. You'll be as tall as Mark soon," she said, smiling proudly.

"Oh, Ma," Billy said, slightly embarrassed in front of his big brother.

"You give me a kiss too, Mark, you're not too old for that either. You going down the beach with the gang today?"

I walked over and gave her a kiss. "Actually it's just gonna be me and Lena. Everybody else is busy today."

"Well, have a good time, it's supposed to be really hot."

"I know, I heard the forecast on the radio yesterday." Then my mother's tone changed, and her face took on a more serious expression.

"You know how I told you that you have to start helping Joanne with some of the things around here?"

*Oh god*, I thought, *she's gonna ask me to stay around the house tomorrow to take care of Billy and Ginny. I can't, it's my last day.* "Yeah, I remember."

"Well, Friday, Joanne wants to go into town early with Shawna, so I need you to stay with Billy and Ginny till I get home. I'll be home early that day but not till after one, so I'll need you to feed them lunch also. I know you like to go to Lena's early, but you'll have to take care of your brother and sister till I get home."

"Sure, no problem, Ma, I can do that." You realize I was quite relieved when I heard this. I should be history by then, so it won't affect me—well indirectly you could say it would. I should be gone by Wednesday, so by Friday my past self would be staying at home and feeding Billy and Ginny lunch while I am back in the year 2014. The critical day, tomorrow, my last day here, I want to be with Lena for as long as possible before Ron retrieves me.

Just then, Joanne came through the door. "They didn't have chocolate, but they had chocolate chip."

Joanne had gone down the store for ice cream for my mother. Apparently they were having a birthday party for one of the girls she worked with.

"That's fine, you got a half gallon though, right?"

"Yeah, that's what you asked for, that's what I got." Joanne pulled it out of the bag to show my mother and then handed her the change.

"Good, thanks, Joanne. Oh, and I did talk to Mark about Friday, you're all set," my mother said as she looked over at me.

"Thanks, Ma," Joanne said then turned her gaze on me with a bit of a frown and said, "I could use a break around here," letting me know it was about time that I helped out with some of the responsibilities in the house. It was then I remembered I never did help her with the cleaning last week like I said I would.

"Have a good time Friday. Mom said you were goin' into town with Shawna."

"Yeah, is that okay with you?"

"Take it easy, Joanne," my mother said, jumping in, "he'll be home, he's gonna help out."

"Well, I'm just sick of doing everything myself with no help from him or John."

"Joanne, that's going to change, I've already talked to Mark about this," my mother said as she looked back and forth between me and Joanne.

"I'm sorry I didn't help with the cleaning last week after I told you I would. I'll um, I'll start doin' more—I promise."

"All right, I'm sorry I got upset, but I haven't got much help in the past, and I'm just tired of it."

"Like I said, this is going to change, Joanne, right, Mark?"

"Yup, I'll do my part," I said then apologized once again to Joanne.

"All right then, it's settled, water under the bridge as I say," my mother added to further smooth things out. "Mark, would you go get me that little cooler from the cellar so I can get this ice cream to work without it melting all over the place."

"Yeah, sure."

# Chapter Two

My mother was gone ten minutes later, and Joanne had retreated to some other part of the house. With Billy and Ginny outside, I had the kitchen to myself, so I decided to give Lena a call before I ate breakfast.

"Morning, Mark, you're calling early."

"Morning, Lena. Yeah, I thought I'd give you a call before I ate."

"It's nice hearing your voice, I'm glad you called early, I was just thinking of you."

"Oh yeah, what were you thinking about," I said, smiling, wishing she were actually here with me so I could feel her close to me.

"Just how we're gonna spend the whole day at the beach together." Then she paused. "Alone, just me and you."

"Yup, just me and you, and I can get down there real early if you want."

"How early?"

"It's eight thirty now, let's see. Say around nine thirty."

"Yeah, I could be ready by then."

"Okay," I said. "Let me eat my breakfast, and I'll hop on my bike and be down there by nine thirty." Then I remembered the bank. "Oh, wait a minute. I forgot. I have to go to the bank first, so better make it around ten, maybe a little earlier."

"Good, ten's fine. I'll see you then, I love you. And, Mark, be careful riding down."

"I love you too, and I'll be careful. See you in a bit."

"Okay, bye."

"Bye, Lena."

# Chapter Three

I was out of the house by nine. I stashed my towel and change of clothes, the certificates with the paperwork and the note about not cashing them until 2014 on the bike rack behind the seat.

Once at the bank, the whole process took only twenty-five minutes, so I knew I'd make it to Lena's before ten. I tucked the receipt for the safe-deposit box and that new, shiny key deep in the right front pocket of my shorts, and off I went.

I pulled up at Lena's house at five of ten and stowed my bike around back. As I returned to the front of the house, Lena was opening the slider and met me on the steps. She looked so happy to see me, and this made me smile. I was that young boy who desperately wanted to be with his girlfriend. Once again, my future self had been pushed aside to allow room for my former self trying to regain control. My hormones were raging as I looked at Lena's well-developed fifteen-year-old body clad only in her bikini. I wanted to take that thing off right there and kiss every part of her. I pulled her close and tight to me. Lena expected a peck on the lips, but when I opened my mouth and began french-kissing her, she responded but then pulled away quickly.

"Mark, take it easy, my mother's right inside the house!"

"Sorry, couldn't help it, you look so sexy in your bikini," I said as I caught my breath, smiling, feeling cocky like I'd just got away with something, something that I enjoyed immensely.

"Easy, we'll have all day at the beach. Go get changed so we can get goin'. I'm all set."

We were at the beach by ten thirty. This time we had Lena's mother's umbrella with us. Lena decided to humor her mother and take it; besides, it was supposed to be a scorcher today. It didn't have the screw-in base like modern-day beach umbrellas, just a metal shaft. I dug a hole and planted it firmly in the sand, and we set up underneath. It was actually rather large and would provide adequate shade for both of us.

The water seemed a bit warmer today as we made our way in. "Come here," I said, and Lena waded closer. I pulled her to me. We were in waist-deep water with small waves gently splashing us as they made their way to the shore. The sun made the water on Lena's body glisten. She was so pretty, and I was so happy she was mine. This time when I french-kissed her she didn't pull away. We were far from her house now, and no one was near us in the water.

After a few minutes, Lena broke the embrace.

"Last week you didn't wanna kiss me, and now you're jumpin' my bones."

"Really," I said, puzzled. "I barely remember that. It seems to me that I've always wanted to kiss you."

"Don't you remember last week, that talk we had? I said it didn't seem like you wanted to french kiss me anymore, and I was worried that you didn't like me enough to continue going steady."

"Yeah, kinda," I said. Of course, my former self would not remember much of that conversation because my future self had then just recently arrived, taking charge of the body. But now the boy was in charge.

"Kinda? I think your memory is going. I mentioned that last week too, but you wouldn't remember that either, right?"

"It doesn't really matter, does it—you know how much I like you right now. I mean…you know I love you, Lena." As I said this, Lena smiled, and the conversation ceased. I pulled her tight to me, and we began kissing once again.

We stayed close, not swimming much, just holding each other and kissing. And when we weren't kissing, we were talking and laughing.

By the time we got out and back up to the umbrella, it was approaching noon, and we were both hungry.

# Chapter Four

After eating lunch, we lay in the sun, but not long after retreated to the shade of the umbrella where it seemed to provide a sense of privacy. And that sense of privacy allowed us to pick up where we left off down in the water. We spooned into each other's bodies, lips once again touching, breath quickening, heaven once again descending upon us, replacing the more common, everyday feel of life.

Eventually I rolled over and fell asleep while "Rocket Man" by Elton John played on Lena's transistor radio near my head. This wasn't typical in my earlier years. In fact, I had never fallen asleep while with Lena at the beach. This was due to my older self still having a hold here in my past, my older self who was much more apt to take a nap on the beach.

I dreamt of Ron again, apparently still worried about getting home, notwithstanding the reassurance from Ella. When I awoke, my future self was back, and I wondered if I had talked in my sleep, revealing anything to Lena.

"Hi," I said as I shook the sleep off.

"You fell asleep for a little while. You really do get relaxed on the beach, huh? That's the second time in about a week that you fell asleep here at the beach."

"Yeah…I um…I guess I'm just so comfortable down here with you."

Lena leaned down and kissed me. "Thanks, Mark, I'm comfortable with you too," she said, looking into my still-sleepy eyes.

I pulled Lena down on top of me, closing my eyes once again, not to sleep this time, but to kiss the girl I loved. And while kissing Lena, the sad thought ran through my mind that I most likely wouldn't be here by this time tomorrow. This made me break our embrace. I told Lena that I was hungry, masking the melancholy that had seeped in. We both sat up, and Lena grabbed a couple of apples from her bag.

"This is all we have left," she said and then handed me one. "We have plenty of lemonade left too if you're thirsty."

"Sure, I'll take some lemonade," I said as I crunched into the apple. Lena poured the lemonade into Dixie cups for both of us then sat back down next to me in the shade of that big umbrella. We sat there like two Indians with our legs crossed under us.

"Lena, I know you love me, and I know right now it would be the furthest thing from your mind, but I just need to say this—"

"Say what, you sound so serious," Lena cut in, and the expression on her face changed dramatically.

"If one day you did happen to fall out of love with me and we broke up—"

"That's not gonna happen, I—"

"Just hear me out, okay?"

"Okay, but I don't like where this is goin'."

"Would you still think of me in some small way...could you somehow keep me in your heart, and always remember that you would remain in my heart forever?"

"You'll always be in my heart because we're never gonna break up—I mean...how can I answer that, Mark...it's like admitting something about myself that I know I'll never do." Lena was becoming defensive and understandably so. I was questioning the very strength of her love for me, but I needed to hear this before time ran out.

"I don't like this whole idea, even if it's only a *what-if,* but I'll answer you—yes, yes! I could never forget you, you would remain in my heart forever." Then Lena turned away from me obviously upset.

"I'm sorry...I'm sorry I brought this up. I know you love me and—"

"You know I'd never break up with you," Lena said, visibly upset now as tears started down her cheeks, and with the tears she began to sob, "How could you even think—how could you ever think that that might happen? How could you ever—" Lena could no longer speak as she cried openly.

"I'm sorry, I'm sorry," I said quickly, thinking now that I never should have opened my mouth. I wrapped my arms around her convulsing body. "Shhh, shhh, it's all right, I'm sorry. I know you won't break up with me, I know." I held her tight, and slowly Lena's sobbing subsided. I waited a minute then gently lifted her chin so that our eyes met. "I love you, Lena, and I'm sorry I brought that up. I really am." Gradually she calmed down. "No worries, right?" I said, and the beginnings of a smile formed on her face. I dabbed at her tears with a napkin.

Lena sniffled then took the napkin from my hand and wiped her face more thoroughly. Then suddenly she balled up her hands into fists and began pounding my chest halfheartedly. "You jerk!" she said, kind of smiling through the hurt left over on her face. "Whyja even bring that up? You know I'll never break up with you, you should know that!"

"Because I'm stupid...and I'm sorry, I shouldn't have. Will you accept my apology?"

"I don't know, you're gonna be in the doghouse for a while though, that's for sure—what do you think about that, buster?" Lena said with a smirk.

"I deserve it, I know. But will you let me in at night, I get lonely?" I said, and Lena laughed. "Why don't we go swimming, change the mood?" I said.

"Yeah, I think that's the first good idea you've had all day," Lena said then jabbed me in the side, catching me unaware.

"Owwww," I howled.

"Well, you deserve it," Lena said, smiling now.

"Truce, okay, I'll be good."

"Promise?"

"I promise."

# Chapter Five

While back in the water, I began thinking about tomorrow again. I wanted to be with Lena alone. I wanted to be holding her the moment Ron retrieved me.

"What do you think about just me and you again tomorrow?"

"You don't wanna hang with everybody tomorrow, we weren't with them today?"

"Yeah, just one more day alone," I said as I moved closer to Lena, interlocking my fingers in hers.

"Well, I don't know what everyone's doin' tomorrow anyway. I guess we could tell 'em we're busy."

"I'd like that, one more alone day," I said as I pulled Lena closer.

We then kissed tenderly while the sun beat down on our wet bodies and the waves lapped against us. I held her tight while thinking about how little time remained. We kissed as my hands roamed the curves and contours of Lena's back, my fingers pressing into that soft flesh, now touching and feeling all the parts of her body that I dared touch there on the beach, in public, memorizing every detail of Lena with all five senses acutely aware. We finally broke our embrace and slowly made our way to the shore.

The hot sun worked its way through the hazy sky above, but it didn't feel quite as hot or humid as they said it would be. Of course, at the beach it never really did feel that way. It was warm of course, but not unbearably so, and the humidity was not as oppressive down here near the water. Cooling off in the water and enjoying, at minimum, a gentle breeze while out of the water seems to always keep the stifling heat at bay.

We lay down in the sun and dried off to Bill Withers's hit from 1971, "Ain't No Sunshine." God, I just loved the music from this era, I thought. It's just so much more meaningful than the music that would come after it, especially that horrid disco crap.

I propped myself up on my elbows as I looked around at the other people scattered about the beach, then across the water at the prison, a minimum-security facility. The inmates in that old brick structure were so close but so very far away from enjoying what we were enjoying here on the beach. It was located on what was called Deer Island. Not an island anymore as it once was, it was connected to Point Shirley long ago when the small channel called Shirley Gut that separated Winthrop from Deer Island was filled in. Although physically connected, hooking around so you could look at it from the beach, Deer Island was its own entity, owned by the City of Boston. Eventually the prison would be torn down, making way for an expansive, state-of-the-art sewage treatment facility that would serve a multitude of communities surrounding Boston, including Winthrop.

"What are you lookin' at, Mark?"

"Oh, I was just lookin' over at the prison and thinkin' about those poor bastards in there."

"Well, they deserve to be there, don't you think?"

"Yeah, I guess so," I said, but I still felt sorry for them. Then I lay back down, looking out from under the umbrella at the sky above the water and realized I hadn't seen a plane fly overhead in a few days. The wind had remained on shore, out of the east, keeping the high temps down a bit here at the beach and the planes away—just as well, it was lot quieter without them roaring overhead.

Before we knew it, it was closing in on five o'clock, so we packed up and headed back to Lena's house. The day had sped by so fast, and tomorrow was quickly approaching—the *endgame* was here. We arranged to meet after supper, not sure who was going to be around tonight.

# Chapter Six

After eating, I took the bus down to The Point with Jamie. It turned out that it would just be us, the two couples: Lena and me and Jamie and Trisha. We would spend most of the night down at The Weeds, as usual.

After getting settled down there near the water, Jamie pulled out the pack of Winstons, and we lit up. I hadn't had one in a few days, but I hadn't thought about them either. I took a deep drag, exhaled; then looking over at Lena, I said, "Did you get those pictures developed that we took last week on the beach?"

"Oh wow, I forgot, Mark. The roll's still in my camera."

"Why don't you give it to me tomorrow, I'll take care of it." I was a bit miffed knowing it was too late now to get them developed, so I'd just bring the roll back with me and try to find someplace that still develops that type of film. In doing this, I would mess things up here a bit, but screw it. It was the only way now that I could bring any pics back.

Then I looked over at Jamie and said, "Girls, you just can't trust them to get anything done." Jamie let out a chuckle just as Lena poked me in the ribs like she did at the beach today. "Owhhh," escaped me as I tried leaning away from the assault.

"That's not fair, Mark, you're the one who forgets everything. Last week you weren't even sure if I had a camera," Lena pointed out.

"I was just kiddin…jeez, what's all this poking me lately—you're really dangerous you know," I said, half wincing and half smiling.

"Yeah, guys are the ones who forget birthdays and other important dates," Trisha added.

"Hey, I remembered yours this year," Jamie protested while gently pinching Trisha's side.

"That's true, but you forgot your mother's."

"Yeah, and my father gave me hell for not gettin' a card."

"It's true, I guess we're all forgetful at times," I said, looking over at Lena and smiling. "Truce, no more poking me in the side."

"Okay, truce, but you be good," Lena said as she wagged her finger at me.

"I'll be good," I said, taking hold of her finger and leaning in, giving her a peck on the lips. Jamie and Trisha seemed amused, both smiling at our little exchange.

As the night drew on, we separated as usual, but not before setting up a time to meet at the bus stop later. Jamie offered me a cigarette before we parted, but I declined.

I tried to just enjoy the night alone with Lena, but my mind kept thinking ahead, thinking about tomorrow. Finally, I pushed it away, or was it really the younger me who accomplished this?

When we realized there was a full moon coming up behind us, across the park and over the water beyond, we turned to face it. It was beautiful, completely full, taking on a gorgeous yellow hue as it hung low in the sky. We sat there holding each other while staring at it, mesmerized, not unlike staring into a campfire, being drawn in hypnotically, unable to avert one's eyes.

"It's beautiful, isn't it, Mark?"

"Yeah, sure is," I replied then leaned back in to kiss Lena. I guess the poets could have come up with something pretty romantic here—two young lovers kissing by the light of a beautiful full moon rising before them.

As the night progressed, I found myself holding Lena more than kissing her, as if by holding on tight we could never be separated. Oh god, I didn't want to leave her tomorrow. I wanted to stay here forever. I longed to stay here—touching her, feeling Lena close to me, smelling her sweet fragrance, and seeing my love and hearing her voice, none of which I could ever possibly tire from. But I was also fully aware that Ron would retrieve me tomorrow.

I was existing now in that second week of time travel where my former self and future self had virtually an equal pull on me. I was, simultaneously, the older scientist who knew it was time to go back and the younger me who wanted nothing more than to be with Lena.

"I talked to Joan and Trisha earlier tonight about us spending tomorrow alone again."

I kissed Lena's forehead tenderly then moved to her mouth where our lips touched, both of us responding slowly and ever so gently. I released my lips and whispered, "What did they say?"

Lena let out a sigh and said, "Joan was a little pissed. She wanted to get together tomorrow. Trish was cool with it."

"Really. I talked to Jamie about it on the bus, he was cool. I didn't expect him to get upset about it anyway. He's gonna see what Roy's doin' tomorrow." Then I thought, *Why is it always the girls that get upset over these things?*

"She'll get over it," Lena replied.

I smiled, kissed Lena again, then said that I was sure she would.

We started for the bus stop at ten of eleven, stopping here and there to kiss, but made it a few minutes before the bus arrived.

"Hey guys, I didn't think you were gonna make it," Trisha said.

"Yeah, we stopped a few too many times along the way," Lena said, looking at me with a smile on her face. I squeezed her hand, letting Lena know that I appreciated all those stops along the way, and then smiled back.

"We made it though, bus should be comin' any minute, huh?" I said.

Jamie looked down at his watch and was about to say something when the bus turned the corner and came to a stop before us. We gave our girlfriends goodbye kisses, jumped on the bus, and headed for home.

# Chapter Seven

*Wednesday, 25 July 1973*

Everyone except my mother thought it was strange when I hugged them this morning, especially John and Joanne. Why wouldn't they, I wasn't that affectionate the first time around, but I knew I'd be leaving soon and wanted to show them how much I loved them.

I stayed with John the longest, knowing he wouldn't even be alive on my return to the future.

"Okay, kid," he said after I told him I loved him and then tears formed in my eyes as we parted.

I ate and got changed quickly knowing how little time remained. I then got on the phone with Lena and arranged to meet her at nine, the earliest I would be down The Point since I'd come back. I wanted to take my bike because I had so much nervous energy to burn off, and when I arrived, I realized that I had never made it down there that fast—ever!

Lena let me in at ten of nine. "Wow, did you fly down?"

"I guess I was movin' pretty fast on my bike," I said.

"I guess so, huh," Lena replied, then after pausing, "All right, I'm gonna run upstairs and pick up my room then tell my mother we're leaving."

"Sure, no problem."

I made myself comfortable in the living room for a while but couldn't sit still, so I walked out to the front room. My mind went back to my leaving this place, or should I say, this time. I was looking across the water at the planes taking off and landing at Logan and the Boston skyline beyond that would look totally different in a few hours—at least to me. Then I heard Lena's voice bringing me back from my reverie.

"Well, I'm all ready," Lena said as she walked into the front room. "It's obviously not a beach day, so what do you want to do?"

"I was thinking of taking a walk, then just hangin' out in the park."

"What about lunch, whataya wanna do about that?"

I told Lena we could get something to eat at Surfside even though I knew that the future me would no longer be here by lunchtime.

"Okay, sounds good."

I glanced at the clock in the living room before we left so I would know precisely how much time I had left. I cursed myself, thinking that I should have bought a watch when I first arrived. I never wore one when I was young and realized now that I'd really like to have one with so little time remaining. I wanted to be constantly aware of the time, especially as it got close to noon. We stepped out the door at nine twenty-five.

I took Lena's right hand in my left, and we began walking. I thought that I'd be doing most of the talking considering the circumstances, but I found myself content just to listen to her voice and hold her hand. When we got to the end of her street, we stopped for a while, sitting on the wall facing the airport across the channel. It was cloudy and unseasonably cool today, but it felt refreshing after all the hot days.

"You're pretty quiet today, Mark, you okay?" Lena asked as she nudged me with her shoulder.

"Yeah, I'm fine…I guess I'm just a bit tired," I said, trying to deflect my true feelings.

We then embraced and kissed. I usually closed my eyes when we kissed, but this time I kept them open. I wanted to see everything, to remember everything. I eventually pulled back, laying my head on her shoulder, pressed in close while I held her tight.

"Mark…you sure you're okay?"

I sighed deeply, close to tears now, and thought of Diana Ross's song "Touch Me in the Morning."

*Wasn't it yesterday we used to laugh at the wind behind us?*
*Didn't we run away and hope that time wouldn't*
*try to find us (Didn't we run)*
*Didn't we take each other to a place where no one's ever been*
*Yeah, I really need you near me tonight*
*'Cause you'll never take me there again*

I lifted my head off her shoulder and brought my face to hers.

"I was just thinking…you know…how much I love you, how much I really do love you, Lena."

Lena smiled radiantly and kissed me, then pulled back quickly and said, "I love you for loving me. I never knew I'd find someone like you, Mark."

"Really, you really love me like that, that much?"

"Yeah, of course." She leaned back in, and we kissed. This time I closed my eyes and let the softness and gentleness of the kiss wash over me like a warm shower.

I don't know how long we sat there on the wall as I lost all track of time. I was no longer thinking about how much time I had left. I was caught up in the moment. I was thinking about how happy I was with Lena. I just couldn't imagine how anyone could be any happier, any more content than I was. And it came to me that this was all that really mattered. We are born and live our lives for one purpose and one purpose only—that is to find love. To find someone to journey through life with, someone to combat the loneliness and difficulties that we encounter in life, problems that can seem devastating to face alone. Unfortunately and tragically, many relationships deteriorate, and some are very short-lived like ours would be. Then that old cliché came to mind: *better to have loved and lost than not to have loved at all.* It was of course an overused expression, but it was also very true.

We finally moved on, walking leisurely around Point Shirley, past houses and streets and other people, but none of this really registered with me as my focus was on Lena. We then made our way down to the beach, and as we strolled along hand in hand, I suddenly realized that there couldn't be much time left.

"What time is it, Lena?"

Looking down at her watch, she said, "It's quarter past eleven."

"You hungry," I asked.

"No, not really, how 'bout you?"

"No, not yet." We continued our walk down the strand until we reached the Deer Island prison property line where we turned around. "Why don't we head down the park?" Lena agreed, and we started back.

# Chapter Eight

After settling in at a picnic table under the shelter at the park, I asked Lena for the time.

"Whataya got a date?" Glancing at her watch, she said, "It's eleven forty-five."

"Yeah, with you," I said, and then, "Just time conscious today I guess."

We snuggled in close on the bench and chatted as the minutes ticked by. I wasn't going to ask Lena for the time again, so I held her hand and kept an eye on her watch while we talked. At three minutes till noon I leaned in and we began french-kissing. This was it, my time here was up, and I wanted to be one with Lena as I was brought back. I didn't want to go back, but the *older* part of me knew I had to. We kissed long and deep. I ran my hands over Lena's body as we kissed, acutely aware of both her and the time, waiting for the transformation to happen, but when I broke the embrace just after noon, I was still here. *Okay,* I thought, *anytime now—crank it up, Ron, let's get this over with.* But the minutes crept by, and nothing happened.

I was still here at twelve fifteen and at twelve twenty. Shortly before twelve twenty-five, Lena asked if I was hungry yet.

"What?" I replied.

"I was asking if you're hungry," Lena said as she wrinkled her brow, noticing that I was distracted.

"Yeah, I am," I said. "Let's go over to Surfside and get some lunch." At this time I realized there could be a problem, but most likely Ron was just slightly behind schedule.

After lunch I was pretty sure there was a problem. Ron was punctual and kept to schedules. It was not like him to be late or behind schedule with anything he did. It was now quarter past one in the afternoon and I was still living here—in the year 1973!

We had made our way back to Lena's house where we broke out the board games and settled in for the day out in the front room. My concentration waffled back and forth between our game of Sorry and me getting back to the present. Regardless, the afternoon passed quickly, and before we knew it, suppertime was drawing near. Lena walked me out to get my bike, and I told her I'd be back down right after I had eaten supper.

On the way home, I didn't have to conceal my worry, so I focused on the myriad of possibilities that could have conspired to keep me here in my past. Something had definitely delayed Ron. It was now well past 5:00 p.m., more than five hours after my retrieval time. *Fuck it*, I thought. *Get home, eat, take a shower, and get yourself back down here to see Lena, and be glad you have some extra time with her. There may be a problem but nothing too serious…I hope.*

# Chapter Nine

I took the bus down to The Point solo and met Lena outside her house at seven forty. She gave me a quick peck on the lips as we sat down on the front steps.

"Is that all I get?" I said.

Lena frowned, saying, "That's all you get here."

"I know, I know, I was just jokin'," I replied.

"I was talking to Roy earlier, and he wanted to know if we all wanted to play poker over at his house tonight. He called Jamie but found out he'd be stuck at home."

"Yeah, I know about Jamie, I called him before I left. Poker sounds good." As I said this, I remembered our poker games and the fun we had playing.

"I called Joan, she's comin' over and said she'd call Trisha."

"Good, we'll have a good group to play with."

"See if I can be the big winner again," Lena added.

"How much did you win the last time?"

"Almost fifteen bucks, remember? It was about three weeks ago."

I said I did, but I really couldn't recall that particular game of poker. I do remember that Lena usually lost money when we played.

We set up in a rather large room facing the street on the second floor. Roy called it their spare living room. There was one on the first floor also. It was a comfortable and spacious room that took up the front half of the second floor with large windows that afforded a spectacular view. In fact, the sun had just set, and the sky and clouds had taken on beautiful shades of orange and pink.

"All right, anybody need change?" Roy asked as we settled in at the card table. Lena brought a bunch of change with her, but the rest of us needed some. There were five of us playing. Trisha decided to play even though Jamie couldn't make it tonight.

When everybody had plenty of change, Roy went over the rules we played by including the amount of money that was bet. The ante and initial betting was five cents, and we played with a two raise limit of ten and fifteen cents. We usually played five- and seven-card stud, five- and seven-card draw, and a three-card card game called guts with a pot limit of ten dollars. The dealer would choose the game, and the deal rotated around the table after each game. Roy dealt first, and he chose five-card draw as the game.

# Chapter Ten

By nine fifteen, the girls were all out. They had lost all their money, and Roy and I had it. We battled back and forth, exchanging wins, then at quarter till ten—since Lena had to be in by ten o'clock—we decided to play one final game, one big game.

It was my deal, so I decided to play seven-card stud where we each threw five bucks in the pot to start the game and upped the betting also. It would now be twenty-five cents for an initial bet then fifty for the first raise and a dollar for the second and final raise.

In the first round of seven-card stud, three cards are dealt to each player: two down and one up. Roy and I both got an ace for our up card, so I knew this had a chance of being a big pot. I peeked at my down cards and discovered, to my delight, I had another ace and a Jack in the "hole." Roy started the betting when he threw a quarter in, and I raised it to fifty cents. He looked up at me, saw nothing on my face to reveal my good hand, then threw fifty cents in without upping the raise. This told me Ace high was all he had. I got another Jack for my second up card, and Roy got an Ace. He threw a quarter in, and I raised it to fifty cents. With a big smile on his face, Roy then picked up a dollar bill from his pile of bills and change, put it in the pot, and said, "Let's make it a dollar." I was pretty sure Roy just had that pair of Aces, and I don't think he knew just how good my hand was already. The pot was growing, and the girls broke from their conversation and started paying attention when they picked up on this.

I don't believe Roy's third and fourth up cards helped him at all. My third and fourth up cards didn't improve my hand either, but I was still sitting on aces and jacks. Roy couldn't contain his excitement when he saw his final down card, so I knew he had a pretty good hand. Then I peeked at mine. I couldn't believe it. I just dealt myself another jack. I was now sitting on a full house: three jacks and a pair of aces. I maintained my poker face as Roy started the betting. He raised, just as I thought he would, and I raised again. Roy threw the last dollar in the pot that now contained close to twenty-five bucks and said, "I call."

His mouth hung open in utter astonishment as I laid my hand down in front of him. "Full house," I said, letting a full smile show on my face.

"No fuckin way," he said and then repeated it three more times. The girls all showed surprise on their faces as they thought Roy had me.

"Yeah, fucking way," I said and pulled the large pot toward me.

"You asshole, I thought I had ya."

"I got the third jack on the last card," I said as the smile widened on my face.

"You lucky bastard, I had ya, damn. I had aces and kings," Roy said while shaking his head and throwing down his hand.

"No hard feelings, right, Roy?" I said, looking at Roy then at Lena. I was still smiling, and so was Lena.

"No hard feelings, but you're still an asshole," he said then smiled and shook off the loss.

"It's not like you lost everything. You still have some money in front of you," I said in consolation.

"Yeah, but I'm about where I started."

"Still better off than the girls, they lost everything."

"Yeah, it's true, but shit, I really thought I had you there in that last hand."

"You can get me next time," I said, and Roy just shook his head.

Lena reminded me that she had to get going as it was just about ten, so we said our goodbyes and made for the door.

"Beach tomorrow, Lena?" Joan asked as we headed out.

"Yeah, probably, I'll call you in the morning," Lena said over her shoulder as we walked down the stairs, leaving our friends.

We didn't have much time for a long good night kiss, but we made the best of it in the shadows on the side of Lena's house. Then as I turned to go, it hit me that this could be the very last time I would see Lena. I hadn't thought about it the whole time we were over Roy's, and now it came back to me like a hard slap in the face, so I turned and ran back to my girl. I startled Lena as she was walking up the steps to her house. I led her back into the shadows, pulled her close, and we french-kissed again with an intensity and urgency that I had never felt in myself before. I then broke the embrace slowly, looked deep into Lena's eyes, and told her once again how much I loved her.

"I love you too, but I really gotta get goin', Mark. I'm gonna get in trouble if I don't get in that house right now."

"Okay, yeah, you're right. I just had to kiss you one more time—sorry."

"Don't be sorry," Lena said, tilting her head as she smiled. "Okay, gotta go, see you tomorrow," Lena said, sliding from my arms and running for the house.

I got the ten twenty-five bus, and all I could think of the entire ride was *I hope Ron doesn't bring me back now.*

I was home before eleven, and the house was quiet when I got in. I washed up and brushed my teeth then quietly climbed the stairs to the bedroom. I was tired, but it took a while to get to sleep because I kept thinking that at any moment I could be pulled back in time. As I was drifting off to sleep, my last thoughts were that just maybe I'd still be here tomorrow and I'd get to see that Jim Croce concert with Lena.

# Chapter Eleven

*Thursday, 26 July 1973*

Iawoke at eight o'clock and immediately realized that I was still here in 1973. I wondered what the hell was going on. *Ron, why haven't you brought me back, what's happened?*

The man in me was worried, but the boy that was in the process of reclaiming his body was content knowing that he'd soon be with Lena and they would be together to see one of their favorite singers in concert tonight—Jim Croce!

As I made my way downstairs, the boy began to take charge: hungry for breakfast and eager to see Lena today.

I poured some milk into a bowl of cereal and sat down at the kitchen table with my mother and sisters. Billy was up early as usual and gone from the breakfast table, and John was still asleep.

"Tonight's the night, huh, Mark?" my mother said as she peered over a hot mug of coffee.

"Yup, Jim Croce in concert, can't wait," I said.

"So Lena's mother's taking you in and picking you up, right?"

"Yeah, Lena's mother will probably pick me up over here, but I'm not sure what time. I would think around seven, but I'm not sure."

"And what time should I expect you to get home tonight?"

"It gets over at eleven, so I would think no later than eleven thirty."

"All right, you be careful in there, things can get wild at concerts, Mark."

"They say Jim Croce concerts are pretty low-key—you know, folk music, not hard rock, Ma."

"Well, you be careful anyway."

"All right, Ma, I will."

"I just found out Elton John's coming in the fall," Joanne said as she got up from the table. "Shawna and I are planning to see him."

"I'd like to go to a concert," Ginny said, chiming in. I laughed as my mother told Ginny she was too young for concerts. "Well, when I get big, I'm gonna go to one."

"All right, sure, Gin," my mother said, "when you get older."

"That should be a great concert, Joanne, I love his songs," I said.

"Yup, I'm not gonna miss that one," Joanne said as she left the room on the way to the shower.

I enjoyed the casual conversation with my mother and Ginny while finishing my breakfast, waiting to get in the shower. I discovered that my mother took the day off from work and didn't have any classes scheduled either, so she planned on bringing Ginny to the Aquarium in Boston today.

"Ma, what time are we leaving?"

"About ten o'clock, Gin."

"Can I go out and play until we go?"

"Yes, but don't get dirty and stay right out front, okay."

"Okay, Mom," Ginny said as she bolted from the table. Just then I heard Joanne exiting the shower, so I excused myself and headed that way.

After showering and getting changed, I called Lena. We planned on meeting at the beach at ten. I told her that I'd call Jamie to see if he wanted to come, and by nine fifteen I was heading out the door to meet him at his house. We'd be back tracking to get to the bus stop, but I was anxious to get out of the house and get to The Point.

# Chapter Twelve

We got to the beach just after ten. Lena and Trisha jumped up off their towels as they saw us approaching. Lena gave me a quick peck on the lips as Trisha wrapped her arms around Jamie.

"I can't wait to go to the concert tonight, that's all I've been thinking about since I woke up," Lena said.

"What concert," I said, smiling as we walked over to Joan and Roy.

"Whataya mean *what concert*," Lena said. Her face wrinkled into a semi-smile as she teasingly pushed me.

As I regained my balance, I leaned into her, smiled, and said softly that I was just joking. "I can't wait either."

Roy was sitting up Indian style adjusting his transistor radio, and Joan was lying on her beach towel, reading a paperback.

"Hi guys," she said as we reached them.

Jamie and I were returning the greeting when Michael Jackson's "Ben" crackled to life on the radio. Joan and Lena both yelled out in unison that they loved the song as Roy tuned it in.

"Eh, it's okay, I wouldn't call it a great song—it's about a rat, you know?" Roy replied, and Jamie laughed.

"It's so sweet, I love the song," said Joan, and Lena seconded it.

"Whatever," Roy said as he put the radio down and looked up at me and Jamie. "What's happenin'?" to which we replied, "Not much," our typical response to that question. "You and Lena are goin' to see Croce in concert tonight, huh?"

"Yep," I said as I looked over at Lena smiling. Lena returned the smile when she heard the concert mentioned while talking to Trisha. "Should be a good one."

"He's okay, but I wouldn't see him in concert," Roy replied, and Jamie agreed. They were both the Aerosmith and Led Zeppelin types while I preferred the ballad singers like Jim Croce, Harry Chapin, and Gordon Lightfoot.

"Whatever," I said, looking down at Roy with a smirk on my face.

Roy smiled back at me as he got up. He grabbed his football and asked if we wanted to throw it around. We all agreed and headed down to the hard-packed sand closer to the water. The girls stayed behind, chatting and catching up on things.

# Chapter Thirteen

L ena and Trisha brought food for all of us, and we ate around noon. Shortly after lunch, we headed down to the water.

It cleared up nice overnight and was warm once again here at the beach—partly cloudy in the eighties, but of course, the water was cold. We managed to stay in for a while though, mainly wading around in the shallows and talking. The planes were coming in over our heads today, so at times we were screaming to make ourselves heard.

"What time's the concert tonight, Lena?" Joan asked.

"It starts at eight, we're gonna leave about seven-ish."

"I was meaning to ask you what time your mother's picking me up, but now I know," I said.

"Yeah, we should be over your house just after seven," Lena said. She was standing behind me nestled in close with her arms wrapped around my midsection. It felt good with her body pressed against mine, but my shins were aching from the cold water.

As I was shuffling my feet around to warm up my lower legs, a plane roared overhead. As it passed, I suddenly was filled with a sense of dread. The memory came back slowly but powerfully as my older self took hold and recalled a horrific event that would occur soon here in 1973: on July 31, just five days from now, shortly after eleven in the morning, a plane would crash at Logan Airport while attempting to land in heavy fog. It would be the worst air disaster ever at Logan.

The crash would be, in part, attributed to unfamiliarity with the aircraft's guidance aid or what is called a Flight Director. Exactly one year prior to the accident, Delta and Northeast Airlines merged to become Delta Airlines. Because of the merger, the two former Northeast Airlines pilots were flying a converted Northeast Airlines DC-9 aircraft with a similar but different model Flight Director. They were flying an instrument approach, meaning they were flying blind, relying on navigation instruments including the Flight Director to guide them to the airport in the extremely thick fog. Inadvertently, the mode selector switch of the Flight Director was dialed into the wrong position for the approach; therefore, the information they were receiving was unreliable, dangerously unreliable.

After receiving late clearance to land, they were coming in too fast and too steep. They eventually passed underneath the glide slope, slamming into a low cement wall that separated the airport from the water of the inner harbor that surrounded it. The plane virtually disintegrated on impact, killing everyone on board instantly save two passengers. One of the survivors lived for about two hours then died, and another managed to live almost five months with burns to over 80 percent of his body. All told, eighty-nine passengers and crew died as a result of that horrific crash.

As I stood there, I realized that all those people who perished were still living and breathing right now, with no way of knowing what lay ahead. It was chilling to think about, to have this knowledge that no one else possessed. Then I shivered from the cold water and this dreadful memory that I had dredged up.

"You okay, Mark" Lena asked as she realized I was shivering.

"Freezing," was all I could say, then managed, with teeth chattering, to ask her if she wanted to get out of the water.

"Yeah, sure, you wanna go lie on the towels?"

"No, how about a walk on the beach though?" I needed to move and clear my head.

"We're gonna take a walk, guys," Lena said, letting our friends know that we were leaving for a while. She then rubbed my arms and shoulders to warm me up, and as we started walking, I began to feel a little better.

# Chapter Fourteen

When Lena and I returned a half hour later, our friends were back up at our spot in the soft sand and Roberta Flack's "The First Time Ever I Saw Your Face" was playing on the radio. I didn't care much for the song the first time around, but as I got older, it reminded me of Lena, so listening to it now with Lena next to me was a whole different experience for me. The impassioned lyrics, slowly and patiently drawn out, describing so eloquently the depth of one's love for another—what a powerful song.

*And the first time ever I lay with you*
*I felt your heart so close to mine*
*And I knew our joy would fill the earth*
*And last till the end of time my love*

I didn't realize that I was standing there mesmerized, staring at the radio, until I felt Lena tugging on my arm, pulling me down to her level on the towel.

"What are you doin?" she said. "You look like a statue?"

"Oh…I was just listening to that song," I said as I snapped out of it. "I like it."

"I didn't know you liked Roberta Flack," Lena said as Joan looked over smiling. Lena then pulled me closer so she could kiss me. She kissed me slowly and deeply, her tongue gently exploring mine. I closed my eyes and was sure I felt heaven itself—it was perfect. Lena then pulled away slowly, smiled, and said that she was learning something new about me every day.

Roy cleared his throat to get our attention and then told us to save it for the concert. Lena and I both told Roy to go screw himself then looked at each other and laughed. Roy laughed along with us.

"Hey, Roy, find that girl with the big boobs yet?" I asked.

"Not yet, but I'm still lookin'," he said with a wide smile. We all laughed except Trish, who had sort of a puzzled look on her face. Joan filled Trisha in on our conversation from the other day while Roy listened.

"Jeez, Roy, you really said that?"

"You know me, I tell it like it is."

"That's a little too much information, a little vulgar, Roy, don't you think?"

"No, not really," Roy replied matter-of-factly, and Trisha just shook her head. Then Jamie rolled over and told Trisha not to be so serious, which resulted in Jamie getting punched in the arm.

"Hey, hey, hey," Jamie protested as he fended off the second blow from Trisha.

"At least you could agree with me—jerk," she said semi-playfully as a smile broke out on her face.

"Hey, hon, you gutta let Roy be Roy—ya know," Jamie said.

"Yeah, Roy's Roy I guess, but he's still a pig."

"Easy over there, sunshine," replied Roy. Then Trisha feigned throwing an apple she had in her hand at him, and Roy ducked. "You gotta control that woman," Roy said to Jamie as Trisha cracked up.

"No one's controlling me, right, Jamie?"

"You heard it, Roy, nothin' I can do about it."

"That big-boobed girl I find won't be as sassy as you, that's for sure," Roy told Trisha.

"You're the boob, Roy," Trisha said, and they both laughed, and the friendly banter subsided.

We went swimming again then returned to our towels for a snack and more small talk. By four thirty Lena and I started packing up.

"You guys are leaving already?" Joan said.

"Yeah, we're having supper early tonight because of the concert."

"Oh yeah, I forgot."

"Jamie, you stayin'?" I asked.

"Yeah, I'll get a later bus, I'm gonna stay a while longer with my sassy woman," he said, smiling. Roy started laughing as Trisha gave Jamie a playful nudge. As we left, everyone told us to have a good time at the concert tonight.

We were back at Lena's house by five o'clock, had our kiss, and said our goodbyes. As I was walking away, Lena called out, "It's gonna be great tonight."

I turned around and smiled, saying, "Yeah, it's gonna be a good show. See ya at seven."

"A little after that, Mark, we're gonna leave here at seven."

"Okay, see ya then," I said then made my way to the bus stop. The boy was in control now as he was most of the day today. Except for that horrible memory that my future self recalled, the day was enjoyed the way a fourteen-year-old would enjoy it. And the boy wasn't aware of the fact that his older self could be pulled back in time at any moment.

# Chapter Fifteen

I was home by quarter of six, took a shower, and made it to the supper table right as everyone was sitting down. We were having hot dogs and beans with brown bread, a staple in our family growing up. As I ate, I kept looking over at the clock. I just couldn't wait to go. Then I thought of something.

"Hey, Gin, I got somethin' for ya," I said then asked to be excused from the table.

"What do you have for me, Mark?" Ginny said as the cutest little smile formed on her face.

"I'll be right down," I told her as I ran up to my room.

I wanted to give her the money I had won in the poker game last night. I grabbed the paper bag filled with change from my junk drawer, plopped it down on the bed, then reached for my wallet to get the bills that I had put away. As I was pulling the bills out of the wallet, the reminder note fell out. Wondering what it was, I unfolded it and read. Needless to say, my future self grasped its meaning and he was back in charge. I didn't want to dwell on my predicament though. I'd put it in the back of my mind as much as I could and enjoy the concert with Lena tonight. Ron would come through. It's gotta be just a matter of time.

I ran back downstairs with the money realizing that it must be getting close to seven o'clock. Ginny was waiting in the hallway at the foot of the stairs.

"Here's something for your piggy bank, Gin," I said.

Ginny's expression was priceless—mouth agape, eyes wide. "All that?"

"Yup, all for you. Go get your piggy bank and meet me in the living room." I glanced at the clock in the kitchen—it was six forty-five—as I walked into the living room.

Ginny was back down in a minute, and we both began putting the coins and bills in her bank. Before we had it all in, I told her she could finish; I had to get going. She then stopped and gave me a bear hug, nearly knocking me over.

"Thanks, Mark, thanks a lot," she said. She seemed so happy.

"No problem, Gin," I said, smiling. "You can get a lot of ice cream with that. Just ask Mom before you buy anything though, okay?"

"I will," Ginny said as she began putting the rest of the money into her piggy bank.

I went back to the kitchen to let my mother know that I was going outside to wait for Lena.

"Okay, have a good time tonight, and be careful."

"All right, Ma."

"Oh, and uh…that was a nice thing you did for Ginny."

"It was just a little extra money I had. I figured it would make her happy."

"Looks like it did," my mother said. Then she said goodbye.

As I started heading out, I realized that this might be the last time I see my mother here in the past, so I turned around and walked back over to her. I gave her a hug and a kiss, saying, "I love you, Mom."

"Love you too, hon," she said with sort of a proud smile on her face as I left the room. I yelled out to everyone else who was still in the house that I was leaving and heard a few goodbyes before I stepped outside.

John was sitting on the porch steps outside, so I sat down.

"What's goin' on," I said.

"Oh, I dunno…lost my job today."

"What happened?"

"Went in late again and he canned me. I'll get somethin' else," he said, shrugging it off. Then I remembered that I still had a lot of the money left, so I pulled two twenties from my wallet and gave it to him.

"Wow, I could really use this. I don't have anything till next Monday when I get my last check. I appreciate it," John said, putting his arm around my shoulder. "Thanks a lot."

"No problem, I had a little extra. You don't have to pay me back either." As I was saying this, Lena's mother pulled up in her little Volkswagen Beetle. I jumped up and started for the car.

"Hey, Mark, have a good time tonight at the concert."

"Thanks, John," I said, looking over my shoulder as I reached the car. "I'll see ya later."

"Yeah, see ya."

Lena stepped out of the car with a big smile on her face. She waved at John, and he returned a wave.

"Hello, beautiful," I said. As usual we didn't kiss in front of her mother. We'd wait till we were alone.

"Hi, Mark, do you wanna sit in the front?"

When her mother drove us anywhere, one of us would always sit in the front. Lena's mother thought it looked too much like a taxi service if we both sat in the back.

"Sure, I'll sit in the front," I said.

"Oh, here's the film from the camera," Lena said as she handed me the roll. "Now you can get it developed."

"Oh, good, thanks," I said then stuffed it into my pocket. I adjusted the seat so Lena could get into the back. Then I got into the front seat next to Mrs. Mendleson.

"Hello, Mark."

"Hello, Mrs. Mendleson," I said as she put the car in gear and pulled away from the curb.

"All right, so I'll plan on being around the front entrance of the theater at eleven. If there's any change in when the show finishes, find a pay phone and give me a call, okay?"

"All right, Mom, we will."

"You two have a good time tonight, and be careful." We assured her we would as she sped down the street.

Mrs. Mendleson was not what you would call a timid driver. She once told me that she liked to zip around town in her little "bug," and it was true. She zipped around at a pretty good rate of speed. She made quick work of navigating through the evening traffic, and we were at Sanders Theater in Cambridge in less than twenty minutes.

# Chapter Sixteen

We were seated by seven forty-five. As I looked over at Lena and smiled, I felt overwhelmed with excitement and anticipation for the show that was about to start. She smiled back at me and squeezed my hand.

The fourteen-year-old boy in me couldn't have been any happier being here at the concert and with the girl that meant everything to him. At the same time, I still retained the presence of mind, knowledge, and awareness of the older man that still resided in this young body.

Our seats were fantastic, located in the lower mezzanine level with a clear view of the stage, which couldn't be more than fifty feet away. We held hands and smiled as we waited impatiently for Jim Croce to come on, and when he did, the crowd roared. Lena and I leaped to our feet, as did anyone else that wasn't already standing when he walked onstage.

When the applause died down, he said, "Hello, I'm Jim Croce. Glad you could make it tonight, thanks for coming." He looked and sounded like a regular guy: a young man dressed in a cotton pullover shirt and faded dungarees. He had that recognizable mustache that gave his face character and, of course, the acoustic guitar slung over his shoulder. *Man*, I thought, *he's really here, he's alive—sitting on a stool onstage about fifty feet away from me. Jim-fucking-Croce!*

He introduced his backup guitarist Maury Muehleisen and then made mention that it was an honor to play at Sanders.

"I understand that President Teddy Roosevelt, Winston Churchill, and Martin Luther King all spoke here. Well, I don't know if I can compete with the likes of them, but let's give it a try," he said, and the crowd erupted once again.

Jim Croce opened with "Time in a Bottle." This was extremely ironic given my situation but not really unusual considering it was one of his most popular hits. A dreamy, wistful type song about saving time in a bottle so those precious moments could be relived once again. When he finished, he told us that the song was written for his son, A. J. Croce, who was not yet born at the time of its writing.

*If I could make days last forever*
*If words could make wishes come true*
*I'd save every day like a treasure and then,*
*Again, I would spend them with you*

His next song was "These Dreams," and when he finished that one, he went on to play one of my favorites, the hauntingly nostalgic "Photographs and Memories."

*Memories that come at night*
*Take me to another time*
*Back to a happier day*
*When I called you mine*

After each of these songs, Croce talked to the audience. He came across easygoing and sincere as he told us the stories behind each song. He spoke just like any other ordinary guy, creating a strong connection with us, his fans. Lena and I sang along to the songs we knew, as did the rest of the audience. He was relaxed up there: singing songs and telling stories as if he were sitting comfortably with his friends.

*Massachusetts General Hospital*
*Saturday, 21 June 2014*

Ron and Jessica were finishing the rest of their Chinese food when Trivia appeared at the door.

"How's my favorite patient and his girl doin'?" she said with a big grin on her face.

Looking up, Ron replied, "Hey, Triv, doing great."

"Hi, Trivia," said Jessica, her face lighting up.

"Feeling all right, Ron?"

"I feel as healthy as a horse except for my ribs still bothering me a bit. Hey, want some Chinese, we've got plenty?"

"No thanks, honey, I just ate before I came in," Trivia said as she walked over to Ron's bed. "Do you still have that gap in your memory, Ron?"

"Yeah, that little piece is still missing—May twenty-third to two days ago when I woke up, the um…the nineteenth. Jessica's been trying to jog my memory, but nothin' yet."

"It's only been a couple days, give it some time. I think it'll come back to you."

"Yeah, I'm not worried, something will break sooner or later."

"Jessica, you gettin' enough sleep now, I know you weren't sleeping much when Ron was out of it?" Trivia said while gently laying a hand on Jessica's shoulder.

"Yeah, I've been catching up the last couple of days. In fact, Ron made me leave early last night," Jessica said, smiling as she squeezed Ron's arm.

Feigning a hurt look on his face, Ron responded by saying, "Hey, that's not fair, just trying to look out for my girl."

Trivia smiled. "I see they got all the gadgets off you, just the IV now, huh?" They had also taken the bandaging from his head.

"Yup, all that crap's gone, just the IV and some lighter bandaging around my chest."

"You're scheduled for some more tests with the neurologist Monday, right?"

"Yeah, that should be it they said, and if everything goes well with those, I should be released the following day."

"Good, that's good, Ron. You do look a lot better."

"Thanks, Triv, you don't look so bad yourself," Ron replied with a playful grin on his face.

"Hey, now don't be comin' on to me, I got me a man at home," Trivia replied, and they all laughed. "All right, I better get goin', I'll see you two later on." Jessica and Ron said goodbye as Trivia left the room.

After Jessica took care of the trash and organized the leftovers from their meal, she went back to sitting on the side of Ron's bed.

As she stroked his hair, thoughts began to form in Ron's head.

"You know, I still haven't been able to get in touch with Mark… it doesn't make any sense…he'd be here if he knew I was in the hospital."

"Maybe he had to go somewhere unexpectedly before the accident and had forgotten to call, that would explain him not knowing you're here," Jessica replied.

"Yeah, but why hasn't he called me back yet? I wish I knew his ex's number. I'd call her to see if she knows anything. I don't even know where she lives. Anyway, when he goes anywhere for more than a couple of days, he lets me know—I don't have a single message on my phone and…" Then it began to come back to Ron. It came back like a veil being slowly lifted from a concealed object. *Mark must be time traveling!* Ron said to himself.

"And what?" Jessica replied, turning quickly to Ron, wanting him to finish the sentence.

"Get that calendar off the wall, Jess. Bring it over to me please."

Jessica unhooked the calendar from the wall near the door. She brought it over and laid it in Ron's lap.

"Here you go hon," she said, eyeing Ron intently.

Ron flipped the calendar back to May and began thinking out loud as it all came back to him. "We met on the thirtieth of May, I remember this now—"

"That's great, Ron, you—"

"Hold on a minute, Jess," Ron said, holding up his hand, stopping Jessica in midsentence. He then flipped the calendar back to the current month of June. "My accident was on June thirteenth, right?" Ron meant the question to be rhetorical, but Jessica answered in the affirmative. Then he began speaking again. "Mark—" Ron stopped himself from completing the sentence again. He knew the date. It was the tenth of this month that Mark left, and if he wasn't back yet, it meant that he'd been gone for over eleven days! He should have come back yesterday, after ten days, but *I don't think he has*, Ron thought. *I've been calling him since I woke up two days ago, and all I'm getting is his voice mail.*

"Oh, shit," he said out loud then said it again with even more emphasis.

"What's the matter, Ron? Mark what, Ron?"

"Jessica, grab my phone, I wanna try him one more time." Jessica handed Ron the phone from the nightstand and he made the call. "Voice mail again, shit! Jessica, I have to get out of here—right now! Your car's in the garage, right?"

"What do you mean, you have to get out of here, you can't leave the hospital, Ron."

"You're gonna have to trust me with this, Jess."

Jessica stood there speechless for a few seconds with a *this is crazy* look on her face but then acquiesced. "All right, what do you want me to do?"

"Close that door, then see if there's a Band-Aid over there on the dresser with the rest of that medical stuff?"

Jessica returned with a Band-Aid after closing the door.

"Open that up, I gotta take this IV out."

"Jesus, Ron, why don't we just get Trivia?"

"No, she'll never let me leave," Ron replied as he pulled the tape from his arm that held the catheter and tubing in place. "You ready, Jess? There shouldn't be much blood but get ready with the Band-Aid."

Jessica showed her disapproval by shaking her head but let Ron know she was ready.

Ron slowly pulled the catheter tip out of his arm. A trickle of blood and fluid appeared at the insertion site, but Jessica applied the Band-Aid, and there was no additional flow. He then got up off the bed, staggered a bit, then regained his balance and went right to the dresser. Ron found his clothes and personal belongings then went into the bathroom to change.

"Ron, your shirt…it's ripped apart!" Jessica remarked as he exited the bathroom.

"Yeah, they must have cut it off me when they brought me in. Anyway, it's all I've got, and we have to go," he said, then peeked out the door. Closing the door quietly, he turned to Jessica, "You're gonna have to drive—my ribs are still bothering me."

"Okay, but why don't I go first, I can get us out of here quicker, you've never been off the floor." Ron agreed so they switched places. "Okay, Ron, the stairway is only about ten feet away. It's closer than the elevator, and we won't have to wait around. It's to our right down the hall, then it's four flights of stairs to the lobby."

"Okay, good, we'll take the stairway. Let me know when it's clear."

Jessica poked her head out the door then pulled it in. "Looks good, you all set?"

"Yeah, let's roll," Ron replied, and they bolted for the stairway.

They descended the stairs, cut across the lobby, and were out the main entrance in pretty good time. Ron was experiencing pain in his ribs, but it was manageable. The two-story parking garage was a short distance from the main entrance, so they were in Jessica's car and driving away from the hospital before anyone noticed that Ron was gone.

"Where to, Ron?"

"Straight ahead, Jess—to my office at Harvard."

Jessica glanced over at Ron while she drove them across the Longfellow Bridge and into Cambridge. Traffic wasn't too bad for an early Saturday night.

"Are you going to tell me what this is all about?"

"I'm worried about Mark. I want to go check his lab, but first, I gotta get the key from my office."

"All right, we'll go check his lab."

"You can't come to the lab with me, Jess."

"Why not?"

"His research is extremely private. He doesn't let anyone in the lab except for me."

"Okay, so I'll wait outside the lab, and if he's not there, I'll help you search other places or make calls or do whatever I can do to help."

"Jess, I'd rather you go back to the hospital and wait there. I won't be long."

"Ron, I understand he's your friend, but you're in no shape to do this alone. He could be anywhere."

"I'll be all right. I'm feeling much better, Jess. I want you to go back to the hospital and reassure Trivia or anyone that's looking for me that I'll be back soon. If I can't handle driving my car back on my own, I'll give you a call."

Then Jessica relented. "I don't like this, Ron, but I guess I can't stop you. Please be careful, and call as soon as you know anything, all right?"

"I will, Jess, I promise."

They pulled up in front of the Science Center at just after seven o'clock.

"You sure you're going to be all right?"

He leaned over, wincing slightly, and kissed Jessica. "I'll be fine."

"I shouldn't let you leave," she said, shaking her head. Then Jessica noticed the bag in the back seat and grabbed it. "Here," pulling a sweatshirt out of the bag, she said, "it'll probably fit you, it's a 2-XL, and it will cover that hideous shirt you have on."

"What are you doing with a 2-XL sweatshirt," Ron asked as he carefully pulled it on right over his torn shirt, trying not to aggravate his injured ribs.

"It was a present for one of my brothers. I'll get him another. Hey, it looks pretty good on you anyway."

"Harvard sweatshirt, huh…well, I'm a Harvard man, so I guess it's appropriate, a little corny but appropriate. Thanks, Jess," he said then leaned over and gave her another kiss. "I'll call in a little while… don't worry, okay."

"I love you, Ron Sarno. You're crazy you know."

"I love you too," Ron said as he opened the door and gingerly got out of the car.

There were quite a few people coming and going as Ron made his way to the Science Center. As he was approaching the main entrance, a student recognized him.

"Professor Sarno, hi, my name's Janet Ian. I was in your algebraic number theory class last semester."

"Oh, hi there." Ron remembered the face but not the name. "How are you?"

"Good, thanks. I heard that you were in the hospital…you okay? I see you have a cast."

Ron looked down at his right hand and noticed the cast was visible.

"Oh, little accident—I'm all right now," he said, wanting to end the conversation and get to the lab. "Listen, I'd love to talk, but I'm in a bit of a rush—I'm sorry."

"Oh, yeah, no problem, I won't hold you up. It was nice seeing you, Professor. Oh, and nice sweatshirt, sir," she said, smiling.

"Thanks," Ron said, a bit embarrassed. "Nice to have seen you too, good night now," he said as they parted company.

Inside the lobby, Ron flashed his ID at the security guard and then headed for the elevators. His office was on the third floor, and once there he went straight for his desk. He sighed. The key to my private lab was where it was supposed to be, in the top desk drawer, and now that he actually had it in his hands, Ron was relieved.

"Good—okay, Mark, almost there," he said out loud to no one.

With key in hand, Ron left the Science Center and proceeded to the Gordon McKay Laboratory of Applied Science right next door. Past security once again, Ron took the elevator to the basement where the lab was located. Although he had never used it, the key turned smoothly in the lock, sliding the deadbolt back, allowing the heavy metal door to open freely. Ron switched on the lights as he closed the door. He flipped the thumb turn, locking the door, and walked as quickly as his injured body would allow to the time machine at the back of the lab.

*Sanders Theater*
*Thursday, 26 July 1973*
*8:25 p.m.*

Lena and I were making out when Jim Croce began playing "Operator," a rather sad song about a guy trying to call a former girlfriend from a phone booth. I pulled back from Lena so I could see and hear him play that song. How many times had I heard it played before, whether on the radio, CD, or the original vinyl, and now I was witnessing it live! *Jesus, Ron,* I thought, *don't take me back now.* When he finished, Jim Croce went on to tell us how he was inspired to write "Operator" from his time spent in the National Guard. The crowd listened respectfully but eagerly awaited the next tune.

"Okay, here's one you might like," he said then played the hugely popular "Bad, Bad Leroy Brown."

"I love this one," Lena said as she squeezed my hand and strained to hear the vocals through the roar of the crowd.

After that, he went on to play another good song, "New York's Not My Home," and at nine o'clock took a short break.

At nine fifteen, Jim Croce walked back onstage. "I'm gonna pick it up a little here," he said then started in with the up-tempo song "Rapid Roy (The Stock Car Boy)," and that really got everyone going again. People were up on their feet, and some were dancing to this fast-paced song. Lena and I got up too. She looked good, keeping the rhythm, but me, I could never really dance. I looked like a washing machine spinning out of control, but I sure as hell was having fun.

"Okay, this one's called 'I Got a Name.' It'll be coming out on my next album with the same title. I hope you like it." Tragically, Jim Croce would die on September 20, 1973, before the album was released, not even two months from now. I was the only one in the theater that knew this, and I wish to God I didn't!

*Like the fool I am and I'll always be*
*I've got a dream, I've got a dream*
*They can change their minds, but they can't change me*

*I've got a dream, I've got a dream*
*Oh, I know I could share it if you want me to*
*If you're going my way, I'll go with you*

A sadness for the man washed over me, and his next song did nothing to improve the melancholy I was feeling. It was called "It Doesn't Have to Be That Way." You see, it's about a man wandering the city-streets around Christmas, a lonely man whose feelings don't match the cheery Christmas sights he's seeing. He's contemplating stopping by his former love's place to rekindle what he once had. This made me feel painfully aware once again that eventually Ron would retrieve me and I would be without Lena. I turned to her, putting my arms around Lena and pulling her close to me. I told her that I loved her. She smiled, and our lips met. It made all the sadness go away—in fact it made everything go away except me and her. We stood there kissing, and as we did, we slowly lowered ourselves into our seats without breaking our embrace or ending the kiss.

And as we kissed, it happened. I felt a sudden jolt of pressure on my entire body as I grew light-headed. Then she was gone.

*The Lab*
*Saturday, 21 June 2014*
*7:29 p.m.*

I stood there in the lab, getting my bearings, my mind transitioning to the reality of my new surroundings. Then I heard a voice calling me.

"Mark, Mark—you all right?"

I turned in the direction of the voice, and it was Ron. *I'm back*, I said to myself, then out loud, "Ron, I'm back! Yeah, I'm fine," I said, looking over at my friend. It was good to see Ron again, knowing that I was safely back home, but at the same time I felt depressed knowing Lena was gone, but I didn't let on.

Ron stepped away from the console and walked over to where I stood. He then startled me by lifting me off the floor with a typical Ron Sarno bear hug. He winced as he slowly lowered me back down then said, "Shit, I shouldn't have done that." Ron took a breath and went on, "I'm sorry I was late bringing you back, buddy." He then paused while looking me up and down. "Jeez, your shirt's a little small, huh?"

I looked down at my clothing and immediately unbuttoned those slim-waisted dungarees that I had on; they were killing me. "Shit, that feels a lot better," I said, and then added, "Yeah, got my fat body back—shirt no longer fits too," I said as I smiled. "I feel fine, Ron. It's good to see you—thanks for bringing me home. Why don't I go get dressed and then we can talk."

"Yeah, go get some clothes on that fit you," Ron said, grinning, "then I'll explain what caused the delay in bringing you home."

I pulled out the roll of film and my old wallet from my pants pockets before taking them off. My younger self would wonder where the wallet was and, of course, never find it, but I didn't think that was a big deal. It had nothing really important in it. I'm glad Lena had given me the film before we left for the concert. I couldn't wait to get the pictures developed. My private lab was unlike the other lab in that it not only had a locker room with shower stalls but also a kitchenette where Ron and I sat down and toasted my return with a couple of beers.

"So you left the signaling device behind."

"Yeah, as a matter of fact, I was just wondering where, exactly, I left it." I got up and walked over to the console, but it wasn't on the surface. I began to look around and eventually found it behind the console, wedged against the wall.

"There it is, I must have knocked it off the console and then forgotten about it when I left. That should never have happened— never!" I said with a frown as I shook my head. "I was nervous at first, knowing I left it behind but knew you'd bring me back. I just didn't expect you to be late doing it." I reassured Ron that no harm was done by delaying my retrieval and that the ten-day maximum stay allowed for mishaps like what had happened.

Ron explained the accident that caused the delay. I winced as he told me about the many injuries he sustained and the resultant coma. He went on to explain the amnesia and how he slowly recovered his memory then, with the help of Jessica, snuck out of Mass General to get back to the lab.

"So who's this Jessica, how come I'm just finding out about her now?"

"We met less than two weeks before you left. I hadn't had a chance to tell you about her, never mind introducing her to you."

"Don Juan, continuing his conquest of the female species."

"No, Mark," Ron said with a straight face, "it's not like that… she's not just another girl. I mean…I feel totally different with her, I really do—I'm in love with her, Mark, and I can't wait to introduce you guys," he said enthusiastically.

"Really, Ron, you surprise me, and I do look forward to meeting the only woman that could take the great Ronald Sarno out of the game." Ron laughed when I said this, and when he did, I could tell right then that he was truly happy. Then I paused and took a more serious tone. "Ron, you didn't reveal anything about the time machine to Jessica, did you?"

"No, not a word. She thought I was crazy leaving the hospital and of course wanted to know why I was doing it, but I didn't reveal anything regarding time travel. I hate keeping anything from her. I really care about her…but I knew I couldn't tell her about your time traveling."

"Okay, good," I said, then paused. "I'm sorry, Ron, but you know how I feel about this getting out."

"No, I understand, you don't have to explain yourself. I'm just going to have to come up with something to justify my crazy behavior when I go back to the hospital. Oh, would you give me a ride back, my ribs are still bothering me."

"No problem, Ron, I don't mind driving you over to the hospital, I really want to meet Jessica anyway."

"Thanks, buddy, now tell me about your trip."

"It was fun…well, not right away," I said as I took a swig of the cold beer. "I was self-conscious and uncomfortable at first with everyone, especially Lena until the transformation began—until I began feeling like my younger self again. Remember me explaining this process to you, Ron?"

"Yeah, you said that as your former self gradually reclaims its body, you would begin to feel like the boy from your past. I'm just glad I got you back in time to prevent the complete reclamation."

"Yeah, me too," I said, smiling. "Anyway, once I became comfortable, once I started feeling like the kid again, it all felt so natural. It was great seeing my mother so healthy and talking with my brothers and sisters when we were all young again. And Lena, boy was I attracted to Lena, I was with her all the time. We spent hours together and with our friends on the beach, having fun and listening to all the old songs I still love from that era. We drank, we went to a movie, played poker, and the last night, Lena and I saw Jim Croce in concert at, get this…Sanders Theatre."

"Sanders Theatre—here in Cambridge?"

"Yup, do you believe that! And also, the day we came into Cambridge to get the tickets, we stopped in at this little curiosity shop on JFK street. The owner, an old woman named Ella, read our tea leaves and knew that I had come back from the future."

"Did you let on she was right in knowing that?"

"Yeah, I didn't see any harm in letting her know. So I had Lena go get us some sandwiches, then I told her everything. She loved it, she was fascinated and wanted to know about the future. She wanted me to come back some time to visit her," I said with a warm smile on my face as I thought of that quirky old lady that reminded me of my grandmother. Then suddenly I remembered Ella pointing out the number eleven in my tea leaves.

"It just came to me, Ron. She saw the number eleven in my tea leaves, and now I realize the significance of that. You brought me back eleven days after I had left. She had reassured me that I wouldn't have a problem returning home, and the eleven turned out to be the day that I would return. Wow, she was good—I never believed in that stuff before, but now I definitely do."

"Yeah, that's right—the eleventh day. Well, it sounds like you had a great time, Mark."

"Yeah, and that concert topped it all off. To see one of my favorite singers in concert, something we regretfully missed out on the first time around. That's where we were when you retrieved me, Ron, at the concert, in our seats making out when you brought me back," I said with a faraway look in my eyes as I thought again of Lena.

"Anyway," I said, snapping back to the present, "let me get you back to the hospital, I want to meet this Jessica."

"Yeah, I better get back, but let me give her a call first, let her know we're on our way."

"All right, Ron," I said then started checking my voice mail and messages on my phone while I waited.

*Massachusetts General Hospital*
*Saturday, 21 June 2014*
*8:57 p.m.*

It was just before nine o'clock when we arrived at Mass General Hospital. Jessica and Trivia were talking when we entered the room. Trivia had her back to the doorway, so Jessica noticed us first. When Trivia realized that Ron had just come into the room, she turned and let him have it.

"What's got into you, boy? With your injuries, you just stroll right outta here? You're not fully recovered, you know that, Ron," she said with hands on her hips and her face set in a scowl.

"I know, I know, Triv, but I had to help a friend," Ron said, holding his hand up in a defensive gesture while looking at Trivia then over at me. Trivia stood there frowning as Ron continued, "Anyway...Trivia, Jessica, this is my friend, Mark, a colleague of mine at Harvard. I am relieved to say that I found him safe and sound in his lab over at the school."

"Well, it's nice to meet you," Trivia said as she shook my hand. "Must be a strong friendship you two have, but I'd say he was a bit of a fool tonight." She was looking back at Ron, slowly shaking her head in disapproval.

Jessica then reached out her hand, and I shook it. "It's very nice to meet you, Mark," she said.

"Nice to meet you, Jessica...you didn't tell me how pretty she was, Ron," I said, making Jessica blush.

"Well, Ron, you get that Johnny back on and get yourself back into bed or ol Triv will see to it herself," Trivia said, pointing over at his bed.

"Yes, ma'am," Ron replied, feigning the appearance of a young schoolboy who had just been chastised by his teacher. He went over and kissed Jessica on the cheek and then headed for the bathroom.

"I don't have to post guards outside your room now, do I, Ron?"

"Yes, ma'am, I mean no, ma'am," Ron replied with a smile on his face as he closed the bathroom door.

With Ron now safely back in bed and Trivia gone to make her rounds, we talked, and I got to know Jessica. She came across as very pleasant, and I was happy for both of them. We decided to tell Jessica what she had already thought happened: that I had gone away and had forgotten to call Ron, therefore knew nothing of his accident.

Jessica told me that she had mentioned this to Ron but to no avail and also complained about Ron's insistence on looking for me alone while she returned to the hospital. She didn't pry about my lab being off-limits to everyone save Ron, and I didn't bring it up. I did mention briefly my time travel research.

At just before ten o'clock I started wondering why we weren't told to leave. "How come they haven't kicked us out of here yet, it's pretty late?"

"Jess gets to stay as late as she wants. Trivia doesn't mind," Ron replied.

"Really," I said.

"Yeah, when I was in my coma, Jess was…well, Jess was afraid for me and real emotional," he said, looking over at Jessica. "Triv let her stay as late as she wanted that first night, then it just continued. She comes across like an SS officer, but she's really a softy. She's got a big heart."

"Yeah, she's super-nice, Mark. We both really like her, so you can see why I didn't want Ron to skip out on her tonight. I'm very happy he found you safe though, he talks so much about you."

"Thanks, Jessica—yeah, the big lug's always worried about me, but actually…that's what I like about him," I said as I turned to Ron.

"He's a good friend and, well—you've got a hell of a guy there," I said, now looking back at Jessica.

"Well—thank—you—pilgrim," Ron replied, sounding more like John Wayne than John Wayne himself, making us all laugh.

"He sounds just like 'em, doesn't he, Mark?" Jessica said, smiling happily.

"Oh, yeah, just like *The Big Duke,*" I replied, and we all laughed again.

"Which John Wayne movie's your favorite, Ron?" Jessica asked.

"Oh, I dunno, I like 'em all, but if I had to name one, I'd say *True Grit.*"

"I know that one, the one with the girl that hires him to track down her father's killer."

"Yeah, that's the one."

"Why that one, Ron, why's that one your favorite?" I asked.

"I liked how he looked after that girl and how he saved her life in the end. You know, he's a tough guy, but he's not ruthless. He might be rough around the edges and at times crude, but he's fair. He plays by his own set of rules, but those rules are backed up by a code of honor and a degree of integrity that makes the audience want him to succeed. In the end of this movie, he does everything in his power to save that girl's life, including riding the horse they're on to its death. Ultimately she is saved, and once again good triumphs over evil. And we all win because we all really want the same thing, we all want good to prevail… It's just a great movie."

"That was quite a speech," I said.

"Well, you know how much I admire *The Big Duke.* He was someone I looked up to as a kid, and I wanted to be like him.

"You were a bit like *The Duke* today, Ron, when you broke out of here and went in search of your friend," Jessica said while rubbing his shoulder.

"Well—thank you—young lady," Ron replied, giving us his best John Wayne again.

We talked some more, enjoying the late hour together, but by quarter to eleven I had to excuse myself. I was beat. I told Ron I'd stop by tomorrow then said good night to my friend and Jessica.

As I drove away from the hospital, I was thinking how strange it was that this morning I woke up as a fourteen-year-old boy in 1973 and shortly I'd be going to sleep as a man in 2014. I then began thinking of where I might want to go next, to what time period I'd like to visit, perhaps to some pivotal historical event where I witness with my own eyes history being made.

# The Endgame

S unday, the first full day of summer, was spent readjusting myself to life in the present. I awoke early to a beautiful blue-sky day with the forecast promising comfortable temps in the lower seventies. I threw open the window over the kitchen sink and let in that cool, refreshing morning air.

After breakfast and my first cup of coffee in over a week, I returned my phone calls, including one from my daughter, Hannah. She was now out of school, so we planned on having lunch and seeing a movie together on Tuesday.

I let the department head, Kevin Costigan, know that I was around if he needed anything, although with the semester finished over a month ago it was doubtful anything would come up.

I got out of the apartment at around ten and decided I'd walk over to Harvard. I had the film with me and happened to find a camera store that still develops that old type of film. I dropped it off and was told that it would be ready tomorrow.

Remembering how good I felt as a kid, I decided that I'd begin walking a lot more and getting my weight down. I got over to the lab and ended up spending a good chunk of the day there, working on redesigning the console of the time machine with built-in safeguards to prevent the possibility of leaving without the signaling device ever again.

In the late afternoon, I drove over to Mass General and visited Ron. He was antsy about getting out of the hospital, but I reminded him of what he had already told me: that he'd be released on Tuesday if everything went well with the tests tomorrow.

It wasn't until Monday morning that I remembered the stock certificates. While sipping my morning coffee, it came to me. I put down the mug abruptly, without spilling too much, and began searching for the safe deposit key, which now should exist and be found somewhere in the apartment.

The most likely place would be in my bedroom. I'd check my desk first. I sat down and pulled open the small top drawer, which was a junk drawer that contained an assortment of items, mostly not used anymore but kept for nostalgic reasons: like an old watch that no longer worked, tie clips that haven't been worn in years, and a padlock with no key to it. I really should just toss all this crap, I thought as I fingered through it. I even had an old key chain with several keys no longer used on it—but no safe deposit key. The bottom two drawers held mostly work-related odds and ends.

I checked the file cabinet next to the desk knowing it probably wouldn't be in a file folder, but I wanted to be sure. It wasn't there either.

I then swiveled around in the desk chair and looked over to the wall opposite my bed where two rather large, matching mahogany bookcases stood. These were nice pieces that I had salvaged from my marriage. The one on the left contained science books, mostly in my field of physics along with textbooks, journals, and various other scientific publications. The other bookcase held your typical assortment of novels. The top two shelves were reserved for the classics. There sat *War and Peace, Les Miserables, The Mayor of Casterbridge, Martin Eden*, and many others. The lower shelves held contemporary novels from the likes of Stephen King, Daniel Silva, and Ken Follett.

My eyes drifted down to the lowest shelf, where next to a pile of old magazines was a large shoebox that once contained a pair of hiking boots. I had forgotten about this box. I hadn't looked through it in years. In it contained old documents including a tattered birth certificate that was issued in 1976, an old social security card, an outdated passport, and assorted certificates and diplomas accumulated through the years. As I removed my undergraduate diploma, which I thought was the bottom-most item, I uncovered, at the very bottom of the box, a plain white envelope. I put aside the diploma and slowly picked up the envelope. Before I could read what was penned on the outside of it, I could feel the solid weight of a small item within. My heart rate quickened as I read the outside of the envelope: *WSB safe deposit key*. I tore open the envelope and quickly had that old key in my hand.

As you could imagine, I was a bit excited, so I hurried to get out of the apartment. I quickly picked up the kitchen, took a shower, and had locked the front door in less than twenty minutes' time.

Before I left Cambridge, I stopped at the camera store and picked up the photos from my trip. I decided I'd wait till later to look at the pictures. I was rather anxious to get to the bank. In fact, I found it difficult to keep the car under the speed limit, and that's saying a lot for the conservative driver that I am.

It was beginning to warm up, so I lowered my window, letting the fresh air fill the car. As I crossed over the bridge into Winthrop, I was overcome with a sense of déjà vu: only last night (forty-one years ago) I had crossed this same bridge heading out of Winthrop with Lena on our way to the Jim Croce concert. Now turning onto Woodside Avenue and into the heart of Winthrop Center, I slowed the car, letting a couple of teenage girls cross the street. I then passed The Pizza Center and bore right onto Bartlett Road, parking in front of number twenty-five—the address of the Winthrop Savings Bank.

As I entered the bank, I once again experienced déjà vu: the memories of my recent trip were very vivid, including the day I obtained the safe-deposit box. The bank was exactly the same size as it was in 1973—no additions, nothing like that, but it obviously had been renovated through the years. It was brought up to date cosmetically and also brought into the computer age.

After showing proper identification, I was taken to the rear of the bank inside the vault by an attractive and fairly young bank officer. The safe deposit room was located at the rear of the vault past a rather impressive safe, massive in size, which happened to be open. Funny, I didn't recall seeing the safe the first time in the bank, but it must have been in the same spot. Perhaps it had been redesigned somehow, or I missed it completely in my haste to get down to The Point that day. We proceeded past the safe and into the safe deposit room. The young girl inserted her guard key into box number 201 and instructed me to do the same with my key, which I did. She then opened the panel, pulled out the four-by-ten-by-twelve-inch safe-deposit box and placed it on a viewing table located in the center of the room.

"I'll leave you here now. Just open the door when you're done and it will signal me to come back. Take as much time as you like," she said.

I thanked her as she closed the door, and then I sat down at the table. Taking a deep breath, I pulled the box close to me and slowly opened the lid. There they were. The note I had written about not redeeming the stock until the summer of 2014 sat on top of the certificates. It was a dried and yellowed version of the note that I had written in 1973. I removed the note then gingerly slipped the seven stock certificates out of the metal box, exercising more care than was really necessary. I then pulled out the paperwork that came with the certificates and set it aside. Except for some minor yellowing and a bit of creasing—from the bike rack when I brought them here—they were in very good condition. The heavy stock paper was of course quite durable, so they held up pretty well, and the ink had retained much of its bold and vivid color too, so they appeared pretty much as I had left them (forty-one) years ago.

I couldn't help smiling and had to suppress laughter so as not to attract the attention of the girl. I sat there for a few more minutes taking it all in. There in my hands I held seven pieces of paper worth well over two million dollars, and it was hard to put them down. I finally slipped them back into the safe-deposit box, closed the lid, then opened the door, thus summoning the bank officer. I watched as she slid the box back into its compartment and closed the paneled door.

As I exited the bank and walked back to my car, I decided that I'd make a call to find out what the stock was worth today and to arrange its liquidation. The person who came to mind was Dave Henchard, a friend I went to MIT with who had changed careers several years ago and now worked at Charles Schwabb in Boston. I thought since I was already in Winthrop, why not drive down The

Point and make the call from there. I hadn't been down there in years...well, not in my present life anyway.

I settled in on the beach wall overlooking Yirrell Beach, sipping a bottled water. Again, déjà vu: the beach looked the same as it did in 1973 minus my friends and girlfriend down there on the sand. Oh, and the prison across the water was gone too. In its place was that state-of-the-art sewage treatment facility. I rather liked the look of the old prison building instead of what was put in its place.

It was just past ten in the morning, and there were several people on the beach already, but none in the water. I really couldn't imagine anyone venturing in today, a mild day, but not warm enough for that cold water this early in the season.

Dave was surprised when I called him. It had been a while. We exchanged pleasantries and caught up from the time we last spoke. When I brought up the stock, he was flabbergasted.

"You have Coca-Cola stock purchased in 1973!" he said. "Jesus Christ, how much?"

"Six hundred and fifty shares, and I'd like to know what it's worth, Dave."

"You know you're sittin' on a fortune. Coke split a bunch of times since then. Why didn't you ever mention this before?"

"Oh, I dunno, it was supposed to be used for college, but I forgot about it. When I rediscovered the stock, I decided I'd just put it away for a while, and then I forgot about it again," I told Dave, thinking it sounded convincing enough.

"Well, right now Coke's at $41.73 a share. Let me look at the split history. When did you say you purchased it?"

"Well, actually, my mother purchased it for me in my name. It was July of 1973." I knew basically what he was going to tell me but listened patiently.

"Okay, the first split after you purchased it happened in May of 1977, and there were five more splits to date. The split in 1986 was a three-for-one, all the others were two-for-one. Let's see...you started with six hundred and fifty shares." There was a pause as Dave did the math on his computer. "My friend, you have the equivalent of 62,400 shares, and at the price of $41.73 a share, your stock is currently worth exactly $2,603,952 bucks.

"Wow, that much!" I said, trying to sound excited but knowing that I pretty much had it figured out. I just wanted to hear the exact figure: the price per share had come down about twenty-five cents since before I went back in time, but I was able to purchase fifty more shares than I had expected, so I made about $200,000 more than I originally figured—not a bad payday. The capital gains tax would be pretty steep, but still it was nice knowing I had that much money at my disposal.

"Are you thinking about liquidating the stock, Mark?"

"Yeah, I'd like to set something up, do you have anything on Wednesday morning?"

"How 'bout, um, ten fifteen."

"That sounds fine, Dave."

"Okay, good, can't wait till I see those certificates. I haven't seen many paper stock certificates—you know it all went electronic years ago."

"Yeah, I know. They're rare. They actually look pretty cool."

"I bet they do. Anyway, I better get goin'. I'll be looking forward to seeing you on Wednesday."

"Okay, Dave, thanks a lot, talk to you later," I said, ending the call.

As I put down the phone, I picked up the pictures there next to me on the wall. I took them out of the envelope and set it aside. I smiled and laughed a bit as I looked through them. The first one was of Jamie and me throwing the tennis ball here at the beach—*Jeez, look at us, how young we were*! I thought. The next one was a picture of all of us on the beach. Lena had given the camera to a woman nearby who snapped this one. We were all so young, so full of life, so happy. The next was of the girls that I had taken just after they had come out of the water. Then a couple from the Longfellow Bridge, the day we went in to get the concert tickets. The pictures were all good and would forever remind me of that memorable summer and my return visit there.

The last picture in the pile was of just me and Lena outside her house. I put down the others and held this one close, staring at that image.

"Oh, Lena, we were so much in love," I said then realized I was talking out loud. I ran my index finger over her face in the picture, and I could almost feel her again, as if she were right here with me. "You'll always be in my heart," I whispered then carefully slipped the pictures back into the envelope.

I took off my shoes and socks, rolled up my pant legs, and walked down to the water's edge. I let the cold water wash over my feet then began slowly walking along the shoreline.

In the distance I noticed a young couple walking hand in hand. They looked about the age Lena and I were in 1973. I smiled as I continued along, thinking again of that special time long ago. It was then I realized how blessed I was to be given the talent to create a machine that allows me to travel through time. No one could do what I had just done, to have leaped back in time and returned safely to the present, to have had a little fun revisiting a very special time in my life, long ago and so very far away.

~ The End ~

# About the Author

Mark Pimentel lives in Goffstown, New Hampshire, retired from American Airlines as an aircraft fueler. Mark has had a lifelong interest in the concept of time travel, loves history, and enjoys reading historical fiction. In his first novel, Mr. Pimentel writes about the intensity of young love, using adventurous science fiction and history as a backdrop for his story.